LANCA LEY LIBRARY

D0433541

Scorper

SCORPER

Rob Magnuson Smith

GRANTA

Granta Publications, 12 Addison Avenue, London W11 4QR

First published in Great Britain by Granta Books, 2014

Copyright © Rob Magnuson Smith, 2014

Rob Magnuson Smith has asserted his moral right under the
Copyright, Designs and Patents Act, 1988, to be identified as
the author of this work.

Lines from 'Preludes', from *The Complete Poems and Plays* by T.S. Eliot,
published by Faber and Faber Ltd, reproduced with kind permission.

All rights reserved. This book is copyright material and must not
be copied, reproduced, transferred, distributed, leased, licensed
or publicly performed or used in any way except as specifically
permitted in writing by the publisher, as allowed under the terms and
conditions under which it was purchased or as strictly permitted by
applicable copyright law. Any unauthorized distribution or use of
this text may be a direct infringement of the author's and publisher's
rights, and those responsible may be liable in law accordingly.

A CIP catalogue record for this book is available
from the British Library.

1 3 5 7 9 10 8 6 4 2

ISBN 978 1 78378 044 0
eISBN 978 1 78378 045 7

Typeset in ITC Golden Cockerel by Lindsay Nash

Printed and bound by CPI Group (UK) Ltd

LANCASHIRE COUNTY LIBRARY	
3011813094838 7	
Askews & Holts	24-Feb-2015
AF GEN	£14.99
SOR	

For Michael and Kitty

One thinks of all the hands
That are raising dingy shades
In a thousand furnished rooms.

T. S. Eliot

1

You're on your way to Ditchling. It's a Thursday afternoon in late March during the unfortunate year of 2012, the year the bookshops are closing and the libraries are downsizing and the Internet attempts its final stranglehold on the written word. You're an American. You're on vacation in the land of your English ancestors. The US economy teeters on the edge of another recession, and you'd better be back at work in a couple of weeks or you'll lose your job.

Leaving Heathrow, you find yourself in the hands of your rental car's satellite navigator. She guides you out of the parking lot. She directs you to the motorway. Two hours in the company of her authoritative female voice pass without incident. Then, deep in Sussex, she tells you to exit the motorway onto a series of narrow roads. A sign says *South Downs National Park*. It's difficult to see because it's raining. At a roundabout you miss your turn and go around in circles, clinging to the outer lane like a sock in a dryer.

The navigator loses patience. She orders you through a maddening sequence of additional roundabouts, up a steep hill, and down an empty road toward a patch of gravel.

'You have reached your destination,' the navigator says.

You leave the engine running and step outside. After the eleven-hour flight from Los Angeles and the long drive in your rental car, being out in the elements has an invigorating effect. The rain needles your face, soaks your shirt, and finds its way into your shoes. A fence, maybe a gate, waits in the distance.

Your khakis flapping in the wind, you make your way to what is indeed a metal gate. You place your hands on the cold crossbar and hold on. A derelict chalk pit stretches before you – mounds of grass, pitted with white craters. This is an abandoned place, the bed of an ancient ocean. Rainwater fills the craters and overflows luminescent and milky white, like lava bubbling out of volcanoes.

Your conception of time expands. Recently, you turned thirty. Naturally you feel old in the company of children, but often you feel too young, especially in the company of more mature men, the ones with respected professions, wives, or domestic partners, not to mention children or pets. You've always wanted a respected profession. A partner remains improbable. In the past, your friends have said you're not bad looking, but these were your adolescent friends, the ones you are no longer technically friends with. Recent acquaintances have told you to your face that you are, at best, a Stone Age throwback.

It has to do with the size of your head. Some cows have smaller heads. You're tall, six foot six to be exact, and your dirty blond hair sticks out in tufts and clumps. At the holiday office party, a female co-worker came over to you in her heels. She stood up on her tiptoes, a glass of red wine in one hand and a glass of white in the other, and she drunkenly surveyed your face. 'Tell you what,' she said. 'You're like Frankenstein – but cute.'

You get back in your rental car and drive away from the gate, back down the hill. At the nearest petrol station, you park and run inside for directions. The man at the counter has never heard of Ditchling.

'Ditch-ling,' you say, a little louder. 'Maybe it's my accent. Ditchling. Any chance you can you help me find it?'

The man nods. 'Ditchling. It's nearby. That bone ash works, I think.'

'I'm sorry?'

'The bone ash works. I think.'

'Bone ash works? For what?'

'We sell road maps,' he says, pointing at the stack beside the register. 'I think Ditchling's just after the bone ash works.'

You buy a map and return to your car. After unpeeling the plastic wrapping, unfolding the pages and prying apart the unwieldy tight creases, the thin plastic spiders down your wrist. You cannot rid yourself of it. You smash the map with repeated blows of your fist and leave it crumpled on the seat beside you.

The windows of your rental car have steamed up. Your forehead against the steering wheel, you give yourself a moment to relax, to return your breathing to normal, then set out again.

You obtain directions from farmers and postal workers. Everyone you encounter is just as polite as you'd heard they would be. Even though you're lost, you cannot deny that it is slightly thrilling, speaking English to people in England.

The sign BONE ASH WORKS appears, along with a picture of a small truck. Then there is a sign for a nature reserve, followed by a smaller wooden sign that points to a gap in the hedgerow: DITCHLING.

You hesitate on the road, your signal flashing. The gap is barely wide enough for your car. Slowly you turn into the narrow lane under an archway of trees. The sun, for a moment, disappears. The road sinks further, and further still, and the horizon falls away as you plunge down into the darkness before emerging into the sunlight again. There is a stone war memorial. Behind this memorial stands the village – the church with its conical spire, the High Street bordered by flint walls, the Tudor houses and shops below. The surrounding hills are misty and green and dotted with sheep. There is a windmill, a beacon.

You drive slowly past the war memorial. The cobblestones under your tires have been pounded smooth by centuries of rain. You drive tentatively, shoulders hunched over the steering wheel. A sign beside an empty pond says, DO NOT FEED THE DUCKS. The sign has a picture of a duck, and an outstretched human hand with a line drawn through it.

All the houses along the High Street have their curtains drawn. Iron railings protect their gardens. The shops under the Tudor houses seem to huddle together – a jeweler's, a greengrocer's, a post office, a café. The church oversees a sprawling and well-populated graveyard. At the end of the High Street, a pub called The Lantern occupies its own corner. The pub has a chimney, tar-blackened walls, a swinging sign of a glowing, handheld lantern. There are pots of flowers around the perimeter and small circular windows that look like portholes.

The road rises up to a Village Hall, then splits into even narrower lanes. You turn back around, over the cobblestones, searching for your B&B. Yours is the only moving vehicle on the road. A few pedestrians scurry into their homes or disappear along the footpaths between stone walls. Ditchling seems designed for ducking and whispering.

You park on the shoulder of the High Street near the jeweler's. When you step out of the car and close the door, the electronic beep of the alarm ricochets against the walls. Which direction does one walk? Your wet shoes slap against the 'pavement', no matter how carefully you tread. Up in one of the houses, a hand parts a curtain.

Near the church, you reach another sign:

DITCHLING MUSEUM:
CULTURE AND CAKE, ART & LOCAL
HISTORY
Winner of Heritage Lottery Fund!

The sign, in the shape of a hand, points to an opening in the flint wall. You escape onto a narrow footpath, and soon you are walking unobserved under a canopy of lime trees. Rows of headstones appear. Up to the left are the main grounds of the church, and this footpath to the museum apparently takes you through an overflow for the dead. The gravestones are orderly and legible. Some of them lean toward each other, as if conversing.

It's been a long journey. You wouldn't be blamed for skipping the museum for now and turning back, maybe going for a pint at the pub. But you've come all this way to make sense of your malaise. It isn't exactly the time to go into it. But these conspiratorial gravestones seem to be inviting you to go into it. If you don't press forward *now*, the gravestones seem to be saying, you'll find an excuse not to press forward in the future.

Under the dripping lime trees, you hesitate. At work – copy-editing print ads – you've started to slip. You haven't been formally reprimanded, but you've come close. Ordinary phrases have lost their meanings. Slogans like 'Eat Healthy' and 'Nature's First Fruit Bar' present you with endless hours of bewilderment. Maybe it's because you work in a cubicle decorated with a cheap calendar of safari animals, or maybe it's because your agency handles the last remaining print publications in existence. At home, reading novels, or books of poetry, you've caught yourself staring at a single word until the letters become hollow, drained of ink.

'Take some time off,' Dr Craft advised. She is an obese and persuasive psychologist with offices in Beverly Hills. 'Some people searching for meaning in their lives,' she said, gazing out the window at the palm trees in her courtyard, 'find it helpful to trace their ancestors. You know, to see how you're connected. This English grandfather of yours, for instance. Where's he from?'

'Sussex. A place called Ditchling.'

'Ditchling. Ditch-ling. What an interesting name. You might make a pilgrimage.'

The gravestones urge you to remember Dr Craft's advice. Objects have always communicated more clearly than humans. You continue under the lime trees until you reach the end of the footpath, where you come to a one-story wooden structure with a porch and front garden. At the door, birdbaths and ceramic flowerpots are overflowing with rainwater. A flyer is posted on the front window:

Winner, UK Heritage Lottery Fund!
Refurbishment pending council planning permission.

You wipe your feet on the doormat and go inside. The bell on the door jingles, and you enter a gift shop – books on local history, pictures of the South Downs, tea towels of Ditchling's church, mugs printed with images of the museum itself. There is a black-and-white antique print of chickens in an enclosure with the caption, **Ditchling Common**. The carousel of postcards creaks as you spin it around.

The woman behind the counter has short brown hair cropped like a monk's. She backs up slightly as you come toward her. This sometimes happens because of your height. As a teenager, you learned to limit any public discomfort by speaking softly and clearly, and generally keeping speech to a minimum.

'Hello. May I visit the museum?'

The woman replies, but she speaks softly, too, and you cannot be certain of her words. She blushes as you take out your wallet and offer her a ten-pound note. One of her eyes starts to twitch, and she covers it with a handkerchief.

'May I please buy a ticket for the museum?'

'We're only open,' she says, 'for another hour.'

'That's all right.' You put the note on the counter.

The woman picks up the money and gives you the change. In the course of this transaction her embarrassment infects you, and by the time you leave the counter, you are blushing as well.

You pass exhibits on flint and local types of chalk. Then it hits you – an overpowering smell of creosote and ink. An antique printing press stands in the corner with broadsheets curling under it. A wooden cabinet has open drawers of letters. Engraving tools hang from the ceiling like weapons – hammers, spikes, scalpels. Stone tablets and headstones lean against the wall.

You come to a darkened booth, where a man sits motion-less on the other side of the glass. The exhibit has a placard:

This man is Eric Gill (1882–1940), best known for his
typography and fonts that bear his name. Gill was an
engraver and sculptor who emphasised sensual qualities in
sacred art. In 1914, he helped to form the Guild of Saint
Joseph and Saint Dominic, a group of Catholic artisans
who modelled themselves after the arts and crafts guilds
of the Middle Ages. The Guild moved from Ditchling village
to the Common where they established artists' studios,
raised animals and worked in close relation to nature.
Each day they rose before dawn and devoted themselves
to holy work and prayer. Eric Gill is part of the museum's
interactive exhibit. Push the button and watch him work!

You push the button outside the booth. A light goes on over the man's head, and he starts to swivel on his stool. There are blocks of wood around him, bottles of ink, loose sheets of paper. He takes up a carpenter's tool and turns to his worktable. He's middle-aged, with a thick beard, round spectacles, and a four-cornered paper hat. He wears a roughly hewn tunic and belt, knee stockings, and rope sandals. Piano music comes out of the speaker, followed by a recorded male voice:

'*Watch me make a woodcut of this lovely woman with plaited hair.
I use boxwood because it grows very slowly, and the growth-lines are
near together, making the hard surface ideal for engraving. See how I
create the longest hairs with a continuous fine line, and the shorter hairs
with little flicks of the engraving tool? I thrive best when celebrating
the human form. When I am finished, I will dab the block with ink and
press a sheet of paper on top. I wear this monastic robe because I dislike*

modern clothes. On my head is a traditional stonemason's folded paper
hat, designed to keep chips and dust out of my own hair.'

At first Eric Gill has his back to you as he engraves. Then
he turns to face you, his mouth open in a smile. The model
is very lifelike. Though you know it's absurd, you cannot
help feeling that he is aware of you watching him. Each time
he picks up a different tool from his table, he glances at you
behind his spectacles with his probing, predatory eyes.

You leave the exhibit in something of a hurry. When
you turn around, Gill has returned to darkness behind the
glass. The next exhibit holds woodcarvings of nudes posing
seductively on letters, erotically adorning various forms of
typography. A book is opened to an illustration of couples,
men and women holding hands, walking in sequence over
a hilltop. In the sky are flocks of birds. Underneath the
drawing is an inscription in calligraphy:

DITCHLING IS RULED BY GOD'S BROTHERS AND SISTERS.

Also in the glass cabinet, there is a child's alphabet
reader. The raised O sails high above its fellow letters like
a moon. The T, with its gimlet shaft, warns you not to look
away. You've always been drawn to letters. It was probably
your mother's doing. 'Each word was once a poem,' she'd say.
'What if each letter was once a word?'

Thinking of this makes you dizzy. You are tempted to
retreat to the tearoom for a wedge of carrot cake. You could
sit quietly on a padded chair amidst the cups and saucers.
Then you see a letter at the bottom of the cabinet, written
by someone named Philip Hagreen. You squat to read it. The
handwriting runs level across the page like a row of bricks.

Dearest Hugh:
It is good news that you are carving bits of wood. Wood carving
requires devotion, and those who devote themselves to art
are worthy.

The opening lines read like a challenge. When have
you ever devoted yourself to anything? You've drawn some
sketches, tried a few poems – but would Hagreen consider
any of your attempts 'good news'?

Wood carving requires a few tools. For end grain work you will
probably find a rather fat spitsticker and perhaps a square
scorper or small chisel. You can get a fine finish with a scraper.
I enclose a double ended one.

How pleasant to find words like 'spitsticker' preserved
behind glass for children to smudge their fingers against.
You wonder where you might stumble upon a spitsticker.
You don't even know what one looks like.

I have no spare spitsticker or square scorper. W. Lawrence of
1 West Harding Street, Fetter Lane is the man to get them from.
All I can find in the way of fine wood to experiment with are
the enclosed pieces of pear, hawthorn, and hornbeam.

Hornbeam. The name of this wood deserves its own
poem, if one hasn't already been written. You wonder what
it would be like to carve something from pear. You picture
the author hunched over his woodcut with his scorper, listening to the radio. Someone's cellphone rings.

'Hello? Let's meet at The Lantern, yeah?'

You peer over the partition to the next exhibit. A man
has a phone to his ear, practically shouting.

'The Lantern! Yeah. The pub's called The Lantern,' the man says, a little louder. 'I'll be there in an hour, mate. Yeah. I'm at the museum where we're doing the rebuild. Killing time.'

Killing time – you've always hated that expression. You return to your own exhibit, back to the letter. It hurts to squat, so you sit on the ground on the damp flagstones.

Ill health does not permit me to visit Ditchling village of late. Meanwhile the enclosed scorper should keep you busy with useful labour.

Yours faithfully,
Philip Hagreen

PS I think it is a good thing, as well as a convenience, to carve with as few tools as possible. This limitation will provide unity.

What if you had been raised here, taught by the likes of Eric Gill and Philip Hagreen? Why did your grandfather ever leave Ditchling in the first place, only to die on his way to California, when your father was just a boy? If he hadn't left England, he might have guided your hand toward a spitsticker. The two of you would have reclined in twin armchairs beside the fire, legs crossed, scorping hornbeam.

A voice announces five minutes until closing. You are reading the letter a second time when the woman from the gift shop appears. She hovers over you on the flagstones. Her expression has become slightly bolder – rather than looking away, she stares. Confectioner's sugar trails down her chin.

'Time to go, sir. The museum's closing now.'

The lights flicker over her head. For a moment you are

disoriented, but you scramble to your feet and follow her, past the illustrations and woodcarvings, and Eric Gill in his glass booth. Darkness has come – you can see it creeping toward the museum door. The day ended while you were distracted, while you had your back turned. Even Leather Jacket with the cellphone has headed to the pub. The dead artists of Ditchling wait out in the churchyard, in their communal underground guild.

At the door you hang back, feigning interest in the carousel of postcards. 'We have a website,' the woman says, jangling her keys. 'Visit our museum online.'

Now you must turn your face away, so that she cannot see your tongue, involuntarily working its way to the back of your mouth. It's these detestable words: 'website' and 'online'. Back in your cubicle, in front of your computer, you will only be able to return to Ditchling for remote 'online visits', squinting at exhibits electronically represented, pixilated, divorced from their mediums.

The woman opens the door and guides you outside. You linger on the porch, and the two of you look down at the birdbath spilling over with rainwater. 'You staying in Ditchling?' she asks.

'Yes.' The sky has cleared. You are grateful for this brief conversation.

'We don't often get visitors from America.'

'I'm tracing my ancestors, actually. The museum's going to be rebuilt?'

'We've been given money to expand. Closed from next week, for almost six months.'

'I'm just in time, then. I wonder – can you tell me where the B&B is?'

'You'll be staying with Bobby and Sheila Swift?'

'Yes.'

'Take the lane back and turn left on the High Street. Just a few houses down on your right.'

'Thank you.'

'You might visit the churchyard tomorrow. Some of our memorials are pieces of art in themselves. I'll leave the light on so you can see your way.' She closes the door behind you and turns the key in the lock. The museum at your back, the headstones and lime trees await.

The church bells ring five o'clock. This is the kind of rush hour you could get used to – no traffic lights, no horns, only the occasional passing car. The Ditchlings walk silently past. Their shoes barely scuff the pavement.

Beside them you drift along, light-headed, excited, sleep-deprived. The villagers bump softly against your sides like fish. Up close, they are even smaller, these Ditchlings. You tower above them as you amble forward, taking care with your elbows and knees.

Inside Savage Greengrocer's, a balding man stands behind the counter in an apron. An elderly woman carefully lowers a head of lettuce into her netted bag. The post office on the corner is closing. A boy in school uniform stands at the counter, watching a man with plastic tongs remove nibs of licorice from a jar. On the wall outside the post office, a Community Notice Board has various flyers:

British Apples: A Talk by Mr Lawrence Savage
Ditchling Village Hall

DITCHLING ANGLING CLUB TO FORM
See Kevin Pollard, Bridge Lane

Chalk Walks with Malcolm Ketteridge-Wilson
Archaeology, Landscape and Exercise
Meet at The Lantern

The next shop along the High Street has a clothed female mannequin in the window and a revolving glass case of knick-knacks. The sign says, *ANIMALS IN DISTRESS.* Posters show emaciated dogs with mournful eyes and kittens peeking out of a cardboard box. Inside the shop, a woman stands behind the counter in jeans, a sleeveless top and red streaks in her hair. She smiles at you through the window.

The bell jingles as you open the door. A radio behind the counter is turned to the news. *'A precipitous decline in birdlife has alarmed residents in the southern counties. Ornithologists are advising the public to maintain diligent record-keeping and bird diaries to monitor the situation...'*

The shop smells of decaying books and musty clothes. More photos of abused animals hang on the walls. You sneak a glance at the woman's nametag as you pass the counter: *Rhiannon.* She smoothes her hands down the sides of her jeans as you walk by. Her staring so disconcerts you that you nearly run into a rack of women's dresses. At the bookshelf against the back wall, you scan the tattered paperbacks.

There are two other customers in the shop – a young boy and his mother, going through some shirts. 'How about this striped one?' the mother says.

'I don't know.'

'Suits you down to the ground, it does.'

The boy breaks away and runs to the counter. He reaches

14

for a stuffed animal by the till and knocks over the donation box. Rhiannon scoops up the spilled coins and starts
plunking them back in.

'Where's that money go?' the boy says, leaning over the
coins. 'The dogs on the pictures? The ones with no legs?'

'Yeah.'

'Why would anyone want a dog that can't walk properly?'

'It depends.'

'Where do you get all these clothes?'

'Where do you think?' Rhiannon says. 'People die, don't
they?'

'Yeah.'

'Okay. When they die, their clothes get donated.' She
stands the donation box back up and leans towards him.
'Sometimes little boys like you die, then other boys wind
up wearing your clothes.'

The boy squeezes his mouth into a small circle. His
mother glares at Rhiannon, snatches her son's hand, and
takes him outside.

You wander over to a rack of men's jackets, blazers, and
plaid coats.

'Not sure you'll find anything in your size,' Rhiannon
says.

'I'm just browsing.'

She shifts toward you. 'You an American?'

'That's right.'

'Lucky. I once asked a Canadian if he was American, and
he didn't like it one bit.'

You study her from the paperbacks. Without knowing
what to say, you open your wallet and stick a five-pound
note into the donation box on your way out.

Outside, you can smell the warm pastries from Sprinkles Café. Through the window you can see the cakes and pies and sausage rolls. There are tables of people inside.

Everyone stares as you open the door. They stare, and keep staring. You pretend to be interested in the water-colors for sale on the walls. The pictures are of the South Downs, the Ditchling Beacon, and fields of sheep. In the foregrounds, figures sit on folding chairs, or on the grass, eating sandwiches and drinking tea.

As you remain at the counter, people resume their con-versations. There is a faint clink of teaspoons and forks on china. Some of the Ditchlings sit around tables, while others are propped against the wall, directly under the paintings. They breathe without seeming to move. These real Ditchlings have sneakily mingled in with the painted Ditchlings, incorporated themselves into the canvas. They have adopted the studied poses of the figures in the paint-ings, as if advertising their suitability for English art.

You continue to wait at the counter, but nobody seems to be working at the café, and none of the patrons offers any guidance. You suffer their glances and outright stares. Soon you retreat, back outside, without your sausage roll.

The Lantern stands in the near distance. The curved walls resemble the hull of a ship. Smoke rises from the chimney, and as you wait in the cold you convince yourself that this pub might be an inviting place. Maybe you can meet someone – a visitor as lonely as you are, a local who might share a pint and conversation beside the fire. You dart around the people-fish on the pavement. You cross the road, straighten your shirt collar, comb your hair with your fingers.

A thin strip of wood above the doorway announces,

PAUL TANNER, LICENSED PUBLICAN. The door is made of heavy oak. Pushing it open takes two hands. Inside, there is a smell of burning wood. Your eyes adjust to deeper levels of darkness. Bookcases line the walls. Two empty armchairs wait beside the fire. The ceiling is crossed with dark wooden beams.

Your footsteps thunder across the carpet as you approach the bar. The tables are unoccupied except for a young girl sitting alone, her back to the hissing radiator. She wears a school uniform and sips a fizzy drink from a straw. A half-eaten chocolate bar, still in its wrapper, sits on the table in front of her hands: *Chocolate Nut Feast*.

Three men on stools have their backs to you. They sit hunched forward at the bar, shoulders around their ears, pencils pointed at crossword puzzles.

'Good afternoon.'

In unison, the men turn. They might nod, but then again they might not. Before long they return to their crosswords.

The silence intensifies. You wait for the barman to return from wherever he is. You are thirstier than you thought, and you long for a pint and packet of 'crisps'. The intermittent scribble of pencils on crossword puzzles becomes a special kind of torture, and you stifle an urge to scream.

As you stand there, you wonder if a barstool carries greater social value than a tourist. Maybe you'd be ignored even if you were raised here. The British, after all, are noted for their cultivation of privacy – and this privacy evidently extends to pubs. Did your grandfather leave because the country is dysfunctional? Or is the dysfunction simply being British, a kind of virus that has wormed its way into your own constitution?

You pull nervously at your fingers. These men might be your distant cousins. Strange inner voices enter your head and propagate – the voices of your childhood, from all the books set in England, about England, by English writers – the A.A. Milne stories and Byron poems and Shakespeare plays and D.H. Lawrence novels. The voices become so deafening that you cannot silence them. On a nearby wall, a framed black-and-white photo shows The Lantern from your exact vantage point. The photo is of the bar, where three men drink on stools. The date on the bottom says 19 November, 1920. In the photo, there is a framed picture on the wall – possibly of The Lantern, at an earlier date – but the details are too grainy to make out.

You turn and catch the schoolgirl staring. Her cheeks flush to the roots of her blonde hair. 'Hello there,' you say.

Slowly she lowers her drink, and the condensation drips down the sides of the glass. *Go home*, the melting ice tells you – *go back to America while you can.*

The girl stands. She has a triangular nose and enormous blue eyes. She leaves her drink and Chocolate Nut Feast on the table, and she runs behind the bar. Soon, you hear footsteps upstairs.

The ice inside her glass continues to melt. *Get back to Los Angeles*, the ice says, *inside your cubicle with your calendar of safari animals thumbtacked to the gray partition, and keep copyediting magazine advertisements.*

You want to explain to the ice what happened, a few weeks back. You'd just finished editing a series of spots for a clothing company, and you'd earned a short break. This is how you spent it: there was dust inside your in-tray, coating the sides of the black plastic where the papers never touched. You ran your index finger along this plastic until a clump collected, and you held it up to the fluorescent light. Growing up, where did it say that your love of literature would bring you to *this*? An hour later, you still hadn't moved your index finger. Some of your co-workers had gathered at the edge of your cubicle, and they were whispering.

You want to tell the ice the rest of the story, but you hear boots on the stairs. A man enters the back of the bar with a hammer in one hand and a rag in the other. He has the same triangular nose as the girl's, except larger. It looks like someone's placed a Dorito in the middle of his face.

'Sorry,' the barman says. 'Just fixing the toilet.'

'You're Paul Tanner?'

'That's me.'

With his help, you identify the strongest beer. No crossword men glance in your direction, though you suspect they've all been listening.

You take your pint to the fire. The beer is good. It tastes like a field of wildflowers. The wings of the chair enclose you, the cushions thick and soft. It was only last week that you took the elevator to the eighteenth floor of a parking garage, leaned over the concrete barrier, and imagined yourself a smudge on the sidewalk below.

Sip your pint. Try to relax. Peruse the books in the case beside your chair: volumes on sculpture, weaving, letter design. One of the titles makes you jolt forward: *Scorper: A Brief Account of My Apprenticeship with Eric Gill*. The author's name is John Cull, the same as your own.

2

The narrow, three-story building has a fresh coat of white paint. A front window looks onto the High Street, curtains open, revealing a table set for breakfast. You climb the steps between double black handrails. Beside the door, a B&B operator's certificate sits over a brass nameplate:

BOBBY AND SHEILA SWIFT, PROPRIETORS

The door opens right after you knock. A woman in a cardigan stands before you – middle-aged, with hair colored a shade of yellow.

'Sheila?'

'Yes.'

'I'm John Cull.' There is a long silence. You wonder if you might have misspoken. 'I have a reservation...'

She opens the door and steps out of the way as you make your way inside. 'Goodness me,' she says, brightening. 'John Cull, is it? From California?'

'That's right.'

'You've made it. Please – come inside.'

You duck under the doorway, and she giggles a little at your height. You want to tell her how you shot up too quickly in adolescence, with no understanding of what to do with your obscene lankiness – a condition that remains the case to this day.

In the hall there's a coat stand, a table and telephone, a sign-in book. There are some Eric Gill postcards from an exhibition at the Victoria and Albert Museum – nude sculptures, drawings of couples copulating, elaborate letters composed of intertwined snakes. Sheila takes your key from a row of hooks.

'That's Bobby in the lounge there,' she says pointing through an open door.

Inside the next room, there is a smell of fried bacon. On a low brown sofa, a man watches television. He is nearly bald, and his small mouth hangs open as if waiting to be fed. He has his hands on his knees, and the colors from the TV have made his face a strange shade of blue.

Sheila opens the heavy door to the dining room and holds it ajar for you to peer in. The only set table is by the window. 'Here's where you'll have breakfast. Eight o'clock. Do you have any dietary restrictions?'

'No.'

'You'll be wanting a full English, then? Eggs and bacon? Sausage? Fried tomato and mushrooms?'

'I think so,' you say, unprepared to discuss breakfast.

Sheila sneaks a hand under her cardigan, feels for her bra strap and gives it a tug. 'He's on the full English,' she calls through the door of the 'lounge'. Bobby nods without looking up from the TV.

'I'll show you to your room, luv.'

She trudges up the carpeted stairs. One of her stockings has fallen down her ankles, and you resist the urge to pull it up. You hold your bag in front of your waist as you climb, elbows tucked at your sides to avoid knocking the picture frames on the walls.

Your room is on the top floor. Sheila unlocks the door and switches on the light, taps the wheezing radiator. The climb seems to have rejuvenated her. She stands at the door, breasts heaving in her cardigan, looking you up and down like a mother.

'Can't be much in that bag of yours.'

'I travel light.'

'We get the odd rambler in the summer when the weather's nice. Otherwise you'll be quite alone with us. The village hasn't much to offer, I'm afraid.'

'That's all right.'

'You sure you're staying two whole weeks?'

'Yes.'

Sheila smiles at you, as if you're joking.

'My grandfather was from Ditchling, you see.'

'Are you a churchgoer?'

The question takes you by surprise. You haven't been to church in years. 'Sure I am.'

She holds out the room key. 'Services are half nine, Sundays. Join us.'

'Half nine, you say?'

'Sound early?' She passes her eyes over you suspiciously. 'It's not often you meet churchgoers these days.'

'I know. A difficult time for people of faith...'

'Anything you need, be sure to let me know.' Sheila places the key in your palm, closes the door behind her and clumps downstairs.

You lock the door and look around. There is something familiar about this room, with its single bed and checked quilt, its wooden chair pushed under the tiny desk against the wall. It reminds you of your childhood, and the nights you spent upstairs in your room, reading with the door closed as your parents watched TV downstairs. You pace the room, running your fingers along the flower print wallpaper. The Victorian crown molding, the yellowing lace curtains – at long last, you've made it into a real English home. It doesn't matter that you're paying for the experience. You can pretend you've been adopted.

On your dresser, a small kettle sits on a tray. The ceramic bowl holds individual tubs of milk. Another bowl holds sugar packets and tea bags, a stack of paper napkins. There are two porcelain cups. One of them has a slight chip – in another life it might have been you who caused this, back when you were a boy. You were too hasty, weren't you, shoving the cups in Mummy's cabinet during the washing up? You must learn to be less clumsy, John.

The curtains run across an elastic line above the window. The curtains are yours to part wide, or to draw as tightly as you wish. That's it, go and see what's happening outside your home. Shift the outer curtain and stick your nose through the thin white net, the inner membrane. Peer down at the High Street in the dark.

It's three in the afternoon when you get up. The jet lag and the drive must have done it – you've slept past breakfast.

In the bathroom you crouch naked in the quaint but cramped shower stall. Hunched over, with your ear pressed to the soap tray, you point the hand-held sprayer over your head and wait for the dribble of water. By the time you've managed to clean yourself, have a cup of tea, and get dressed, it's almost four o'clock.

A brochure with a picture of a young boy petting a lamb leans against your tea tray:

> The village of Ditchling has much to offer: ancient buildings of charm and note, museum, country park, specialist shops, pub and tearooms. It was the Saxon Dicul and his folk who gave their name to the village and it is possible that the burial mound on Lodge Hill was Dicul's own. Saxon looks and Saxon ways stamped the village for centuries to come.

Tearooms, shops, a country park? A Saxon burial mound? You hurry downstairs to explore. The TV is on in the lounge. The door is open, and you stick your head inside. Sheila and Bobby sit side by side on the little sofa, a tea tray on the table in front of them.

'Sleep all right?' Sheila asks.

'Yes, thanks.'

'We thought you might have perished.' Her hands in the pockets of her cardigan, she glances in your direction and looks back at the TV. It's a chat show – the host, with his toothy malicious smile, prowls the stage with his mike, lecturing his guests on parenting skills.

'I must have been more tired than I thought. After the flight—'

'You missed breakfast,' Sheila says.

'I'm sorry.'

'Bobby had to eat it. You're going to give him indigestion if you keep missing meals.'

Bobby sits motionless on the sofa. He does have something of a gut, but you can imagine the discomfort an extra breakfast might cause. 'I won't let it happen again.'

'You going out now?' Sheila asks.

'Yes. Researching Ditchling's Saxon heritage.'

'Have a good day,' Bobby says, without looking up. He laughs at the screen. 'That's what everyone says to each other in America, isn't it – have a good day!'

Sheila laughs, too. 'Here comes the paternity test,' she says. On TV, the host is holding up a sealed envelope.

You hurry outside, down onto the High Street. It's overcast and nearly dark, but at least it's not raining. Your rental car is still parked across the road in front of the jeweler's and the bank. To the left is Savage Greengrocer's, then the post office, Animals in Distress, Sprinkles Café, and the pub. Also to the left, across the road, are the gravestones and church.

Straight ahead, there is a footpath between the jeweler's and the bank. It looks like it might lead to Lodge Hill, where the Saxon king Dicul is supposedly buried. Maybe you can get your bearings in the last of the sunlight and walk along the grass.

The path cuts between houses. The first front garden just has chickens, but in the next garden, a group of boys are playing soccer, using overturned flowerpots for goalposts.

'Excuse me.'

The boys stop playing and turn toward the fence. There are six of them – young lads with windblown faces, wearing school uniforms with ties.

'Sorry to bother you – is this the way to Lodge Hill?'

The boys continue to stare silently across the fence.

'I'm looking for the Saxon Dicul's burial mound?'

It's your accent, undoubtedly. They stare as if you're from another planet. Finally one of them kicks the ball through the flowerpots and watches it roll to the far fence. 'Dick Dicul,' he says, and laughs. 'Dick Dicul in Ditchling.'

'A stranger threatens our bloodline,' a boy says, staring at you.

'Whoever buries his hand rules the rest,' another boy says, and he laughs. The rest join in – and as this laughter rises, your mind goes blank and your ears ring, and the next thing you know you are running fast. You pass laundry drying on clotheslines, cats perched on walls.

The lane comes to a clearing. A trail winds up a hill, past a couple of overturned trees and a murky pond. You climb a wooden turnstile, squelch your way over the muddy grass, and scramble to the top of the hill. The whole walk takes about ten minutes. Dicul's mound is a small promontory, suspiciously round, perhaps purpose-built for his burial. Crows peck at the patches of muddy grass. Sheep nibble their way across the nearby grazing lands. Here you are with the animals, still panting a little, your back to the blowing wind.

Farmlands stretch in the distance, and what looks like the Bone Ash Works. Chimneys rise from a cluster of factory buildings behind a barbed-wire fence – animal bones crushed for glue and ceramics. When you turn in the other direction, facing the wind, the tidy village lies beneath you – the church with its conical spire, the rabbit warren of narrow lanes and shops, the chimney-topped Tudor houses and Village Hall.

This bird's eye perspective reveals the central question: What in the world are you doing here, on top of a hill?

This trip to England may be futile. Because your father and mother, with their cloying Anglophilia, have already claimed the family's monopoly on all things British, without ever bothering to visit the island itself. Their obsessive affection for the English language meant you were given dictionaries and word-finder games, not to mention books on colloquialisms, euphemisms, and word origins for birth-day presents. With their unapologetically antiquated views of 'heritage', your parents made it impossible for you to dis-cover anything for yourself about England. In Los Angeles, a city that defines itself by reinvention, you grew up under the influence of the Old World, so that your desire to visit the motherland was always simultaneously encouraged and discouraged – encouraged because it was England, of course, and the fount of goodness – but discouraged because of the inherent dangers of dispelling your parents' myths and revealing your origins to be more prosaic than desirable. In visiting your 'ancestral seat', you have placed yourself at considerable psychological risk.

Yet there is no need to panic. You are not here for your parents' welfare, you are here to gain a better understanding of yourself. You have come to a place you've never been to before because a psychologist has suggested it. The boys playing soccer will never know this feeling of rootlessness. They won't think twice about their origins. They'll call their sport football, and all their lives they will mock the Ameri-cans who call it soccer. They were laughing at you just now – and until they die they will laugh at Americans while learning to be increasingly subtle in their ridicule.

They can laugh all they want. You'll show them. That's it, jump up and down on the burial mound – prove to Dicul who's boss. He's not the only one who'll make the brochure. That's it, jump. He's dead, you're alive. Jump up and down, right on top of his remains.

At a certain point a man has to stop dilly-dallying. He has to stop wasting time, to take himself by the hand and get to work. If a man wants to make a mark, he can't just let villages like this exist, day in, day out, sleepily carrying on as if they had all the time in the world to decay. It's a little village, but you're a big tall American, and you can see things as they are from these commanding heights. Keep jumping. Stamp your feet. Men like Dicul, men like you – they enter the fray, make people remember.

All that jumping makes you stumble. Flesh and bone. Trip, tumble to the grass. Don't mind the sheep as they turn their heads.

While on the ground you find your composure. Gather yourself for the journey down the trail. Bend forward, place your hands over Dicul's bones, gather up the Saxon's strength.

Inside The Lantern, the crossword men are on their stools. The little girl sits at her table against the radiator, only now she's got a spaniel with her.

You walk to the bar. Paul Tanner gives you a nod of recognition. The girl and her dog watch you take a pint to your armchair beside the fire. *Scorper* waits for you on the bookshelf. Take it down, open it up.

> My name is John Cull. I am a scorper and a scrappy man at that if anyone seeks the truth of it. For two years, I worked as an apprentice to the famous engraver Eric Gill. What, you may ask, is a scorper?
>
> Scorper (Oxford English Dictionary): A gouging tool for working in a depression, as in hollowing bowls,

butter-ladles, etc. Also used in removing wood or metal from depressed portions of carvings or chasings after outlining or engraving, so as to leave only the drawing in full relief.

You lower the book and peer around. He would have come here, your grandfather, to drink his ale and wipe his mouth. From your back pocket, you remove the printout of your genealogy research. There he is, right on the family tree. Born in Hassocks and married in Ditchling. Moved to America, dead at twenty-nine.

> The style or character of the work shall be greatly influenced by the shape of the point used. It is desirable that the belly part of the scorper be sufficiently rounded.

The roundness of your own belly serves as confirmation. Yes, you are decidedly of scorper stock. Like your grandfather, you dwell in the depressions of letters. *Amend this page,* your supervisor tells you, *tighten that margin.* Each day you peer at the white, scrape at the edges, bring the ad into full relief.

> The modern engraver selects the kind of tool which best expresses his artistic individuality. Once a tool is made up, and found to be good, to alter it is not desirable.

Artistic individuality – close your eyes, imagine the possibilities. Whisper it. 'I want to be more than a scorper.'

The words drop out of your mouth and into the fire. When you open your eyes, a man has joined you in the opposite armchair. He is older than you – late fifties, beard gray, fingernails yellowed. His unwashed hair clings to his ears. He looks like he might be a drunk.

'I see you've discovered one of the village books,' he says, winking. Despite his appearance, he speaks coherently. He wears corduroys and crosses his legs like a gentleman.

You sit up straight and smile – it is pleasant, after all, to have someone to chat with. 'I didn't hear you sit down.'

'I hope I'm not interrupting.'

'Not at all.' You glance at the bar, where the crossword men hunch grumpily on their stools, backs turned. 'I was just reading about wood engraving,' you add, hoping to maintain the conversation.

'Oh?'

'Yes. I'm thinking of taking it up myself.'

'We don't get too many Americans in Ditchling. You *are* American, aren't you?'

'Yes.'

'Not Canadian?'

'No.'

'We had a Canadian in Ditchling a few years back. He took offense—'

'I'm American.'

'How long are you staying?'

'A couple of weeks.'

The man laughs. 'You're going to try and take up wood engraving – in a couple of weeks?' He laughs so vigorously, his face turns red. 'Where are you from in America?'

'Los Angeles.'

He lurches forward. 'My favorite program is *Friends*. That and *Law and Order*. And *CSI: Miami*.'

'I don't watch television.'

'But you've got Hollywood right there!'

'There are over ten million people in Los Angeles. Not everyone is immersed in the television industry. Not everyone drives around in convertibles.'

'All right, mate. All right. No need to get defensive.'

'It's a common misconception, that's all.'

'*You're* not common, then. You don't watch telly.'

'Not if I can help it.'

'What – too good for it?'

You are not going to participate in this country's unfortunate obsession with class. The conversation has annoyed you, and you turn back to your grandfather's book. You've almost started reading when the man belches. When you look up, he grins.

'I've lived in Ditchling all my life,' he says, tapping his empty pint glass. 'The stories I could tell!'

You want company, the man can sense it. After a moment you place your book on the side table and return to the bar, where you order a couple of ales.

Paul Tanner has changed into a clean shirt. His Dorito nose polished into a shinier triangle, he leans toward you with his elbow on the beer mat. 'Two?'

'Yes, please.'

He stares at you. 'You on a binge, mate? We don't allow any of that in here.'

'A binge – not at all. One pint for me, and one for my friend.'

The barman angles his head, like a dog hearing a strange noise. 'What friend?'

You turn around. 'Him,' you say, pointing at the man by the fire.

Paul nods slowly. 'You're the American researching his ancestors.'

'How did you know?'

'It's a small village,' he says, pulling the pints. 'I'll give you a small piece of advice. Don't put your hand in where it don't belong. The past is the past.'

'Sure it is.'

'Don't let any of that Eric Gill nonsense over there get you in trouble.'

'A fine man,' one of the crossword men says.

'Not in my book,' another crossword man says.

'Ditchling wouldn't be much without him,' the third one adds. 'A good friend to many an aspiring artist.'

While they continue to debate the matter, you take the pints to the fire. Eric Gill of Ditchling – is it possible your new friend is a descendant of the famous sculptor and engraver? What would it be like to have this man as your guide and cultural attaché – a man with whom you might enjoy the occasional pint – witty, modest, dry, in short, a man with deep historical ties to Sussex, and the kinds of artistic connections to help shape your entré into the social fabric of Ditchling?

You hand the man his pint, and he starts drinking before you've had a chance to sit down.

'Mr Gill? The barman mentioned your name...'

He narrows his eyes, the beer wet on his lips. 'You haven't given me your name, Mister CSI.'

'You first.'

'All right. My name *is* Eric Gill. I was christened after my grandfather.'

'My goodness.'

'Or so I'm told,' Eric says, waving his hand absently. 'I don't think my mother knew for certain. Her mother supposedly had an affair with Gill – but then he had plenty of lovers, I'm afraid.'

'Did you ever meet him?'

'He passed away before I was born.'

'Same as my grandfather.'

Eric doesn't appear to have heard you. He takes *Scorper* from the side table and opens it up. 'Look at these old tools.' He stabs his dirty finger at the illustrations. 'The ink roller. The slab. The oilstone for sharpening the gravers. Lovely old things.'

'Everything's digitized these days. Printing presses are finished.'

'I doubt that.'

'I'm a copyeditor. I know what I'm talking about.'

'Maybe in Californ-I-A. Here, people care about the printed word.'

Behind the bar, there's a commotion. The schoolgirl is chasing her spaniel around. The dog runs under her arms and beneath the tables, eventually finding its way to your armchair where it buries its snout in your crotch.

One of the crossword men speaks without turning around. 'Someone should teach that bitch not to be so forward.'

The girl appears beside your chair. 'She's only saying hello.'

'A dog keeps a man company,' the second crossword man says.

'I prefer cats myself,' the third one adds.

You pet the dog a little and try to scoot her away. She leans hard into the inside of your leg.

'You promised me your name,' Eric says.

'Same as the author of that book in your hand. That's my grandfather.'

Eric brings the cover closer and twitches his nose. 'John Cull? Never heard of him. But then my grandfather had plenty of apprentices.'

Very carefully, you reach into your pocket and retrieve the printout of your family tree. 'See – John Cull, born 22 May 1904, in Hassocks and married in Ditchling, Sussex. Our grandfathers knew each other!'

Eric shrugs. 'That's just names printed on cheap A4 stationery.'

'It's been validated.'

'By whom? Lots of people claim associations with the master.'

'What about you? You said you didn't know if Gill *was* your grandfather. Mine's right here in black and white.'

'Don't believe everything you read.' But you can tell by the way Eric looks at the printed names that he's jealous of your evidence. 'I doubt anyone's heard of John Cull,' he says.

'I wouldn't be so sure. His book was shelved in a prominent location.'

The spaniel's snout delves deeper into your crotch. You try to scoot her away. 'She's only saying hello,' the girl says again.

Eric Gill opens *Scorper* and pokes at the tools. '*I've* got some of these old things. Left me by mum. I don't live far – I could show you if you like.'

'When?'

'Anytime you'd like.'

Is it really true – your first invitation to an Englishman's home? You try to disguise your excitement by casually checking your watch. 'It's getting kind of late.'

'Maybe for some.'

'I should order dinner before the kitchen closes.'

'Why didn't you say so?' Eric clasps his hands. 'Come over to our house for tea. My wife's making something special.'

'Really? But – I wouldn't want to impose.'

'Nonsense. Not every day I meet an American.'

'Not every day I meet an Englishman!'

In your enthusiasm, you leap to your feet. The dog growls, and as you back slowly toward the door, you realize everyone in the pub is staring.

You are lucky to be walking side by side with Eric Gill. Ditchling has turned dark. At the top of the High Street the pavement ends, and you take the left fork along a one-lane country road. A car slows, gives you a wide berth when it passes, and the taillights disappear around the bend.

'You're sure it's okay that I'm coming for dinner? I'd hate to disturb you and your wife.'

'No trouble,' Eric says. 'Not far from here.' He's started to veer from the drinking. He slips into some weeds, regains his footing.

'Do you mind if I ask what sort of work you do?'

'Oh, art of various kinds. Pottery, woodwork, sculpture. I've given some poetry readings.'

'Any success?'

'Audiences generally agree I have a way with words. No money in it, of course, but then the best literature never does, does it? For a while I worked as a bus driver.'

'I looked for a bus to Ditchling.'

'They discontinued the service for lack of passengers,' Eric says. 'Suits *me* fine to be made redundant – it's the wife who minds.' An 'off-licence' appears in the distance under a dim yellow light. 'Now we'll just pop in here.'

You follow Eric inside. A man sits behind the counter watching football on a laptop. Eric grabs a four-pack of beer, two bottles of wine, a bottle of gin. 'I wonder,' he says, slinking over. 'Would you mind pitching in a few pounds? The wife would be so grateful for a drink. After cooking all day …'

You reach for your wallet. Somehow, you end up paying for everything.

Outside, you walk abreast of Eric again. In the nearby fields, the shadows of cows huddle together in the drizzle. The dark outline of the South Downs looms against the horizon.

'My grandfather came here to get away from London,' Eric says, opening one of the beers. He drinks from the can while he walks, and now and then he passes it to you to share. 'He wanted to work among the artists here in Ditchling – the painters and weavers, the potters and jewelers and calligraphers.'

'Why did they come *here*?'

'Some say it was the mist. Others put it down to the sheep and the farmsteads. He used to visit the South Downs as a child on family holidays. He wanted to live in the countryside with his animals, set up his studios, work on his wood engravings and sculptures. He could pick raspberries and mushrooms and plums!'

'I like the sound of that.'

'It was only later that he attracted disciples. The young

poets and woodcarvers, the young letter-cutter apprentices like your grandfather, who came to sit at his dinner table and learn. Hey. What we should do if you're interested, Eric says, glancing over his shoulder, 'is make our own book.'

'Really?'

'Really. We could use those tools in my barn. After dinner you can dust them off and see how they work. I could write the text, draw the illustrations, and you...well, you could do the editing. Here, hold this a sec.'

Eric hands you the bag of alcohol. He leaves the road, climbs a stile, and trudges into a field.

The drizzle has turned to rain, and you hurry to catch up. You must keep him close so you don't get lost in this dark field that seems entirely composed of mud. The two of you slop along until suddenly the shadows give way. A barn appears in a clearing. It stands on a piece of level ground, under a tree, with brick walls and a tile roof.

'That's your home?'

'I was born right in there. Lived here all my life.' He elbows your ribs. 'You're going to love it!'

'Hold on.' You clutch Eric's arm. 'I'd really like to collaborate on this book. But – do you think I can do some of the actual writing of it? Maybe help out with an illustration here and there?'

'I thought you said you were an editor.'

Surely he'll understand. If you don't speak up, you'll always be a scorper. 'You said your grandfather was a friend to aspiring artists.'

'Yes.'

'Well, maybe I'd like to try to do something other than editing.'

'Let's talk about it later,' Eric says. He hands you what's left of his beer and starts off again.

You polish off the beer and run after him, bottles clinking. Eric reaches the barn and stops. A sliding door runs on wheels along a track. As he slides it open, a burst of cold air blows out.

'Now let's sit down to dinner. Welcome!'

You step over the threshold. Your eyes water in the blowing wind, and you try to find the light. Something illuminates the back portion of your brain, the brain from before you were born, before you were American or British or even human. You blink, time passes, and instead of a fire and a table of food, you find yourself alone in an abandoned barn.

'Eric?'

Your guide has gone. Half the roof has collapsed into a pile of broken tiles and the cement floor runs with mud. Shivering in your muddy khakis and soaked shoes, you are hungry for the dinner you were promised, a hunger that only aggravates a familiar and desperate confusion. You pace the empty building, searching for clues.

It's like before, in your cubicle at work, with the finger of dust and the fluorescent light. Moments pass – the moments of a man who has become lost to himself.

Clutching the bag of beer, wine and gin, you wander the empty ground. If you don't keep moving, you'll catch cold. Hurry, make it back to The Lantern before the kitchen closes. It's not the end of the world – a man can retrace his steps across a muddy field, climb a few stiles. When did it happen? Where did you make your fatal turn? The pub? Yes, it was by the fire, holding your grandfather's book.

On your way home, you make a mental note to avoid The

Lantern. The pub, with its beer and books and crossword men, can only mean trouble. But what is England without its pubs? As you near the village, you glare at the cows in the fields and curse your decision to leave the relative safety of Los Angeles.

You reach an off-licence. The dirty yellow light guides you inside. Behind the counter, a man is watching a football match on a laptop. He leans back in his chair as you approach. The dark pits of his eyes are watching you closely. He's got an electric heater aimed at his legs, and he's holding a mug of steaming coffee.

'What – back already? Tracking more mud across the floor?'

'I'm sorry?'

'You're not driving, I hope. You're in no shape for it.'

You place a twenty-pound note on the counter. You gather up your nerve. 'Tell me. Am I alone?'

'What are you on about?'

'You saw me, earlier tonight? Was I alone then?'

The man sits forward in his chair. It depresses you that this stranger, with his coalpit eyes, represents your only link to reality.

'Please – tell me.'

'You came in here an hour ago,' the man says, 'and went through this same routine. I can't take your money again.' He pushes the twenty back across the counter. 'Go home, mate. Sleep it off.'

3

Y ou wander the High Street in the dark, past a café, post office, and grocer's. All the shops are shuttered and silent. A small black car waits on the shoulder of the road. It looks familiar. Come closer, peer through the windshield.

It's your rental. Don't be alarmed at your reflection in the glass – the facts come clicking back, as if on a mechanical chain – you drove here from London, yesterday morning. The proof is right there on the dashboard, the rental contract with your name across the top. And there is your packet of airplane peanuts on the passenger seat.

Sit on the hood, slip off your shoes, knock out the mud. Stow the liquor in the trunk. The church bells ring and you count eight. If you have any sense left, you won't go to The Lantern.

Put your shoes back on, brush your hair with your fingers. Don't do it. Don't go – but before you can stop yourself, you are walking back up the road, toward the pub. You have to see it once more, even if you must act like a criminal returning to the scene of his crime. You must revisit the place Eric Gill appeared, the place where you took your fatal turn.

The pub is a primal thing, slumping in the shadows of the village. The faded sign of the glowing lantern swings in the wind. Do not go inside. Do not – but if you do, limit yourself to one pint, perhaps two, together with a hot meal.

You reach for the door when a light goes on, up on the second floor. A shape moves behind the curtain. The shape unnerves you and you hesitate. A moment later the girl steps outside. 'You left this on your chair,' she says, and she hands you *Scorper*.

'This is the pub's, isn't it?'

'But your grandfather wrote it. You said so.' She looks down at the ground, places one shoe over the other.

'I told you this...in the pub?'

'Of course!' She turns to go inside.

'Wait – I shouldn't go in there, not now. Tell me. Is there anywhere else to eat in Ditchling?'

She points down the High Street, over the rooftops. 'The pizza shop on Boddington's Lane.'

'The pizza shop?'

'Yes. A shop that sells pizza. It sometimes stays open late. Otherwise, you'll have to come back.'

When the girl has gone into the pub, you step inside the flowerbed. You make your way to the first round window embedded in the wall like a porthole, stand on your tiptoes, raise your nose to the glass.

The crossword men are in there, hunched on their stools. Behind them, the barman rolls a cigarette with his elbows on the beer mat. The girl has returned to her table by the radiator, the spaniel beside her. The armchairs by the fire are empty.

Did Eric Gill lead you to the fields and sneak away? The truth strikes you, the uncomfortable fact you've known all along and wanted to deny – he might not be a good friend for you after all. He clearly doesn't have your best interests in mind. Who leads a man to a field and abandons him?

Maybe Eric Gill was only being nice to you so he could take advantage of your services as an editor.

The barman licks shut his cigarette. He gestures with it as he speaks to the crossword men. You can almost hear him explaining how they turn up from time to time, these lonely Americans, obeying some ancient genetic code like salmon returning to their spawning grounds to die.

That American did look lonely, the first crossword man would reply.

Yes, the second one says, *lonely and lost*, and the third crossword man would conclude with finality, without even bothering to lift his head, *All Americans are lonely and lost – that's why some of them come to England in the first place.*

You turn your back on The Lantern. The rain has stopped and the fog has lifted. There is a new clarity to the evening, but the clarity only intensifies the darkness. The air smells like wet stone.

Some of the houses along the High Street have their upstairs lights on. Hidden eyes, behind the curtains, are watching you deliberate in the flowerbed. The curtain eyes wonder if you'll have your dinner in the pub or the 'pizza shop'.

You climb out of the flowerbed and walk down the High Street, searching for Boddington's Lane, and you find it after the B&B, a darkened passageway of cobblestones. As you plunge forward, the flint walls rise high above your head.

The further you walk, the more you suspect you'll never leave. A familiar feeling of tranquility comes over you, as it always does during the preludes to your epiphanies and most important awakenings. For too long, your job has been to imagine yourself a 'you' and only a 'you', constantly displacing, sublimating, projecting yourself into advertising taglines: *Your World, Your Way. Are You Ready for Great Taste? Be Your Own Financial Future.* Now you've arrived in the place you were meant to inhabit – a village that subsumes you into its architecture, absorbs you into the rain-pummeled soil.

The red letterboxes are built into the stone. The doors reach the height of your shoulders, and as you walk past them, voices seem to whisper up and down the lane. How can it be that people live on the other side of these walls? You have entered a human tunnel with no discernible exit.

Deeper and deeper he travels, beneath the grass, into the chalk pits.
Watch out – the American wants to eat!
Turn off the telly. Go to the curtain.

The lane turns, and a light appears in the distance. An Italian flag hangs over the lane. The restaurant has glazed windows and stenciled lettering: PIZZA.

The door stands open, so you go inside. The pizza shop is a dim cavern with low ceilings. A woman in jeans and a T-shirt is wiping down the tables. Your shadow falls over her, and she gasps as she turns around. She's young, with lively blue-gray eyes and brown hair curling around her shoulders. Her neck and arms are very pale, as if she's been kept captive.

'Sorry to startle you.'

'You didn't. I mean – you did, I suppose. It's all right.'

'Closing up?'

'I was. But come in if you'd like. Everything goes to waste otherwise.'

She's flustered. Her lips quiver a little when she talks.

43

She relights the candles on the tables, and the place slowly brightens. The walls are made of stone, the restaurant built inside what looks like a cave. In the kitchen, smoke rises into the copper apron of a chimney. Tourist posters of Italy hang crookedly in their aluminum frames.

'What would you like?' she asks, circling behind the counter. She ties her hair back into a ponytail.

The menu lists various types of pizza, nothing more. 'Pizza sounds good.'

'That's funny.'

'Which one is best?'

'I'll make you two of the house favorites.'

'Two?'

'You look hungry,' she says, without a trace of pity.

She takes your money. Her hands are small, rubbed raw, the nails bitten down to the quick. She withdraws into the kitchen behind the counter, and you can see the whole operation from where you stand. In a metal sink she washes up as the steam rises from the hot taps.

When she dries her hands, she catches you still lingering. You retreat to one of the tables, sit down, and open *Scorper*. Over the tops of the pages you watch her roll the dough, slather the sauce, shoot the toppings around like a card dealer. She slides the spatula under the pizzas and takes them to the oven. Then she brings over napkins and cutlery, a basket of bread and olive oil. Her neck has flushed pink.

'Wine?'

'Yes, please.'

There is no doubt about her beauty – yet *she* seems doubtful, or at least indifferent to it. She opens the cabinet against the wall and turns on a stereo. In her presence another man awakens inside of you – unafraid, ambitious, eager for conquest.

'Who knew there'd be pizza in Ditchling?'

'My husband's idea.'

The longing in your chest, the ache you feel just watching her, sinks into a hard pit in your stomach. Of course she would be married.

A rack of wine stands against the wall, and she takes down a bottle of red. With a paring knife, she unpeels the plastic from the neck with one movement of her wrist. You imagine this woman with her husband in Venice, making love in a private *terrazza* overlooking the canals, shaded to protect her pale skin. She puts down the knife and takes up the opener. 'He thought Ditchling needed a decent restaurant. That it would appeal to tourists.'

You wonder how many bottles she's opened like this for him. Maybe he's not very intelligent. What sort of person thinks a place like Ditchling would attract tourists? After ten minutes, you've become deeply jealous of a man you've never met. At the same time, the fact that you are still capable of strong emotions like jealousy makes you relieved, almost hopeful.

'Does your husband cook?'

'Not any more.' She twists the opener and pops out the cork. 'He's dead.'

Dead! The pit leaves your stomach. You feel it traveling back up, resurfacing as an ache in your chest again. Her calm delivery makes his death sound almost pleasant – as if her husband has his best years ahead of him, a man enjoying his retirement in a coffin.

'I'm sorry…I had no idea.'

She brings over your bottle and glass. Your words do not convey the requisite sympathy. They are just words people use. She sits at the next table and stares at one of the crooked posters on the wall. The smell of baking pizza fills the restaurant.

'Is your husband buried in Ditchling?'

Her expression makes you reach quickly for the bottle. You splash more wine in your glass and wish to God you could disappear. Instead, you cannot stop yourself from talking. 'I only ask because – well, I walked through the churchyard yesterday. It's a beautiful place. I have ancestors buried there, supposedly.'

Your voice echoes inside the cave. After a moment, she sighs softly. 'My husband was Italian. The funeral service was over there.'

'Right. What about you? I mean – will you be buried in Ditchling? Or do you want to be buried over there, with him?'

'I think I'll check on your pizza,' she says.

She goes into the kitchen. You finish your wine and pour another glass. You cannot help it – you need desperately to explain. 'I only ask,' you call after her, 'because your church-yard looks like a perfect place to be buried. We don't have churchyards like that in the States...'

She doesn't reply. She bangs around in the kitchen a while and teaches you, by her silence, how to be silent yourself. Finally she brings over your pizzas.

You haven't eaten since this morning, and you're starving. The pizzas are hot on your table. You can't decide which to eat first. One is made with white sauce and the other red. There are vegetables and rosemary on the white one and pepperoni and cheese on the red. The cheese is melting down the sides, and you dig into the red pizza without pause except to drink wine. You've almost polished it off when you look up and find her watching from the counter.

'How do you like it?' she says, laughing.

You make hand gestures that are intended to show your appreciation. She keeps laughing as you continue to eat. 'You must be the American everyone's talking about. The one researching his grandfather.'

You reach for a slice of the white. 'This really is a small village.' Someone from the museum must have mentioned it, or one of the crossword men. Maybe it was Eric Gill. The second pizza tastes even better than the first.

She sits at the table next to yours. She leans back and watches you eat, as if fascinated by an animal in a zoo. You wonder if this is normal behavior for British pizza shop proprietors. Sitting in her company you feel like a guinea pig, or a rabbit that has run into a cave occupied by humans and is permitted to stay. You wish you could be left here throughout the night, and into the small hours of the morning, so that when she opens up tomorrow she'll find you here, content with your wheel and scattering of straw, if only to be allowed the occasional glimpse of her face.

'Do you have a bathroom? Sorry – a loo?'

'Through the kitchen.'

You need time alone to think. She might actually be interested in getting to know you. 'Back in a minute,' you say, and you get up and duck around the counter, squeeze between the giant cans of tomato paste and spices and bags of flour.

A small door opens into a bathroom the size of a closet.

You run the water in the sink and check your eyelids for twitches. It stares back at you – your overlarge and lumpy head. Is it possible this woman actually *likes* you? Maybe you could quit your job, move permanently to Ditchling, help out behind the counter. The restaurant could be your sanctuary. With time she might look upon you as a savior, a consoler in her ever-decreasing grief. Meanwhile you could take art classes, write poems, eat pizza at night as a reward.

You open your mouth, peel back your lips, and run a finger across your teeth. You want to be impulsive, the brash American people expect. Maybe the pizza shop owner will scoot her chair closer, reach for the bottle of wine, and hesitate with her hand outstretched.

'Scorper,' she'll say, noticing your book. 'What's that?'

'A man who carves around the drawing on a woodcut. Or, the tool used for that purpose.'

She'll pick up the book and examine the cover. 'John Cull. What a wonderful name.'

'Thank you. I happen to share my name with the author.'

Late into the night, perhaps over a second bottle, you'll talk about Ditchling's golden years, the legacy of the artisanal guild and its masters of engravings and woodcuts. 'Grandpa Cull,' you'll suggest, 'was probably close friends with Eric Gill, along with all the other famous sculptors and poets.' She'll bring over the tiramisu she perfected during her first, slightly unfulfilling marriage. Sure, you've dabbled in art yourself, you'll confide, and you've always wanted an opportunity to devote yourself.

'Listen,' she'll say, leaning closer, 'your grandfather moved all the way to America, right? There's no reason why you can't move back.'

Splash cold water on your face. Turn off the tap and watch the water swirl down the drain. It's possible you've gotten ahead of yourself during this toilet break. It's as if there are two of you here at the sink – one with hope, and one without. The one without hope decides to make a deal with the other, to fix a deciding sign: you will return to your chair and keep absolutely quiet. If she speaks first, it will mean she likes you.

You leave the bathroom and head back through the kitchen, past a pack of cigarettes and a lighter on the counter. She's still sitting at the table next to yours. She looks even smaller and paler than before, hollowed inside the bowl of her chair, hands in her lap, fixated on the poster of Italy.

You sit down and reach for the last slice of the white pizza. It doesn't taste as good as it did before. It's cold. You chew the crust and you look at Venice. He was lucky, her Italian. You cannot feel sorry for him just because he's dead. He had his time with his English wife, his pale and lovely flower.

The pizza is hard to finish, but you do not want to offend her. When you've swallowed the last bite, she doesn't seem to notice. You start to second-guess the scenarios you imagined in the bathroom.

The silence stretches on. It acquires a kind of shape, a horrible and monstrous physicality in the pizza shop, jeering at you mutely from the ceiling. Sooner or later, she *has* to speak. At the very least, won't she have to ask you to leave?

You have stopped eating because there is nothing on your plate, not even any sizeable crumbs. You have finished almost all the wine. She continues to stare at the Italy poster – the Grand Canal of Venice. She may as well be there now, sharing a gondola with her dead husband, instead of sitting beside you in Ditchling.

Strategically, you settle your own gaze on a section of the wall that holds no posters of Italy, just stone. This section of the wall offers more room for the imagination.

What if she's not thinking of him after all? What if she's just shy? Or even repressed? Of course – how could you have forgotten? You have read about this famous British quality. Now, at long last, you're witnessing it first hand. This shy young Englishwoman is not speaking to you, but it's not because she doesn't like you. She's not speaking because she has repressed her forbidden feelings, and to express them overtly would be improper. She's not a coarse American. It's the national custom, you've heard – deflecting potentially charged emotions with benign conversations on the weather, or simply staying silent. The pizza shop owner can hardly be expected to grip your hands and confess her love for you. What a fool you'd been, making such an impossibly difficult deal with your unhopeful self, the self who needs comforting and encouragement, not stringent preconditions to conversation.

Still, you made the deal and cannot talk yourself out of it. Over time the candles on the tables burn low and hot. One of them snaps, fizzles out. The electric hum of the kitchen fridge seems to grow louder. Her silence lasts far too long for anyone with normal repression. Has she fallen asleep? No, you sneak a glance and see that her eyes are open. She is awake but apparently in a daze. Overworked, no doubt, the poor flower needs to rest. This is another quality you share. The two of you are kindred souls, working hard in the daytime and sailing through your parallel evening dreams.

No words will be needed. No fatal turns to watch out for, no danger of blurted embarrassing confessions.

There is a noise outside. You sit forward in your chair.

'I think,' she says, 'that—'

But you don't get to hear what she might think. She has spoken first, and the bet has been won by your hopeful self, but there is no time to celebrate because a man has appeared in the open door. He's over six feet and stocky. He wears a brown corduroy blazer and jeans tight around his crotch.

'So there you are! Coming home, are we?'

'I have a customer.'

'Thought you might have stepped out for a cheeky fag.' The man comes inside and passes his eyes over the mess on your table. Used napkins litter your plate. Puddles of olive oil surround the breadbasket and wine bottle. 'A little late for dinner,' he mutters, lurking near your chair.

'He's finished, Kev. I'll be back in a mo''.

He takes off his blazer and drags a table over, letting the wood legs scrape across the stone floor. 'I'll take a coffee,' he says. 'Now that I've come all the way here.'

You're sitting between them. It would be the simple thing to leave, so that they can be alone as she closes up, but you don't feel like making it easy for him. He's a hard creature, all muscle and lazy strength, a man of slouching and incontestable authority. His hands are broad and strong, his gold watch clasped tight on his hairy wrist. He opens a packet of gummy bears and pops them into his mouth, one after the other, watching you. Every movement he makes, every violent annihilation of each defenseless gummy bear, communicates his wisdom in the ways of the world – he's seen more in Ditchling than anyone else, nothing surprises him.

'Margaret,' he says. He takes a phone out of his jeans pocket, leans across your table, and sticks it in front of her face. 'Check it out.'

Margaret – you've always loved that name. But you don't get a chance to savor the sound in your head because a revving motor has intruded into the restaurant. On the phone's screen, a Land Rover appears with this man in the driver's seat, his elbow on the door and the window rolled down. He grins at the camera as he revs the car and throws it into gear.

'Ace, isn't it?'

Margaret nods as the video flashes across her beautiful mouth. She has become even smaller in his presence, almost frail.

'Coffee,' the man says.

She gets up, clears away your dirty dishes. There is a small amount of wine left in the bottle, and she dumps it into your glass.

'A bit late for dinner,' the man says again.

You look at him. Your eyes fall submissively to the dimple on his chin. 'I was hungry, I suppose.'

The man puts his phone back in his pocket and stares openly, his thin lips in a sneer. 'You Canadian?'

'I'm from the States.'

'Oh. Right. You're probably offended right now.'

'Not really. It's only the Canadians who care about being mistaken.'

'Where about in America?'

'California.'

'Californ-I-A. The place to be, supposedly.'

'Really?'

'You tell me.'

'I don't know about that. I like it here so far.' You give him your best smile.

'What – Ditchling?'

'Yes.'

He snorts. 'You can have it, mate. You're staying with the Swifts, I bet.'

'That's right.'

'Watch out for Sheila's soup. Famous, isn't it, Margaret?'

The man tips the rest of his candy into his mouth. You can practically hear the gummy bears scream as he waits for your reaction. He crumples the empty packet into a tight ball and releases it onto the table, where the plastic slowly expands. 'No, I've never had any interest in visiting America. Even Californ-I-A.'

What follows is a different kind of silence – a hostile war of unspoken words. Your sanctuary in Ditchling is slipping away.

'I thought we'd watch that documentary tonight,' the man calls into the kitchen. 'The one on fly-fishing.'

Margaret clatters the dishes in the sink and doesn't respond. What is she thinking, associating with this jackass? Then you remember – every woman you've ever fallen for, at one time or another, has associated with jackasses.

She returns with three mugs of coffee, a sugar bowl, and milk. You allow yourself to be happy about this. Margaret wants you to stay a bit longer, to serve as a buffer, to delay the fly-fishing documentary. Soon she will be sitting on the sofa watching men in rubber waders.

'I could manage a holiday in Orlando,' the man says. 'Disneyworld, all that.'

'I don't think theme parks are the best way to explore American culture,' Margaret says. She sits at the man's table, pours a drop of milk into her mug, and sips her coffee.

'Is that so,' he says. 'I never thought America had any culture to begin with.'

'Kevin,' she says, placing her hand on his wrist. Her sweet little chewed fingers rest on his hairy forearm.

You've always hated the name Kevin. You keep smiling as you reach for your mug.

'Everyone says we're going the way of America,' Kevin says. 'Diversicating. If that's evolution, I want no part of it.' He spoons sugar into his coffee and stirs it around.

'Life in America might not be what you imagine,' you say.

'Really? And how do you know what I'd imagine?'

'I mean – America's not one thing. Or even one set of things. It was founded on principles that are intentionally open to interpretation.'

'Is it, then? Sounds like we're back to diversicating. Tell me – if America's so bloody wonderful, what are you doing in Ditchling?'

'Researching his ancestors,' Margaret says. 'His grand-father worked with Eric Gill.'

Your hope surges further. She's already heard the best details, and you haven't had to say a word about it. There was real pride in her voice, or at least admiration.

'The pervert?' Kevin says. 'The one in the robe who ran round Ditchling Common, shagging his own daughters?'

Margaret looks away. You are not aware of these allega-tions. Gradually you lean back against your chair, and your smile disappears.

'Those so-called *artists* gave Ditchling a bad name, if you ask me', Kevin says. 'You know that perv even put it to his dog?'

'Kevin', Margaret says again. 'Enough.'

Your hand shakes a little as you lift your coffee mug. 'My grandfather wasn't exactly an artist. He was a scorper.' You nod toward the book on your table, with its photo of wood-cutting tools on the cover, but Kevin doesn't even glance at it.

'A what?'

'A scorper. He scraped around Gill's drawings to make the woodblocks.'

'Wouldn't have wanted that job. You know what Eric Gill drew on those woodblocks? Naked blokes.' He scans your shoes, your mud-stained khakis. 'Naked. Blokes. One after the other. The man was in love with his own cock.'

Kevin sees your grimace and laughs. 'You didn't know that, did you? Your granddad carved knobs. Knobs and knob ends, every day! No wonder he buggered off to America.'

Margaret slowly stands up. She collects the coffee mugs and the empty gummy bear packet and takes them to the kitchen. She moves with the fatigue of a woman who has listened for years to men like this.

'She's closing up now', Kevin says. He puts his hands behind his head and rocks back in his chair. 'It's high time you cleared out.'

You have become the newest pair of curtain eyes. Below, a street lamp illuminates the pavement, and if any lost tourists appear, you'll track them, perhaps report them to other villagers. Tonight, for the past hour, there has just been empty pavement, waiting under the mist.

Kevin – and probably Margaret, too – expected you to lose your temper. Kevin was 'winding you up', as the British are fond of saying. It will be your pleasure to disabuse them of their expectations and be a gentleman in Ditchling.

You leave the window, sit at your desk, and switch on the lamp. It's time for *Scorper*.

You have to admit you are apprehensive about reading the book, given that it's clearly a cheap, self-published pamphlet, with narrow columns of text and wide margins. But Kevin cannot make you ashamed of your family. If your grandfather scorped Eric Gill's nudes, what of it?

In June 1922 I began my apprenticeship to Mr Eric Gill. I was eighteen and sought practical experience with artists in my desire to become one. Mr Gill has had his share of critics but pray remember that he has since become famous for carving the Stations of the Cross in Westminster. He and his wife Mary had just converted to Catholicism at the time of my employ. They lived ascetic Christian lives with regular chanting and prayers.

When I started the scorping, Mr Gill was occupied mostly with tombstones. He designed for priests and bankers alike, there being nothing like his craftsmanship. He would sculpt the war memorials for village greens. Mr Gill's form of devotion was something I didn't understand at first, but I began as a Catholic in order that I might work with him and learned to devote myself in equal measures to art and God.

He got me started on lettering straight away. We worked at his studio on Ditchling Common, in the workshops, between daily services at the chapel Mr Gill had built. We prayed among the cows and the sheep, then proceeded to our engravings. He taught me how to look at the alphabet with new and wholesome eyes. He showed me a wood engraving of an A and observed me as I put the scorper to it.

'Words form the building blocks of our laws, our poems and our prayers,' Mr Gill would say. 'Each letter should be clear and readable.'

I must have scorped well-nigh ten blocks of As before Mr Gill allowed me to start on his B. My fingers felt they had done very hard work. When I was finished with the alphabet to his satisfaction, he had me assist with the gravestones. He wanted very much for people to admire his inscriptions. Pray remember that most people didn't pay much attention to ordinary tombstones before Mr Gill.

I didn't yet know what kind of art I myself wanted to practise. It is a marvellous thing when I think back, but it required meeting my wife to find out the ways and directions of my life. But I am jumping ahead in the telling. At that time, during the burdensome interval between my youth and my adulthood, I knew only that I wanted to follow in Mr Gill's footsteps and make a mark or sign.

On the wall opposite the desk, a crack in the plaster spiders up to the wooden beams. You want to keep reading, but these are the only words you've got from your grandfather, and when the book is finished, that will be it. What kind of man becomes a Catholic for the sake of art? You hope he will talk about his future wife, the woman who must be your grandmother.

The crack runs up to the shadows of the ceiling, where it disappears at the source, like a river meeting the sea. You are reminded of the hours spent inside your cubicle, staring at the streaks of in-tray dust. Time passes, and the next thing you know, you are still at your desk.

It's almost dawn when you hear the geese. They strafe the B&B with a chorus of aggravated honks, as if they've been created specifically to torture people out of their dearest dreams. You chase after the lingering images in your mind – Margaret, kneeling at your feet, her pale bare arms encircling your calves. Beside her lies a drawing you've given her, a work of art so stunning that it answers her unspoken grief for her dead Italian. She had swooned with a new devotion, declared herself yours.

The geese keep honking. It's just after five, and they seem to be circling, dive-bombing the B&B in waves until everyone inside is forced to run. You have three hours before Sheila's breakfast. Maybe you can catch Ditchling off guard.

You creep downstairs, guided by the nightlight at the bottom of the landing. It feels vaguely criminal, sneaking out of the B&B before the appointed hour for breakfast. You unlock the front door and close it with the faintest of clicks.

The village sleeps in darkness. Have the geese gone? You zip up your coat and sneak down the High Street in the opposite direction of the pub. Past Boddington's Lane a wider road appears and you sprint the length of it, turning now and then to see if any windows light up in the houses, if anyone is watching.

At the end of the road, larger houses wrap around a cul-de-sac. There are more street lamps in this neighborhood, and the front gardens are strewn with children's toys. This is where the Ditchlings reproduce. You cannot help it – you must get closer to their doors and bedrooms. At a low front gate, you climb over without a sound.

In the garden a plastic gnome stands beside a flower-pot. Empty milk bottles, lined up like infantry, wait for the milkman. Here it is at last, the real England – the gnome, the flowerpot, the milk bottles. You pick up the pot and smell the damp soil. You hold a bottle to your cheek and shiver with joy at the coldness, the goodness, the promise of fresh white milk. Even in a world saturated with e-readers, tradition lives on. These Ditchlings have tried to hide the evidence, but you've found it. A man only has to get up early to learn the truth.

You're still at the door beside the gnome when another squadron of geese flies overhead, raising the alarm. *Honk, honk! Honk, honk!*

You spin in a circle, trapped. You put the bottle back in formation and hurry to the shadows behind the gate. *The American is awake*, the geese honk, *he's out in your garden.* You squat on your heels and hope these milk-drinking Ditchlings are heavy sleepers.

When the birds have passed, you jump the gate and run back to the High Street. Overhead, a lone goose lags behind the others. The bird labors in the air, flapping pitifully, its face pinched against the black sky. Its trajectory drops, then drops further still. You must follow this bird. You must find its pond.

Running hard, you pass the War Memorial and down

into the flats. You reach the gap in the hedgerow and emerge onto the road you took two days ago, driving in from London. The goose has become a distant smudge. You run past grazing pastures with cows slowly taking shape in the shadows.

A sign stands over a gravel road:

MOORECROFT NATURE RESERVE
TEA ROOM, APRIL TO SEPTEMBER

There are illustrations of various waterfowl on the sign – ducks, moorhens, geese. This is the poor creature's pond, you can smell it. Across the car park, you find an entrance heading into a wall of trees.

A gate blocks the path, and you climb it without difficulty. You make your way in the dim light, up a short hill. At the end of the tree line, the path emerges onto an open field. The wet grasses and reeds are glistening with dew. In the distance lies the pond.

The geese have congregated. They're quiet now. There must be over a hundred of them down at the water, filling the near bank like tufted brushstrokes of white on a gloomy canvas. You stand back in the tall grass, starstruck. This is what gets you weak-kneed: the sight of birds floating in the water, shielding each other from the wind. The whole scene reminds you of *England* – the pond at dawn, the geese and encircling trees. You have caught nature at rest, long before it puts on its mask.

You come closer to the pond, as close as you dare. The birds are seemingly indifferent to your approach. Perhaps they're asleep. You've turned the tables on Ditchling, and now it's time to turn the tables on the geese.

'Remember me?'

At the bank, you squat beside the water and whisper so the creatures won't be alarmed. Sometimes a man becomes a hunter in his motherland.

'When you flew over, I was the one who woke up.'

You offer reassurances. Inching forward, you court them with whispers until you reach out and snatch the nearest by the throat. The goose flaps its wings and kicks, but you've got it. You wade back into the reeds while the others honk and splash. They fly over to the far bank and resettle there, leaving you alone with your new friend.

'You're mine now.'

You hold its beak down in the reeds. With your other hand you hold its little legs tight. The goose has a frightened black face, pretty white feathers you'd like to pluck. There are holes along the sides of its beak, venting air in wet desperate bursts. You look into its round black eyes and find the Sussex you've been waiting for – the home of sensitive plants and animals, the Albion fields of creatures who love poetry.

The goose struggles to be free. You can feel its warm rubbery skin, expanding and contracting under its feathers. It doesn't understand that you don't want to kill it.

'I listened to you as you flew over. Remember? Now it's your turn. Let me tell you a story. Do you know what I did, the first time a boy at school made fun of the way I looked, and a girl laughed?'

The goose fixes its eyes on you with an expression of sympathy.

'I ran home. I snuck upstairs to my room and I tried to draw a picture of my pain. It didn't look anything like what

I felt, so I tried to write poems.' The goose squirts little gusts of wet air. 'Don't you wish you could read and write?'

You move the beak up and down. It stops flapping and kicking. It's learned how to listen.

'In college, I studied art and English literature. I read Shelley and Tennyson and Byron. I gained a great deal of respect for your people. Almost ten years as copyeditor – and how long can a man do it? You probably think it's silly, me telling you this. But I swear…'

You lower your head over the goose, so that your lips almost touch its beak. 'I swear – you'll soon see what I'm capable of.'

Twigs snap, back among the trees. A man's coming to the pond.

You release the goose and lie flat on your stomach. The sun is conspiring against you, turning the sky ever-lighter shades of gray. What if the warden has come? Pond water penetrates your clothes. Beside you, the faithful goose opens and closes its beak, probably stunned. Maybe it's reluctant to fly away from its new friend. On the other hand, the bird could be acting the part of the faithful companion in order to betray you later. You elbow its wing, and the goose flies off, honking toward its companions on the other side of the pond.

The man has almost reached the water's edge, a stone's throw from your position. He's carrying a fishing pole. Still on your stomach, you track him through the reeds. It's Kevin. He's wearing waders, a mesh fishing jacket, a hat with fur earflaps.

You can't deny that Kevin's handsome. He has a dimpled chin and the kind of nose found on the heads of Roman coins. As the sun emerges over the pond, you turn onto your side, your head in your palm, and watch him tie off. He casts. He whips the line across the water. He makes his lure dance.

In another life, Kevin would have been a typical American. He would have been born into a sporting family from Montana, a dynasty of renegade Republicans who hate government, drive SUVs, and hang stuffed elk heads from their living-room walls. His bookshelves would have proudly held the novels of Hemingway and Norman Mailer, perhaps a biography of Andrew Jackson, abridged for easy reading. It's all becoming clear. Kevin has real problems. Something must have happened to create his sneer. In his role-playing fantasies, he alternates between Land Rovers and holidays in Disneyland wearing mouse ears.

How similar you are to Kevin, after all. You're both Americans in England, poor boors trying to fit in. You had been rather hard on him in the pizza shop, suggesting he had a poor imagination. Wouldn't it do to make friends? It's time to express yourself openly, to dispense with formalities. Kevin casts over some lily pads, his back turned, when you stand up out of the reeds.

'Good morning, Kevin. Beautiful day!'

Kevin ducks as if he's been shot. He lets out a kind of girlish cry, arms thrown up around his head. He stays crouched in the reeds a moment, looking at you.

'What the hell?' He stands up with his fishing pole. 'What are *you* doing out here?'

You point across the pond at the geese. 'They woke me up. I thought I'd go for a walk.'

Kevin looks across the water. It's not fair – all the geese have gone to sleep, and they don't look capable of anything but silence. He comes wading across the reeds. You try to convince yourself, as he comes closer and closer, that he's going to stop soon. When he throws down his pole, you know it's too late to run.

'Liar,' Kevin says. He shoves you down into the reeds. 'What are you doing here? Tell me the truth.'

You squirm at his feet like a snake. 'I am telling the truth.'

'You're up to something. In the pizza shop after hours. Flirting with Margaret. Now you're out here without a hat, spying.'

'Please – I don't have a hat. The geese woke me up, and I followed them to the pond.'

'You climbed the gate?'

'Yes.'

'Without a hat?' Kevin looks around the reserve, gesturing at the trees. 'Who leaves before dawn without a hat? Disgusting bloody artists. You're all the same. Get up and fight.'

'Nobody's ever called me an artist.'

'I'll bash your head in. I'll cut off your hands and bury them in the ground.'

'Please. You don't have to worry about me, Kevin. I won't tell anyone you were fishing in the reserve.'

'You're damn right you won't.' He takes a handkerchief from his mesh jacket and blows his nose. For a moment he looks out over the pond, eyes hardening. He's still flustered from being taken by surprise. Your vulnerability, lying there in the reeds, only eggs him on.

'I'd better not see you here again,' he says.

'You won't. I promise.'

He kicks you in the ribs. Then he kicks you again, so hard

it makes you cry out. 'I won't let you off this easy next time.'

Kevin picks up his pole. He heads back toward the tree line, shoulders squared, head thrust forward with his ear-flaps swinging. Your side feels broken apart.

You try to stand and fall wheezing onto your back. Slowly, your breath returns to your lungs. Up in the sky you see the geese. They have left the pond in an enormous V, off toward the South Downs, in the opposite direction of Ditchling.

Still wet from the pond, you try the front door of the church and find it locked. St Margaret's is twelfth-century Norman, the bulletin board says, built on eleventh-century Saxon foundations. Flint handaxes have been found on church grounds dating to 250,000 BC.

It's almost nine, and you're going to miss Sheila's breakfast. The footpath around the church runs through the territory of the dead – a site where centuries of tribes have come and gone, waged battles over biblical passages, plots of farmland, marital rights. Kevin may be aggressive, but he's just part of England.

The soil under your shoes is densely trodden. How many fluids have fallen, how many strains of blood mixed with rainwater and limekiln discharge? The feet of peasants and lords have walked here, believers and heathens, bare feet and boots. Animals and men, goats, pigs, beetles and bird droppings, species more closely entwined in England than in America.

Some of the headstones are Eric Gill's. The fonts have no serifs – just hard, clean edges. At the grave of a man named Simpson you stop and slide your finger along the capital

S. The letter takes your finger and pushes it back out, as if doubting your capacity to read.

You want to know why your grandfather did it – abandoned tradition, jumped off the island, altered his spelling. As a boy, you were told your blood ran with generations of heroes and poets. You carried your pride to school like a secret.

Why didn't he fight back?
Mud on his shirt and sore ribs.
Why did his psychologist tell him to come?

You sit on a slab until the voices go quiet. Don't be upset – you can't blame the dead for their curiosity. Yes, they're right, you sat in Dr Craft's chair for two months until the insurance caps kicked in. She listened to your troubles with her face turned away, as if shielding herself from the stink of your psychopathology. A photograph of herself hung on the wall beside her diploma.

'I have a secret love of moles,' you confessed. 'If I see a woman with a mole, I'm always tempted to kiss it.'

'You say your grandfather came from this place,' she said, changing the subject. She rolled the word around in her mouth. 'Ditch-ling.'

Ditchling – the perfect place to die.
We are all Ditchlings. We come out of a ditch in birth and
return to a ditch in death.
Forever decomposing into gutters, draining into the
subterranean water table.

Hungry, resting a moment on the damp stone, you wonder, yet again, if you should have come, but it's true and you can't deny it – you'd rather be here right now than anywhere else, even with self-doubt and the torment of voices, because self-doubt and torment have always been part of your inheritance, passed down to you by the dead in this very churchyard.

Get to your feet, take the path between graves, climb to the highest point on the grounds. Stop near the boundary hedge. From this vantage point, you can see to the museum and the lower graves, and in front of you, over a low stone wall, the High Street. In front of The Lantern, a man unloads a keg from a delivery truck. Paul Tanner watches, smoking a cigarette.

The hedgerow disappears on the horizon, over the Weald where the real whisperers dwell. Your ancestors could have come from those hills. Maybe the first Culls worked in the chalk pits. Fish fossils form the substrata of your forehead, you offspring of Ditchling.

The woman from the museum scurries up the lane between the lime trees. She carries an unopened umbrella like a sword. At the door she turns, catches sight of you amongst the uppermost graves. She could be a distant cousin on your genealogical bracket. She studies you a moment, then opens up the museum.

Roam the mounds, search the names. A Cull has to be here somewhere. Artists rise up around you. *Morris, Skilton, Nelson, Helton. Edward Johnston, Calligrapher, Designed Logo and Typeface for London Underground.*

Your father loved his heroes. He loved the dead, especially if they wrote, or fought in wars. Instant immortality, dying before you can fail, dying in battle, dying with your words in ink and your pen in hand. How catastrophic to dredge up the past, to dig up what lies dormant, to uncover the remains and sift through silt.

At the front of the church, you try the door once more. Surely there is a burial registry inside. But the handle doesn't budge. You knock against the closely hewn grains, and it's like rapping on granite. The bulletin board near the door has a crayon version of the illustration from the museum, the one with a long line of couples holding hands and walking over the hill under flocks of birds. And at the bottom of the page, in a child's neat hand, an inscription:

Ditchling is ruled by God's brothers and sisters. A stranger threatens this bloodline – you shall know him by the disappearance of birds in the sky. Whoever buries the hand of the stranger rules the rest.

You take a lower footpath toward the rear of the church, along the dark and soggy ground where older headstones sink into the turf. The graves remind you of your co-workers in Los Angeles. In the mornings, their entire heads are visible above their computers. By lunchtime, you see only hair. At five o'clock, they have sunk so far down, down into the pockets of their ergonomic chairs. Only their wrists and hands are visible on the sides of their computer screens.

There's a low door to the belfry at the back of the church. Above it, a stained-glass window shows Jesus on the cross. You grab the iron spikes protecting the window and hoist yourself up. Is someone in there, sweeping the belfry steps? You make out only formless shapes, wraiths behind glass, bellringers' ghosts.

As you lower yourself to the grass, one of the spikes breaks off in your hand. A weapon? Look to the sky, thank it for this gift. The wind peels back its lips, offers a colder bite.

With your spike, you keep wandering the graves. Here lies a weaver. There lies a painter, a poet, a bookplate maker. The letters have become homes for lichen.

Kneel on the grass, you. Put your arm around my headstone.
Stain your fingers with iron. Breathe life into my faded
epitaph.
Engrave me.

A small square headstone sits alone in the clumps and tufts. It's so buried, you almost trip over it. The lettering where the name should be has faded to the point of complete obscurity. The grave hasn't even had the privilege of being defaced – it's simply blank from time and teeming with lichen. There could be anyone underground.

The boundary hedge lies behind you, sheltering you from the wind. Kneeling, your arm around the headstone, you get going with the spike. The letters, scratched white, come through the carved gray crust. When you're finished you stand up, step back, inspect your editorial work.

JOHN CULL
The American of Ditchling

The rain has come again. Take the most direct route across the mounds, hurry under the eaves of the church. Press your back to the stone. Down on the ground, a cigarette butt lies beside your shoe. It pokes out of the mud, uncurling its fiendish head like a worm.

Water gurgles from the downspout. Dribble and drown. The skies are silent, as if all the birds of Sussex have gone into hiding. Dark clouds pass overhead, bringing an early evening to the morning. Has Sheila given Bobby your bacon and eggs? Will you be blamed for his indigestion? The American has been seen in our churchyard, she'll say. God gives man a spike, he learns how to scorp.

4

When I finished with the alphabet to Mr Gill's satisfaction, I started scorping my own epitaphs for the newly deceased. I worked in my studio out on the Common with a pot of tea, smoked a pipe with each piece of granite. This is not easy work, slow and tiring and the dust gets in one's eyes. I shall be pleased if a hundred years from now, people still read my lettering.

I scorped many headstones before the book illustrations started. We had our own printing press given to us by a German Count, one of Mr Gill's patrons. The Guild of St Joseph and St Dominic introduced its bookplate, a right hand open in devotion with a cross on the centre of the palm. Mr Gill drew the illustrations in pen and ink, then carved them true on the woodblocks. I dug around them so the ink would stick.

In our spare time, Mr Gill encouraged me to develop my own skills of observation. I shall always remember his kind and practical advice. 'The greatest training of an artist,' he told me, 'is to learn how to draw the common things – the chimneys, the ditches, the drains.' In this way I learned to make the common beautiful to the eye.

You would also like to 'make the common beautiful to the eye,' but as you keep reading, the words blur. You can barely distinguish black from white. This morning has made you woozy, and your ribs are still tender, the flesh sore. Kevin will regret what he's done.

The kettle whistles. Get up, put *Scorper* away. It's time to sit behind your curtain with your hands around the chipped teacup. You must take care of yourself. Don't hold a grudge against Kevin – everyone knows England has her Neanderthals, her men of the Stone Age. You frightened him, that's all. It's the Christian thing to turn the other cheek. With time, the two of you might become friends.

Sit quietly; avoid straining your eyes. Pull your chair right up to the curtains. That's it. Stick your nose through the gap.

To take in one's village on a quiet Saturday afternoon – what more can one ask for? Below, the High Street stretches before you. Directly opposite, the bank sits squat in its established position of authority. Next door, the jewelry shop glitters on the bottom floor of its Tudor house. Upstairs, the iron window frames bulge, the white curtains drawn tight.

Point your nose to the left, and you've got a side view of Sprinkles. The sandwich board is out on the pavement advertising today's specials. A little further along, The Lantern sprawls on its corner of the High Street.

Sip your tea. Do as you're told. Angle your nose slightly to the right, where the church and spire rises out of the South Downs. The lane between the lower headstones cuts through to the museum. That's it. Find the tops of the lime trees, rest your eyes on nature, calm down.

With only your nose exposed, you can hide behind the curtains as long as you like. You can daydream of Margaret and imagine all sorts of artwork for her. A chalk figure, embedded in the Downs? A naked warrior with a phallus and an axe? Close your eyes, imagine the possibilities – charcoal drawings of village life, multi-hued sunsets, Impressionist paintings of couples sipping tea on the grass. Perhaps you'll even draw some 'common things' and make them beautiful.

You open your eyes from your reverie. Across the street, there's a man on the pavement. You jump out of the chair and move away from the curtains. He was brazenly staring at you in broad daylight, penetrating your private bedroom.

Slowly, discreetly, edge your nostrils back into the gap. He's by your car in front of the jewelry shop. He's got a sketchpad in his hands, and he's still looking at your window. It's Eric Gill.

He can't fool you. He's put on his grandfather's outfit – the robe, the rope sandals, the four-cornered paper hat – but you recognize him all right, despite the disguise. What's he doing out there, openly drawing *your* curtains, right when you've stuck your nose through the gap?

Hurry to the desk for your sketchbook and pencils. You brought these materials to England for a reason, so go and grab them now, put them to use. You can't let Eric get away with this. He's drawing you – what if you draw him? He's violating your privacy, what if you violate his? Lace up your shoes, slip on your coat. Out the door and down the stairs.

At the bottom of the landing you find Sheila waiting for you. She's facing you in her cardigan with her arms crossed, her left stocking down around her ankle.

'You missed breakfast,' she says.

You slow down for the final step, approach her with your eyes lowered in contrition. She's taken a bath – her pink face is scrubbed and gleaming. You can smell the soap. 'I had to give Bobby your bacon and eggs again,' she says.

'I'm sorry.'

'And the sausage you said you wanted.'

'Tomorrow I'll have my breakfast, I promise.' You continue to keep your eyes lowered before your surrogate mother. Secretly, you don't mind being scolded.

Sheila scratches at her elbows underneath the cardigan. The door to the lounge is closed, but you can hear the TV. The announcer has an American accent:

'ESPN presents pre-season baseball. The Texas Rangers take on the Detroit Tigers in a matchup of last year's American League Championship Series...'

'Bobby's watching baseball?'

'He's absolutely addicted. Maybe the two of you could watch a game together sometime.'

'That would be nice.'

She peers around the lounge door. 'His trousers are hanging on the airer. He's not exactly presentable. Some other afternoon?'

'All right.'

'Would you prefer your breakfast later, maybe? Half nine?'

'Sure – a little later might be better.'

'Half nine, then.' She looks at you. 'Not tomorrow, though, luv – it's church. We'll wait 'til Monday to start the new schedule.'

'All right.'

'You are joining us for church?'

'Yes. I think so.'

'Tomorrow's breakfast at the usual time, then. I do expect you at table. No good having food go to waste.'

'I promise. I'll try and get an early night...'

You try to inch past, like a boy hurrying out to play, but

she makes no effort to move, nor to withdraw the extended leg with the fallen stocking. 'I heard you this morning', she says, under her breath.

'Oh?'

'Sneaking out.'

'I didn't wake you, I hope.'

'I'm a light sleeper. It's Bobby who sleeps through anything. Ever since he was a baby.' She slips her hand beneath the top of her cardigan, finds the bra strap and gives it a tug. 'You share a bedroom with your little brother, you know his habits like your own.'

In the silence, the words sink in. 'Did you say – your brother?'

'Mmm. Do you have siblings?'

'No.' You look at the lounge door and try to imagine the location of the kitchen, the rooms beyond. You wonder if they still share a bedroom.

Sheila nods at the pad in your hand. 'You're an artist?'

'I've tried a few sketches. Portraits, mostly.' You take a small step closer, trying to edge your way past, but she doesn't move.

'That explains you getting up so early. Artists keep such odd hours! Nobody's done a decent drawing of our B&B, you know. Something to think of. You might find your way onto a picture postcard.'

Sheila takes a step toward you, so that you're almost touching. She reaches for your shoulder, and you flinch. 'Take this,' she says, producing a hat from the coat stand behind your back. It's a woman's hat, bright and yellow with a floppy brim. She stands on her tiptoes and settles it down around your ears. 'Rain could come on at any moment.'

'Thank you. Very kind…'

'I'm *well* pleased to have an artist in the house.' Her hand on the small of your back, Sheila steps to the side and guides you out. 'Follow your inspirations, luv,' she says, closing the door behind you.

At the top of the steps you adjust the hat and stare up at the clouds. It's a relief to be finally outside in the brisk air. The village is quiet except for a passing car, and you are all-too conscious of the fact that you haven't yet checked to see if Eric Gill is still across the road. You have the sneaking suspicion that he *is*, but once you confirm this, you will be committed to acting on the information and taking another potentially fatal turn.

Eric Gill is indeed across the road. And he is still drawing in his sketchbook. The Ditchlings pass him as they go about their business, giving the artist room to work. Eric soon sees that you've noticed him. You have verified his identity, as it were, and he flips the cover of his sketchbook shut, tucks his pencil in the outer pocket of his robe, and walks quickly away.

'Hey!' You scamper down the steps. He's walking fast, toward the lane to the museum, and you have to run to catch up. 'Where are you going?'

Eric tries to move by, but you get in front of him on the pavement. 'I saw you just now, looking up at my window!'

'No, you didn't.'

'Yes, I did.'

'You didn't. You only had your nose through the gap.'

'How could you know that if you weren't looking?'

Eric shrugs. 'I hear things.' He pushes his spectacles up the bridge of his nose. They're too big for his face, and they keep slipping. He looks you up and down, begrudgingly acknowledging your existence. 'And what are you doing outside, a sketchbook under your arm?'

'You tell me.'

'Tell me first.'

'No, you tell me, Eric. Tell me your intentions, please, instead of luring me into talking, luring and baiting me so that I end up betraying my innermost thoughts!'

You have become louder than you wanted. Some of the passing Ditchlings have noticed. Eric Gill tugs his earlobe and steps away from you. He straightens his robe, stands a little taller.

'*My* intentions? Please do not try and intimidate me with your rude demands. I am a *permanent* resident of Ditchling, and I don't have to explain myself to anyone.'

This gets you where it hurts, and he knows it. Just like that, you have to grovel, to seek his forgiveness. 'You're right, Eric. Please – I didn't mean anything by it. Forgive my tone. It's just that – I – please, I want to work with you. The two of us. Remember how we planned our book, using your tools and your printing press?'

'That was two nights ago. A fine thing, finding you'd gone, just after I'd invited you to dinner!'

'But it was you who abandoned me!'

'Did I? I don't remember.' Eric sniffs self-importantly. 'Artists can be scatter-brained, I suppose. But I do have an idea for a book – a new idea. Come with me.'

He takes your arm, guides you back up the High Street. There is a narrow clearing between the bank and the jeweler's – a small strip of dirt, littered with beer cans and sandwich wrappers – and he draws you into this area to

hide. The two of you are wedged in so tightly you're practically touching.

'I've had my eye on something, John. I was only *pretending*
to draw your window. So the others wouldn't catch on.'

'Others?' You peer around the wall. He must mean the
curtain-eyes, the Ditchlings. 'What were you drawing just
now? Tell me.'

Eric opens his sketchbook. He flips through the pages
and opens to a sketch of the B&B, drawn roughly but com-
petently, more or less to scale. He taps at the bottom of the
image with his pencil. 'There. Have a look at *that*.'

'That what? It's excellent work, Eric. But I can't quite
make out what that is…'

'There,' he says, tapping the pencil again, 'at the bottom
of the handrail.'

Near the ground, he's drawn something jutting out from
the bottom step, parallel to the pavement. 'What is it?'

'A bootscraper. Welded right into that step – the only
one of its kind in Ditchling!' Eric rubs his palms together
excitedly. 'Here. Let's go and take a look. Be discreet, for
God's sake, whatever you do.'

'I don't understand. You want to create a book on
bootscrapers?'

'There's money to be made in this village. Everyone's after
their share of the Heritage Lottery Fund, and artists are in
high demand. The Ditchling Historical Society already
stole my drawings for their wattle-and-daub picture book.
Last month they did a slide presentation for the village –
charged a fiver a head!'

Eric's spectacles slip down his nose again. 'Paul Tanner's
written his pamphlet on the history of The Lantern, and

now he's launching a second book on local chimneys, followed by a third one on Ditchling's brass bell pulls. Lawrence Savage has his book of vegetarian recipes...'

He peers out into the street. 'Now we'll walk by Sheila's bootscraper, as if we're just out for a stroll. Act naturally, John. Don't stare. Don't stop, or do anything out of the ordinary.'

Eric Gill straightens his robe and crosses the High Street. You follow close behind. A woman walking her dog smiles and nods, and now you see that there are real advantages to being in Eric's company – people notice you've made friends. As we pass the B&B, he angles his head slightly, toward the bottom of the handrail.

Two narrow iron bars run parallel to the bottom step. The lower one looks like it might take the dirt off the sole of your shoe.

'Hold on, Eric. Let's see if this thing works.'

'God, no,' Eric whispers, flapping his arms. 'Get away from there. Everyone will see!'

You hold the handrail for balance and slide the bottom of your shoe along the crossbar. The dried mud falls away in an even slice. There's something faintly erotic about it. You raise your cleaned shoe high in the air.

'Just think of it, Eric. Your wife's inside, reading to your children in the drawing room, maybe ironing the handkerchiefs. She's told you, time and time again – "your shoes had better be clean when you cross that carpet!"'

'Move away from there!' Eric hisses.

'This is my home now. I can use my own bootscraper, can't I?'

You lift your left shoe. Holding onto the handrail, you place the heel along the crossbar and drag the sole along the edge. Another layer of dried mud falls effortlessly away. 'I jsut thought of something. Do you think Margaret might like a book on bootscrapers, Eric? This one is perfectly incorporated into the ironwork. And the rounded divots are a brilliant touch. Something ordinary, beautifully made. Back when people traveled by horse, these things must have been in constant use…'

You scrape your right shoe again. Then you switch back to the left. You can't stop. Boot scraping makes you so happy, you want to scrape off every little particle. 'Imagine bringing home the local artists, Eric. "Yes indeed, Mr Johnston, I'll show you my latest engravings forthwith. First, pray tell me – that piece of horseshit stuck to the bottom of your boot. Would you like to avail yourself of my scraper? Proceed, fine sir. I am considering a pamphlet on these handy items, perhaps a monograph, dedicated to my wife Margaret of course—"'

'What the fuck?'

This new voice is not Eric's, and as you turn at the bootscraper, Kevin stands in front of you. His corduroy blazer is tight on his shoulders, and his chin dimple is aimed at your face like a spotlight. Margaret stands beside him, her arm resting on his.

'I thought you said you didn't have a hat,' Kevin says.

You look for Eric's support, but he's gone. 'This thing?' You flip up the brim. 'It's Sheila's.'

Kevin drops Margaret's arm and comes closer. You can smell his cologne. 'A menace to Ditchling, this one.'

'C'mon, Kev,' Margaret says.

'I've had enough of him. Snooping. Talking to himself in broad daylight like a poof.' He takes the sketchbook out from under your arm. 'Let's have a look,' he says, flipping through the blank pages. 'He hasn't drawn a thing.' He drops it to the ground and kicks it down the pavement. 'Pick that up.'

'Don't do this,' you say.

'Pick it up.'

'No.'

'Pick it up, or I'll break you into pieces.'

'Kev,' Margaret says, 'leave him.'

Inside the B&B, the curtains in the lounge twitch. You know what's coming. They played this trick on you in school – as soon as you bend over, he'll kick you. Across the road, two elderly men have stopped to watch.

You bend over and wait. You hope he won't be too rough.

'Go on. Kick me.'

'I can't be bothered now. You're like an injured giraffe.'

The shame is too much – he's just watching you and smirking. Kevin laughs, the old men join in, and, still laughing, he walks away with Margaret beside him. You stand up, but your knees are wobbly and you fall forward, scraping your chin. You try to stop your hands from shaking as you collect your sketchbook to go up the steps, back home to your parents. The schoolyard bully has gotten the better of you again.

On your chair behind the curtain, in your torn khakis and undershirt, you stick your nose through the gap. Your scraped chin beads blood like sweat.

The High Street is deserted because Kevin has kept everyone indoors with his ungentlemanly behavior. You see it clearly now, the awful truth that everyone wants to pretend isn't true – these Ditchlings are afraid of what an American might do to avenge himself. Across the road, the curtains of the Tudor house shake with anticipation.

He'll go find Kevin.
He's going to get it over with, Cull. He'll clear the way for
Margaret.
Watch him grab the scorper and go to work.

Point your nose over the church and into the hills. It's not even five, and the South Downs have turned black. You've read about Sussex in early spring. Why is everything barren? Where are the birds? Shouldn't the daffodils be out, along with the poppies?

Pull your nose from the curtains. The tea has curdled in the cup. You haven't eaten since last night's pizza. Down in the café, you could buy a sausage roll, or dinner at The Lantern.

The radiator stands cold and mute against the wall, scowling like a disappointed father. Sheila and Bobby haven't switched on your heat. Why would they, with a coward for a son? If you want to get buried in Ditchling's churchyard, inside the memorial garden, you have to prove you're worthy.

Wipe the blood from your chin. Put on a clean shirt. Wear that black one with the long sleeves so he won't see you coming until it's too late.

In your socks you wander the bedroom. Above your desk, the shelf has a few paperbacks for guests: *The Downs at Your Doorstep. Brideshead Revisited. Watership Down. The Penguin Dictionary of Surnames.*

Surnames. Open to C for Cull, stopping briefly at Cornwall. Celtic and Latin, *cornu* for horn and *wealus* for Welsh.
Cornwall, land that looks like a horn and originally populated with
Welsh. Cowan, Crosby, Crisp. Cull – to take away, to thin the population
of, to kill.

Put on your shoes, wear a warm jacket. Slip the spike
down the inside pocket. That's it – down those stairs like a
man, no need to tiptoe. It's time to hit Ditchling on a Saturday night!

Open the front door and step outside. It's almost dark.
There's something strange going on. You thought you'd find
an empty road, but it's crowded. The Ditchlings are walking
up the High Street in steady streams, carrying bottles of
wine, bulging plastic bags, gift-wrapped parcels, framed art.
You stand in front of the B&B, watching them walk right by
your bootscraper.

There really is no end to these Ditchlings. They seem
to have a common purpose. You fall in behind one of
the columns, past the shops and The Lantern. The High
Street gains in elevation, up to the edge of the village as
if toward some distant communal sacrifice. They appear
to be heading to a low brown building on the right – the
Village Hall. People are walking from the opposite direction
as well. There are cars waiting to turn into the parking lot,
blinkers flashing.

In the front of the Village Hall, lights on either side of
the double doors have been switched on. The Ditchlings
trudge inside silently, heads down. They look like the
bearded thanes from *Beowulf* marching into the guildhall
to discuss war and politics over brown bread and horns
of mead.

You hide under a tree near the entrance, beyond the reach of the lights. As the villagers pass, you recognize a few of them – the woman from the museum with hair like a monk's, carrying a stack of books wrapped in red ribbon. The greengrocer is carrying a box of vegetables, followed by a woman with a basket of marmalades and a man with tattoos on his neck pushing a pram full of apples. Another man is holding a box of wine bottles. An elderly woman is the last to go inside. She's carrying a tray of bright flowers in tiny individual pots.

You come out from under the tree. At the open door you crane your neck inside, trying to overhear fragments of conversation.

A door slams down the road. A beer can rolls toward the curb, and a woman runs past you, visibly pregnant, out of breath.

'You won't get far!' a man shouts from an open window. The woman keeps running down the High Street, and he shouts after her, 'Go on then, bitch! Where are you going to hide after it's born?'

The man shuts the window as her footsteps disappear down the street. He doesn't deserve to produce Ditchlings. You can almost hear the baby inside the woman's womb as she runs: *Come with us. Take my little hand and be my Ditchling father.*

You step cautiously into the lobby, past the umbrella stand and leather club chairs. Plaques line the walls. High on the wall, above all the others, there is a gold-plated plaque etched in Gill Sans.

DITCHLING

Is in the Parliamentary Division of Lewes. Its civic affairs are administered by the Rural District Council, excepting local matters which come under its Parish Council. The duties of a Parish Council are chiefly as follows:

(a) The lighting of the village

(b) Keeping a watchful eye on public rights of way, and in this respect the Parish Council may repair same, if they so desire

(c) The administration of Burial Acts

(d) The provision of recreation grounds, etc., etc.

Other plaques commemorate local associations – the Cricket Club, the Rotarians, the Freemasons and Lions, the Lime-burning, Tanning and Brick-making Guilds, the Ditchling Society of Bellringers. Framed photographs of society banquets stretch the length of the corridor, including a 1951 joint tourist initiative between Madison, Ohio and Ditchling. The middle-aged transatlantic tourist boards are dining together at a long table, dressed in suits with their smiling drunken faces turned to the camera. It strikes you that everyone in the photo is now dead.

At the end of the corridor, voices are coming from a lighted auditorium. A flyer is posted above the door:

Quiz Night Tonight! Win Prizes

All Proceeds to Benefit Ditchling Hospice

You peer inside – under the high arched ceiling, teams are assembled at separate tables. Onstage, an overweight man with a moustache sits on a folding chair, a pile of papers in his lap and a microphone in his hand. Around his feet, like presents under Santa Claus, the Ditchlings have arranged their prizes – the tray of flowers, bottles of wine, the basket of vegetables, the pram filled with apples, jams and cakes and packaged toys, sports equipment, dress shirts wrapped in clear plastic.

The crossword men make up one team. Larry Savage the bald greengrocer sits with the woman from the museum and some elderly women who frequent Sprinkles Café. Sheila and Bobby share a table with a female friend. One team is made up of young men in their early twenties, gawking with expressions of ironic amusement. Another team of young women sits together in the middle of the auditorium, laughing, drinking wine in plastic cups. Margaret is among them. Her hair is down around her shoulders, her face slightly flushed. She sees you in the doorway and raises her hand.

'David? Is it really my David?'

An old woman in a flowing shawl comes toward you, arms outstretched. Her eyes are watery, her lips trembling. 'David,' she says, clutching your shoulders with surprising strength. A man hurries over from the nearby table. 'Mum,' he says, prying her away. 'C'mon, Mum.'

'Tell me where you've been, David!'

'This isn't him,' the man says.

'Not David?'

'No, Mum.' The man turns to you, his voice lowered. He's tall, and he pats at the air with his palms. 'She thinks you're my brother, you see. He died a few years ago, and ever since—'

His mother is frowning now, as if blaming you for resembling her son. 'It's not often we get visitors this time of year,' the man says. 'Do you mind if I ask where you're from?'

'The States. Los Angeles.'

Onstage, the Quizmaster taps the microphone and explains the rules – two rounds of questions, with a twenty-minute break in between. The team with the highest number of points gets first pick of the prizes.

'Please forgive us,' the man says.

'It's all right. I understand.'

Patting the air with his palms, he leads her back toward their table. Then he turns. 'Sorry, would you like to join us? We've plenty of fish and chips. And wine, too. We might form a team?'

His mother, now that the quiz has begun, has lost interest in you. The man seems nice enough. 'It's not against the rules?'

'Rules?' He smiles. 'No, it's very informal here.'

You follow them across the auditorium floor. Along the way the man introduces himself – Brian and his mother Eve. At their table, he gives you an answer sheet and a pen, hands you a plastic cup of red wine. The first question comes over the mike.

'What is the third of Chaucer's *Canterbury Tales*?'

You click your pen, record the answer. A few tables over, Margaret waves again, and you wave back.

'Scrimshaw comes from which animal?'

'Who wrote *Under the Volcano*?'

And now you sense that everything you have stood for in life, everything noble and good, has been a preparation for this hour. The Ditchlings cannot imagine what it has taken, what fortuitous calamities have conspired to produce this single joyful evening when you might finally prove yourself.

'The river Severn originates in which county?'

'What city did Edgar Allan Poe call home?'

The fluorescent lights blaze down on your table like rays from heaven. Your pen scribbles the answers before you have time to second-guess yourself.

'Which popular board game was originally called Criss-Cross?'

The game you were raised to play, the Scrabble tiles – you can almost taste them in your mouth. A man can never remove his memories, nor can he object to unexpected homecomings, surrounded by new family members.

The first round's over. Pass your answer sheet to Brian, watch his eyebrows shoot up his forehead. Eve has stopped blaming you for resembling her dead son. She hands you a package of fish and chips wrapped in butcher paper. The smell of the fish and salty chips makes you gulp at the air. Then, just as you seize your plastic cutlery, Eve leans in, her voice low.

'You're American,' she says.

'Yes.'

'Don't let them know that, my boy. Don't let them find out!'

'Mum,' Brian says. He looks at you more closely. 'It is odd. You really do look like David.'

'Your brother.'

'Yes. He spent a number of years in the States, you see. It changed him. He came back full of plans. He wanted to start up a business here—'

Eve reaches for your hand. 'Be careful,' she says, squeezing your fingers. 'Be careful of the Pollards. And the Swifts!'

'Bobby and Sheila? The owners of the B&B?'

A small hand slides down your cheek and cups your chin.

'That's a nasty scrape.'

You turn in your chair. It's Margaret, and she's drunk, you can tell by her pouty lips, the yellow in her eyes. 'Kevin can be such a beast,' she says. 'He shouldn't have knocked your sketchbook away like that. I don't know what to say except sorry.'

'Forget it.'

She sits down, and under the table her knees graze against yours. 'These questions are impossible,' she says. 'How are you getting on?'

A man with a walking stick taps his way toward your table. His silver hair is combed back behind his ears. 'Malcolm Ketteridge-Wilson,' he says through his dentures, extending his hand.

'I'm John Cull.'

A younger woman stands at his side. Her wrists, ears, and neck are festooned with jewelry. Her face is a tapestry of makeup. 'He's the American I was telling you about,' she says.

Malcolm nods. 'We've spent time in Atlanta, Georgia, back in the sixties. You traveled in England much? Been up to Yorkshire?'

Margaret is watching, trying not to laugh. You reach for the wine and drain it. 'Not yet. It's my first time in the country.'

'You Americans travel round England more than we do! The way I look at it, you're really our transatlantic cousins. I conduct the Chalk Walks round here. I'm sure you've seen the postings.'

'I think so – on the bulletin board?'

'They're really landscape lectures. Ask my wife Jilly about it. Used to be more popular when we had our wheatears and spotted flycatchers.'

'Malcolm's a bit of a birder,' Jilly says.

'Some say the North American goose is responsible for the reduction in our native species,' Malcolm says. He taps his cane near your chair.

'Too many insects and tree worms these days,' Jilly adds.

'I've got a photo of my cousin,' Malcolm says, fumbling for his wallet. 'Lives in Atlanta. He says the Americans don't speak English. Not really.'

'I hear your granddad lived in Ditchling?' Jilly asks, adjusting the diamond bracelet on her wrist. 'Worked with Eric Gill?'

'The way I look at it,' Malcolm says, 'people simply evolve over time. Mind you, I've never gone in for religion.' He taps his cane on the ground. 'We hear you found yourself in a bit of bother with Kevin.'

'It was nothing,' Margaret says.

'Kev's a sound bloke,' Malcolm says. 'Went to a minor public school. His dad invented soap dispensers.'

'Automatic soap dispensers,' Margaret says.

'Automatic soap dispensers.' Malcolm taps his cane again. 'That's it.'

'And now managing director of the ash works,' Jilly says. She puts her hand to her mouth and giggles. 'It's just that – every once in a while, he simply goes irate.'

'And there's no warning,' Malcolm says. 'It could be a petition for more parking that he thinks is getting ignored during council meetings. Or if someone looks at him the wrong way when he's talking about his angling.'

'Is it that strange that Kev should want more decent parking spaces along the High Street?' Margaret asks.

'As I say,' Malcolm says, 'Kev's a sound bloke. I know the two of you are close. It's just that temper, that one little hiccup I'm talking about. Sorry to interrupt your dinner,' he adds, noticing your fish and chips.

'I'll leave you to it,' Margaret says, standing up. A make-shift bar has been erected at the side of the stage, and she heads for the queue, swaying a little.

'You married?' Malcolm asks. He sits beside you, where Margaret had been. 'Children?'

'No. Nothing.'

'Your accent isn't too bad, you know. You don't have to tell people you're from the States.'

'If you wanted to pass as a Canadian, he means,' Jilly says. She drags over a folding chair and sits at the table, barely glancing at Brian and Eve.

Malcolm puts down his newspaper. It's a local daily, and the headlines stare back at you, stained with vinegar. *Mothball Threat to Sussex Estates. Hit-and-run Fugitive Caught After Four-week Hunt. British Trust for Ornithology Warns of Invasive Ruddy Duck.*

You search for the wine bottle, but it's all the way across the table. It wouldn't be polite to ask Brian for a refill. 'Excuse me – I need a drink. I'll be back in a minute.'

The queue for the bar has extended. The two men in front of you are chatting as they inch toward the woman pouring wine.

'But my boy's only eighteen. And *he's* working.'

'What's he doing, then?'

'Nice piece of employment. The benefits office, no less – finding other people jobs. Mind you, we're still paying his bills…'

You look around. Stains streak the auditorium's white-washed walls – spilled coffee from Historical Society luncheons, splashed beer from Rotary Club banquets. The ghosts have come out of the churchyard to drift among the living.

I died in a hospice. The money raised here will go to a good cause.
Out in the corridor you'll find me in the Lions Club photo.
I'm beside him, in the back row on the left, wearing the funny hat.

Margaret has received her wine. She gathers her hair in one hand and uncoils it across her back. After a quick sip, she heads back to her table.

Not a bad looking lass.
Cull will soon be dead – he should get her while he can.
He won't be the first to be enticed by Ditchlings.

Up on the stage, the man with the moustache raises his mike. 'Time for the second round!'

The people in the queue peel away. The dangers of drink are paramount – but you drop a fiver in the cup, take your plastic goblet, go back to claim your fish and chips.

'What is the largest island in Japan?'

Back at Brian and Eve's table, you place the answer in its box, courtesy of the geography your father drilled into you during your pre-teen years – punishment, disguised as life preparation.

'This one's dead easy. Who is buried by the winning post at Aintree?'

You glance at Brian, biting the end of your pen.

'Horse racing,' he whispers. 'Don't worry, I've got it.'

The Quizmaster rocks on his chair, hand on the mike. 'Which midfielder had his first start on England's 1966 World Cup team?'

A bit of panic – sports trivia isn't your strong suit. But Brian keeps scribbling. His back is straight, his cheeks pale despite the wine. Maybe you *are* related. Beside him, his mother looks on proudly.

'How many hands are buried in Ditchling Common?'

'A bit of local knowledge,' Brian says, waving in your direction. 'How many are there, Mum – twelve?'

'The word *pandemonium* was invented by which writer?'

Now you're back on familiar ground. In high school, while your classmates hit the beach, or drove the canyons stoned, you read Milton in your bedroom.

'How many sonnets did Shakespeare write?'

Answer logged. The second round ends, the Ditchlings huddle and consult. You hand your answer sheet to Brian, and his eyebrows waggle up his forehead again. He produces the master sheet and passes it to the stage.

The auditorium falls silent while the Quizmaster tabulates the scores. The tension is too much and someone has a coughing fit. Another Ditchling starts to wheeze. The Quizmaster points his pencil at your table and says first prize.

The applause rises to the roof beams. Brian and Eve gesture for you to stand. Out of your chair, you stand tall without crouching. The applause rains down in waves, and you drain your wine, dab the sweat on your forehead, walk dizzily to the stage.

'Anything you want,' the Quizmaster tells you.

It's better than Christmas. What will you choose? A basket of marmalades? A dress shirt?

A framed watercolor leans against the stage. You pick it up, hold it at arm's length. Someone's painted the B&B. There is the front window opened to the breakfast table, there are the front steps faithfully rendered, the double black handrail and even something that looks like a bootscraper. And on the top floor, something has been added to the gap between the curtains. It's a nose.

You turn and narrow your eyes at the assembled Ditchlings, talking and drinking at their tables. Onstage the Quizmaster leans forward on his folding chair, sleeves rolled to his elbows, hands on his thighs, waiting.

'Is the artist who painted this here?' you ask him.

'Donors typically remain anonymous. Please hurry – I have to announce second place.'

The Ditchlings are gathering. A camera flashes, then another. The chroniclers are recording your moment with the offending painting, gathering evidence in case of a future crime. You lean the frame back against the stage. The tray of flowers will do nicely – pick them up, show everyone your choice.

Margaret watches you walk toward her, the faint smile on her face becoming an open giggly grin. She's sweet when she laughs. You place the tray of flowers on the table in front of her, pluck her a tulip and bow, kiss her cheek, linger at her neck, savor the soft white skin. Her friends titter and gasp. This is the real prize, the smell of pale and milky flesh. Then you notice it – a small, beautiful mole – hidden in the underbelly of her chin. And all at once, this wondrous mole puts the lie to Margaret's preternaturally pale complexion. Her character seems to change before you, to deepen and darken, disabusing her of her pale flower identity, transforming her into a person capable of enigmatic subterranean depths and pigmentation portals to ancient *homo antecessors*. She smiles as you linger – perhaps she was trying to keep the mole secret, but now the truth is out.

The cameras flash. The applause continues, even as you return to your table. Margaret's mole is yours and yours alone. Surely Kevin doesn't know of it. He's not the type to notice a blemish in his milk.

When you're back in your chair, away from her table, the moment of victory fades. An old sadness overtakes you, a defeated sense of futility from a lifetime of strikeouts. What if that beast, that jackass and monkey and fool, with his Disneyland sensibilities, actually *knows of Margaret's mole*? What if managing directors of the Bone Ash Works are more than typically observant?

Brian offers you a celebratory cup of wine, and you drain it with a grimace. It will kill you if Kevin knows of the mole. You must believe, even if this belief requires a leap of faith, that Kevin remains unaware of her beautiful nuance, her transcendental Hawthornian mark, her flaw that redeems all of humanity, like Jesus on the cross.

The hunger that raged moments before has been reduced to a cramp. You observe yourself at a cold and removed distance, like a fly on your own shoulder studying its host as it reaches for another plastic cup. The Quizmaster announces second place: the crossword men. The grumpy wordsmiths send their delegate to the stage. He's the oldest of the crosswords, a know-it-all, his long curly hair a remnant from his rebellious days in the seventies, an amateur academic who doesn't appreciate being knocked down by an American punk. He waves a pale hand, churlishly acknowledging the lukewarm applause – he's used to coming in first.

'Take the next step,' Eve says, fixing her watery eyes on you. 'With Margaret.'

Your wine wobbles in your hand. 'Beg your pardon?'

'She's a lovely girl. Do you fancy her?'

'Mother,' Brian says.

'Poor Carlo. They made such an exotic pair. He'd still be alive if it weren't for Kevin.'

Brian swats the air with his palms. 'Take no notice of her,' he tells you.

Kevin – behind Margaret's husband's death? You're about to fish for information when Eric Gill appears at the door. He's wearing his grandfather's outfit again. He's offended and wants an apology. You can tell by the way his legs are spread wide in his robe, the way he coldly and disdainfully looks over the tops of his spectacles at the gathering. He sees you and pretends not to notice.

'Excuse me,' you tell Brian and Eve, 'I must join my friend...'

You cross the auditorium. Eric Gill barely nods when you reach his side, but at least he doesn't abandon you. The two of you stand beside each other, the master and his apprentice, surveying the Ditchlings.

'Sorry about the bootscraper.'

Malcolm is passing in front of you – he turns on his cane.

'Good work tonight,' he says, and you nod in thanks as he continues toward the bar.

'Someone's making lots of friends.'

'I said I was sorry, Eric. About the bootscraper.'

'I should have known to expect the worst from an American. Bull in a china shop. In future, I'll be keeping my plans to myself.'

'If anyone has a right to be offended, it's me. I would never have painted *your* nose without permission.'

'I didn't paint that ghastly piece. I do have some sense of proportion – the nose, as rendered, is far too small.'

Bobby and Sheila have spotted you by the door. They're approaching with their friend, a very tall woman with bleached hair and broad shoulders, wearing heels.

'Here come more of your *friends*,' Eric says, and he disappears up the corridor.

'Our lodger,' Sheila says, 'takes Quiz Night!' She's put on a dress and clean stockings. Her hair clings to her scalp in tight ringlets.

Bobby is beaming. He's holding a paper plate with chips and ketchup. 'On his first go, too.'

'Didn't you like that painting, luv?' Sheila asks. She puts her hand on her friend's back. 'This is Brenda. She's been studying.'

'It was shit,' Brenda says. 'Because he didn't take the picture, did he?'

'Maybe it was that nose,' Bobby says. 'What's the word – cartoonish?'

'It was shit,' Brenda says again.

'Brenda's taking art classes in Brighton,' Sheila says.

'I hope you don't mind me putting that nose in,' Brenda

says. 'I live across the road, you see. The flat above the jeweler's. Right across from yours.'

She's staring you up and down. There is a silence, and Bobby chews the end of a chip. 'You two are almost the same height,' he says.

'No – I'm in heels,' Brenda says, showing you the backs of her shoes.

'I liked your painting, I just didn't think it would fit into my suitcase. I wish I could be taking art classes in Brighton.'

'Come and join us,' Sheila says. 'There's music next. We have wine.'

Margaret is watching from her table. 'I'd like to. But I have an appointment…'

You hurry out of the auditorium. Eric Gill is at the end of the corridor, standing in front of a framed poster, his hand on his chin. You stand at his side, and together the two of you admire the old lettering.

DITCHLING GOOSEBERRY
AND CURRANT SHOW.
The Seventy-Seventh Annual Meeting of
the Horticultural Society, 26 July 1899.
For the Best Pint of Red Rough Gooseberries
(Strigs and Eyes not to be removed),
a Copper Tea Kettle, unless the person has
previously obtained the Kettle, then a Prize
of Five Shillings will be given.

'Life was simpler in those days,' Eric says, straightening his paper cap. 'Don't remove those gooseberry strigs before judging! Look here, John. "Prize for biggest turnip, two shillings." And "For the Best Gallon of Peas, a Duck will be given by Mr John Brown." How nice to be able to live in such harmony with your neighbors. How good it feels to be a native.'

'Please. How can I make it up to you?'

'To grow wholesome crops. To lead a communal English life without the interference of outside strangers.'

'I'll do anything.'

'You seem to be getting distracted. Socially, I mean. Are you sure you have time to spend with me, away from your friends?'

'I just wandered in here. I hadn't planned on staying—'

'That book on bootscrapers,' Eric says, turning to you. 'I might do with an assistant.'

'Really?' You reach for his hand and grip it tight. 'Tell me, Eric. Tell me what you'd like me to do.'

'I will draw the illustrations. And I will write the text. When I'm finished, you can scorp around my drawings. Do a little editing, of course. There might be some production costs involved…if you prove yourself, we'll see about expanding your role.'

'Can I write a word or two? Maybe do a small sketch?'

His arms fly out of his robe, and he seizes your shoulders. His nails are sharp and dig into your flesh. 'You think you can simply walk into the role of an artist? You've got to earn it.'

'Please let me go, Eric. All right, I'll do it. I'll be your scorper.'

'John?'

The two of you turn toward the auditorium as Margaret walks slowly along the corridor. She moves without shifting the air. She comes all the way up to you, looks at the poster on the wall, then back to you, her hair slightly awry, her mascara smudged from laughing, or crying, or both. Her drunken, sad beauty suits her. She has the wide blue eyes of mountains and fields.

'What are you doing out here?' Margaret asks. 'Leaving already?'

Eric lingers beside you, openly leering. It's not appropriate, the way he's gurgling and smacking his lips. You open your mouth, but the words simply won't come.

'You're reluctant to chat,' she says. 'Because of earlier. You're still angry with me because of Kevin.'

Eric is back at it, cackling and snorting. He even points at Margaret's breasts. 'Shut up,' you tell him, and she looks at you sharply, thinking you meant her.

'I don't blame you for being upset,' she says.

'We're creating a book on Ditchling's bootscrapers.' It isn't exactly your intention to reveal it – the secret just comes blurting out.

'A book? Who's creating the book?'

'I am. I'm thinking of including Eric Gill.'

Before you can explain, Eric's got you by the throat again. Because of the constraints of his robe, he can't move as freely as you can. You catch him hard in the ear and chase him out the door. As he runs off down the High Street, you almost feel sorry for him.

Margaret's waiting for her American.
She'll lose interest if he's not careful.
Go on, mate – get over there and say something.

Ditchling's Bellringers are calling out to you from their framed photograph. They're right – Margaret has retired to one of the leather club chairs in the lobby, beside a potted tree. You come toward her, straightening your shirt collar. There's applause and clinking glasses in the auditorium, where a man is playing guitar and singing an old folk song.

You kneel at Margaret's side and reach for her neck. 'We've both had too much to drink,' she says, taking your hand. She gives it a light squeeze and releases it. Up the corridor, a couple of Ditchlings come out of the auditorium, see you and Margaret, and hurry back in.

You remain kneeling beside her. Margaret touched you, just for a moment – she grasped your hand in a way that gives you confidence. The musician starts another song.

'I could keep kneeling here without talking. Or I could tell you what's on my mind.'

'Go on.'

'For years I've been gripped with a desire to create something that people talk about, long after I'm gone. Hasn't everyone felt this, just for a moment? Who hasn't stood in a library, or in a museum, and felt a painful sense of his place in history? Do you remember how you loved to read as a young girl? Do you remember when you woke from your dreams, and you dared to remember the details, and the details were more important to you than anything in your waking life? You recorded your dreams because you didn't want to forget.'

Margaret has sunk deep into her chair. Her face has fallen into the shadows, but you can see that she is staring at you. 'Meet me later,' she says.

You lift your hand, move her hair aside, find the mole.

'We can't do this in public,' she says.

'Because of Kevin?'

Margaret stands up out of the chair. 'It's a small village.' She checks the entrance to the auditorium, then quickly encircles your neck with her arms. 'I don't want people to think I'm up to something.'

'I understand.'

'You're the first American I've met in Ditchling.'

She pulls herself closer, clasps the back of your neck. Your mouth is against her skin. It cannot be – you are crossing the threshold. And you have come face to face again with the mole.

'Tell me – does Kevin know about it?'

'What?'

'The mole.'

There is a long silence. Her arms leave your shoulders, and she steps away. 'What are you talking about?'

You remain kneeling, alone, your arms hanging limp at your sides. 'That mole – the mole under your chin.'

She laughs nervously, finds it with the ends of her chewed fingers. 'I don't know.'

'It would make me sad. If he did know.'

'I should get back to my friends, rejoin my team.'

'What was that question about the hands buried on Ditchling Common?'

Slowly she walks back toward you and leans in, her elbows on your shoulders, placing the mole in front of you once more. You can feel her hand on the back of your neck. 'An old myth. About strangers like you, coming here and interfering with our ways. The birds disappear when the strangers come – so they're caught, and their hands are cut off as a warning.'

'What a heart-warming tale.'

Margaret stares at you with her lovely blue-gray eyes. 'There's this cottage behind the museum. The old school-master's house. If it's clear at night, you can see the stars from the bench in the back garden. Nobody goes there, nobody will see us. Meet me there tonight. Around eleven?'

She doesn't wait for you to agree. She cups your cheek in her little palm and returns along the corridor, swaying slightly from the drink.

5

It is not impossible to imagine Neolithic man in his cave, making use of many chisels and flint carving tools to fashion objects pleasurable to the eye. Likewise the resourceful scorper should not limit himself to a single tool. He may make use of jumpers, points and punches. To remove a goodly amount of stone he may prefer a wider edged implement. For end grain woodwork he is wise to take in hand a finer point or hacksaw blade.

Mr Gill believed art is beautiful in the same degree that we labour to make it so. He did not approve of modern forms of production. 'Industrialisation is to be condemned', he used to say, 'for it reduces the workman to a subhuman condition of intellectual irresponsibility'. In Ditchling Mr Gill was ever fond of sayings that made me believe he could at times be a fellow of pious and rigorous judgment. 'A good life is mortified life. Good taste is mortified taste, that is, in which the stupid, the sentimental, the irrelevant is killed'.

What does it mean, some of us asked, to kill things that are irrelevant? What is the best way to live? The older members took notice of his words and had their own interpretation. They referred to an ancient Ditchling prophecy about strangers and said the artists on the Common should cleave to it in the strictest possible manner.

There are voices down on the pavement. They are loud and raucous, like a lynch mob. Close *Scorper*, place it back on the bookshelf. Could it be that a posse is forming to get you – a citizen's brigade seeking justice for your upcoming date with Margaret?

Stick your nose through the gap. No, it is just a few drunken Ditchlings, returning from Quiz Night. They pass beneath your window under the lamplight, singing and bellowing at each other, and at the end of the High Street they separate, into their homes, lock their doors to keep you out. The so-called special relationship with America is evidently not based on trust.

Margaret will cut through the divide. She'll represent the milder, conciliatory side of her country at your transatlantic summit in the schoolmaster's garden. You'd better dress properly. That's it, go and get a fresh shirt. Tuck it in. Put on a blazer.

A transatlantic summit – but what if the meeting is a trap? What if Margaret isn't mild at all? What if she's pretending to be nice so that she can be the bait for Kevin's hook? You should bring your spike for self-defense. The curtains shake with anticipation.

> *Take some practice stabs.*
> *Make the first one count.*
> *Hurry up, Cull – the church bells are ringing.*

Turn your back to the window, one stab for each chime. Over and over you cut through Kevin's flesh. The bell rings and the spike stabs – and is there some significance to the time she's chosen? Seven. Eight, nine. There is an ominous pause between the tenth and the eleventh chime, making you pause with the spike in the air, uncomfortably waiting, as if by some impossible chance the mechanism is broken. There it is at last. Will eleven stabs be enough?

Take it easy now. Don't get worked up. She's only invited you to sit on a bench, for God's sake. That's it, hide that weapon in your blazer pocket – hopefully you won't need to use it.

But Margaret is a woman. And women have betrayed you, haven't they?

Don't think about the past. There is no need to revisit the minor and supposedly forgettable episodes that make up your limited sexual history. You hope that tonight will be different, you hope that you are beginning a new phase of adulthood – the British holiday romance – but as you leave your room and creep down the stairs, your former girlfriends are waiting at the bottom of the landing. There is nothing positive about this development, nothing to be gained by their presence.

You've had two 'relationships'. And they're *there* all right, the both of them, huddling by the coat stand. As you sneak out of the B&B, they follow behind you, hovering over your shoulder.

Take the little lane to the museum. Elbow the women aside and stride ahead. It's not fair – they won't be shaken off. Natalie takes one arm and Rachel the other, and they drag you over to the graves beyond the lime trees. They have been getting to know each other, here in Ditchling. They whisper and compare notes as they hold you on top of a gravestone. It's not enough to traumatize your memories – your ex-girlfriends want their stories told in the company of the dead.

'A fresh start,' you beg as you try to escape. They jab you with their elbows until you submit to being revisited under the lime trees' gnarled branches and naked trunks.

You met Natalie in *Introduction to Shakespeare*, first year in college. She had come from an exclusive prep school in Maryland, an institution with puritanical Quaker roots that had evolved into a bohemian experimental laboratory for sex. At eighteen, she'd already had flings with a dozen men, including her math teacher. She had shoulder-length blonde hair, brown eyes, long swimmer's legs. What she saw in you, God knows. Maybe it was the fact that you'd been reading Shakespeare closely while she'd been sleeping her way through high school. Maybe it was your terrifying height – another box for her to tick – but you weren't about to protest, and soon you were walking campus together, holding hands.

Then Natalie's father visited from Maryland. He was a famous artist with windblown hair and a haunted expression. He had an exhibition in town, and he invited you both to lunch. Natalie introduced you, and after looking you up and down he seemed to recognize the limits of your soul. He barely spoke to you during the meal. He kept his haunted glances to more important areas of the restaurant.

The snub plagued you for weeks. For the first time, you were unable to make love. Natalie pretended not to be bothered by your impotence and suggested her Quaker education meant that sex didn't much matter. Slowly you felt her shift away. When you went to parties together, she would gaze over your shoulder at other men. She started to hum out loud when you spoke.

One night, you went to her room and found it locked. On

the other side of the door were noises – noises that stopped when you knocked. The next morning she had a new friend, a Russian exchange student named Dmitri, a chain smoker and self-proclaimed nihilist who liked to crush his cigarette butts into the open pages of books. Soon *they* were walking campus together holding hands. From her friends you heard that she took the nihilist to lunch with her famous father. And because Natalie continued seeing Dmitri, you suspected her father found the nihilist to his liking.

The impact of these events lingered. The more you tried to meet other women, the more you suffered psychic aftershocks. To be made impotent by an artist, and his daughter, and his daughter's Russian boyfriend – how could you recover? There passed years of embarrassingly incompetent flirtations and failed one-night-stands. Then you met Rachel, at a bar, almost three years ago. You spoke to her because she was plain and because you wanted to build up your confidence. The fact that you worked as an editor actually seemed to interest her.

You talked about ideas, and you talked about books and paintings, movies and politics. You talked about Los Angeles – its beauty, its youth, its inability to portray nuances to a world that preferred it to advertise superficiality. Then, a few weeks after your first date, Rachel stayed over. You knew it was coming, and you dreaded the inevitable, while hoping it somehow wouldn't happen. After you led her to the bedroom, she slipped under the covers and waited, panties off and T-shirt pushed up to her shoulders. You unbuckled your belt, took off your pants. Then it returned again – the memory of Natalie's father, passing his eyes over you without interest, ignoring you during lunch, the memory of Natalie looking over your shoulder at parties and humming when you spoke, the memory of her walking around with Dmitri. And when you climbed on top of Rachel there was nothing between your legs to speak of. You mumbled an apology, pulled up the sheets, endured the silence.

'Has it happened before?' Rachel asked.

'With my first girlfriend.'

'How many other girlfriends have you had, John?'

This was one subject you had not yet discussed. There was nothing to say, nothing at all. You turned on your side and did not reply – and Rachel, in her intelligence, divined the necessary truths.

'Maybe we'll try again in the morning,' she said. Then she turned on her side with her back to you, and she switched off the light.

Later that night, you heard her masturbating. You pretended to be asleep until she'd finished, and after she fell asleep you lay awake, all night, until the morning came with its promise of a temporary escape from human interaction. Rachel didn't leave, though, until after she'd had her breakfast. It was over your bowls of cereal that she told you her theory.

'Men are impotent,' she said, 'if they never go after what they truly want. John, your only heroes are dead artists.'

You did not reply to this – you simply finished your cereal. Was Rachel implying that you should go after the life of an artist, or go after being dead? You walked her to the door and didn't kiss goodbye.

Lying on top of the grave, you stare at the stars. Natalie and Rachel have left you alone at last, but Ditchling's dead have not.

Surely he's had sex since Natalie. Ten years?
Rachel could have been gentler with him.
Maybe Margaret will be. Hurry, Cull – it's past eleven,
and she's getting impatient.

You leave the graveyard and jog up the lane. A small schoolmaster's cottage stands to the right of the museum. In front of the door, on the broken concrete, remains the faded chalk outline of a hopscotch game. One, two, three, four, turn around, go home, stop pretending, give up.

A path, overgrown with moss and rotting leaves, winds around the side of the house. It's dark and there are worms underfoot – you can feel them squish. You come to a garden behind the cottage, enclosed by stone walls. Ferns drape over the walls. And there is Margaret on a wooden bench under a canopy of blackberry bushes. She's lying on her side, huddled in her raincoat, perhaps asleep.

You walk the wet grass, scanning the garden for Kevin. Margaret sits up suddenly – and before you know it she's left the bench and running toward you, faster than you'd thought she was capable.

'You're sweating,' she says, wrapping her arms around your waist. She looks up at you with her blue gray eyes, and you were out of your mind to think she could have deceived you, that she could be bait for anyone's hook.

'I ran. I lost track of time.'

She stands back and sweeps the air with her hand, still a little drunk. 'Welcome to my school. I played next door every day. Even in the rain.'

The two of you sit on the bench and listen to the owls. A bird feeder with chipped paint hangs from a cherry tree.

Broken flowerpots litter the grass.

'What happened to this place?'

'Not enough children in Ditchling. The schoolmaster's cottage is abandoned, and they turned what used to be the school into the museum.'

A cold wind blows high overhead. You are protected by the walls, and the trees, and the wind travels on its way without molesting you for long. It is a pleasant thing to sit quietly without talking. 'Please don't say anything for a moment,' you tell Margaret.

She nods. The fact that she understands your whimsical and potentially rude request for silence makes you relieved. You reach for her hand. Maybe it's your nerves – you start to laugh. It's the strange act of holding a hand – flesh and bones, a hand that belongs to someone else – inside your own. Laughter is contagious, as they say. Soon the two of you are laughing, still holding hands and losing yourselves in the idiotic mindlessness of laughter.

After you've finished you sit in silence again. Your smile fades. Margaret's smile fades as well. You stare at the wet grass under the moonlight. What was once mindlessness evolves into a horrible awareness, tinged with sadness, of your inability to say anything meaningful. You become so self-conscious, you are wary of shifting even slightly on the bench, for fear of disturbing what remains of your earlier lightheartedness.

'It's a nice night!'

Your words linger in the garden and fade. There is another uncomfortably long silence. You have broken your own contract of not talking, and you want to drink to the health of all the people in the world who are lonely. Your hands are still entwined, but they are so devoid of feeling that they might as well be piles of twigs.

'I shouldn't have said it was a nice night.'

She looks at you. There is nothing to do but try to kiss her. You don't understand why you must participate in this mad enterprise – but your lips briefly touch, and remarkably, she doesn't pull away. You lean back to where you had been before, and you stare in panic at the naked cherry tree and broken bird feeder.

'You mentioned a book,' Margaret says, holding your hand a little tighter now.

'The book on bootscrapers? It's very much in the formative stages.'

'Tell me about it. If you'd like.'

'It's probably going to be a small book.'

'That doesn't matter all that much, I shouldn't think.'

Her words give you confidence. 'You're right – it *doesn't* matter. I'm in the early stages of my career. What does it matter if my first book is small?'

'Exactly.'

'Somewhere between experience and expression – that's where I am. In the past, each time I've tried to devote myself to a piece of art I lose momentum, somehow. But now I'm really about to launch into this project. It might sound strange, but I think it's because I met you.'

A series of loud beeps comes from Margaret's pocket. She drops your hand like it doesn't contain anything, least of all your feelings, and takes out her phone.

The cold wind couldn't touch you, but technology has found its way into the garden. The squished worms on the path scream out with their dying breaths.

Stop talking, Cull.
He'd bloody well better not, under any circumstances, use
the word 'muse.'
Or tell her he's lonely.

'I have to go soon,' Margaret says, reading her text. She puts the phone back in her pocket.

'When you leave, I'll be by myself, of course.'

Margaret scoots further away without seeming to move. 'It's just getting late,' she says.

'I'm used to it. Being by myself, I mean. Don't listen to what I was saying earlier. You shouldn't even pay attention to what I'm saying now, as a matter of fact. It's not as if you're my muse! Was that Kevin?'

'Yeah.'

'That's nice.'

'You must think he's a right dickhead.'

'Not at all. He seems like a really good guy.'

She looks at you. 'He can be. He helped me get on after Carlo died. But I know he also *can* be a dickhead.'

The words 'Kev' and 'dickhead' hover over the bench. You want to ask about the circumstances of Carlo's death. But before you know it Margaret is talking again – partly to you, and partly, it seems, to the garden.

'It's all because of the dough. Most people don't know the difference between hand-made and frozen, but *I* do. I'm up at half four every morning making it fresh, only to come up short every night with a whole lot of uneaten pizza.'

'Are you closed tomorrow?'

'Of course – on Sundays we honor the Lord!' She laughs again, but this time it's full of spite.

'Because if you weren't closed tomorrow, I'd come back. I thought your pizza was delicious.'

'Really?' She turns. 'I liked watching you eat it.' She pushes your shoulders against the bench, and her little hands go to work unbuttoning your shirt. She slips her hands around your waist. She leans in and kisses you, full on the mouth.

'What's this?' Her hands knock up against the spike in your jacket. She reaches in, takes it out. 'What *is* this?'

'Nothing much.'

The spike looks even more menacing in the moonlight. She tests the point with her finger. 'Where did you get this nasty thing?'

'The church.'

Margaret giggles. 'You dirty little thief. Coming to England and taking our relics.'

'I thought it might come in handy. Especially around Kevin.'

'Hah.' She drops the spike back into your jacket and stands up. 'He doesn't like you,' she says. 'But I might. You're the first American I've ever really talked to.' She straddles your lap and finishes unbuttoning your shirt. She leans in again when her phone goes off.

'Oh, for fuck's sake.'

Still on your lap, she wiggles the phone out of her jeans. You wait there with your shirt flapping in the breeze while she leans her elbows on your shoulders and reads the text. The electronic display lights up the ends of her chewed fingers.

'I've got to go.' She climbs off and puts the phone back in her pocket.

'Can't you stay a little longer?'

'No. But come by tomorrow, okay? Ignore the sign that says I'm shut. I've got something to show you.'

'What is it?'

'Something of your grandfather's.' A parting peck on the lips, and she's gone.

For nearly an hour you shiver in the garden. A more sinister stream of cold air finds its way over the walls. It slivers along the grass and snakes up the legs of your trousers.

Margaret has something of your grandfather's? Your father once showed you a photo of the man's childhood home – a tiny cottage, a gray street, an automobile in the driveway. There is a rumor that he spent his infancy in an orphanage.

Strangely, your father has no interest in this ancestral fishing expedition. Not knowing allows a man to cultivate his myths. And that is the way it is with Americans, you reflect on the cold garden bench – they sail away, cut themselves off with weapons and wars and oceans, only to wake up as ghosts, searching for their former selves in Sussex, Holland, Germany, Africa. They reach for their wallets and book their flights. Back at home they share the snapshots, compare ghost stories based on the ribbon from a distant relative's hat.

The longer you sit on the bench, the more you fear you'll never leave Ditchling. The bench-makers of the world have been secretly trapping people for years. People sit down to rest their feet, and the next thing they know, they're dying.

You return along the path of the dead worms. Out in front of the schoolmaster's cottage you move through the faded squares of the hopscotch, back between the lime trees into the sacred garden of headstones. Your hunger is a sharp pain in your side, a turning knife.

Ditchling is quiet – and as you walk under the stars toward Boddington's Lane, you realize you are officially spying now, just as they suspected. There was something suspicious about Margaret tonight. If you can catch a glimpse of her, even her shadow behind a curtain, you might get the jump on her, psychologically speaking.

She thinks she is luring you with this information about your grandfather. She thinks you care about putting together a scrapbook. Doesn't she understand the extent of your dilemma? Does she think you want to go back to America with a handful of souvenirs? You've come to leave your *own* souvenir, reclaim your territory, leave your mark.

Quiz Night has laid Ditchling low. Even the mail slots, embedded in the flint, stay quiet. You tread softly on the cobblestones, and the ancient spirits of the lane flatten themselves against the stone to let you pass. They aren't expecting anyone out and about this late.

'Keep out of the way,' you whisper. 'Don't betray me.'

The lane turns. The walls close in. You've almost reached the pizza shop when a small figure in a raincoat appears in the distance.

It's Margaret. You're sure of it – the quick movements, the shape of her narrow shoulders – you start to call out when she opens a door. A dirty yellow light shines across the lane, and you press your back against the wall. The door creaks shut, and you return to the darkness.

You wait with your neck pressed against the cold stone, watching what remains of the light in the narrow window above the door. If this light goes off, you make a deal with yourself to go home.

The minutes pass, the light stays on. It's so quiet, you can hear murmurs. You creep along the cobblestones, stop outside her door, and lean in. Margaret is in there, consoling someone, her voice faint but audible.

'It's all right. The pain will pass. Things will get better. They have to get better...'

Is she consoling herself? You lean in further, place your ear against the cold wood. The silence makes you worry. It is the silence of a void opening in someone's mind, a cavity created by unspeakable pain.

'Margaret?'

You jiggle the handle. The door opens abruptly, and a sickly woman with long white hair stands in front of you in a white nightgown. Behind her, flickering candles throw shadows against the walls.

'Sorry – I was looking for Margaret?'

The old woman comes at you. She bats you in the chest with her fists. You hold her off as she fills Boddington's Lane with screams.

Margaret's home, like the pizza shop, resembles a cave. The walls are brick, and the stone floor is covered with rugs. A kitchen off to the side has a copper chimney. The little window above the door faces the lane.

You sit at a wooden table in the center of the main room, sipping black tea. Margaret hangs laundry on the radiators. An electric radio is tuned to the late-night news. Margaret has changed into a T-shirt and pajama bottoms. She walks barefoot, her hair down, her shoulders slumped. As she hangs the laundry she consoles her mother-in-law, Dona Matarazzo. 'You'll get better,' she says. 'The pain will pass with time.' The old woman does not appear to be listening. She reclines on a narrow bed in the corner, propped against pillows, a handkerchief in one hand and a string of rosary beads in the other. Her threadbare socks poke out of the bottom of the blankets.

On the wall, and on Dona Matarazzo's bedside table, are framed photographs of Carlo, her dead son. He was handsome, almost pretty, with shoulder-length light brown hair and a strong Italian nose. There are also a few framed photos of the Pope. Incense burns underneath icons on the wall.

Dona Matarazzo mutters in Italian, staring at you with her coal-black eyes. You try to smile at her, but she looks like she wants to leap out of bed and hit you some more.

'What is she saying, Margaret?'

'My Italian isn't very good,' Margaret says. 'But I think you scared her to death.' She bends over, her hands on her knees, taking short gasps.

'What's the matter?'

'Too much to drink. It'll pass.'

'*Capisco bene.*' Dona Matarazzo lifts her handkerchief to her mouth. She coughs without stopping, and with growing ferocity. It is a deep unclearing, as if she has become the mouthpiece for someone being tortured in the center of the earth.

Margaret shudders. She's still bent over, a damp pillowcase hanging from her hand, her face even paler than normal. 'What were you *doing* out there? Opening people's doors in the middle of the night?'

'I was just taking a walk.' You glance at the old woman, at the Pope, at Carlo – they all can tell you're lying.

'I don't know *why* I had so much wine,' Margaret says. She tosses the pillowcase over the back of a chair.

Dona Matarazzo is still coughing. Her feet shake in her socks, and her bed rocks under her shoulders. Margaret is watching you, as if waiting for an honest answer, while the radio blares against the wall.

'In a moment, Gardener's Question Time. First, the weather. Over most of the UK, damp conditions tomorrow, with strong gusty winds in the south...'

Dona Matarazzo takes deep breaths between coughs. She doubles over on her side with her face to the pillow. Something has invaded her, a malignant force intent on squeezing out her lungs. Margaret pads into the kitchen to put the kettle on. She waits for the electric click and pours out the water.

'Mama,' she says, bringing her a mug. The old woman can't stop coughing long enough to sit up. 'Mama,' Margaret says, and crawls into the tiny bed. She sits with her back against the pillows, leans the old woman against her chest, cradles her until the coughing subsides.

There is a loan application open on the table. You're sitting at an angle that allows you to read it.

APPLICANT: Margaret Matarazzo, Boddington's Lane
CO-SIGNATORY: Kevin Pollard, Bridge Lane
PROPERTY ADDRESS: 'The Studios', Ditchling Common
PROPERTY DESCRIPTION: The parish of Ditchling has an area of 3,844 acres, a long, narrow strip little more

than a mile wide, and about 6 miles long from north to south. A ridge runs along the north-western boundary, culminating in the crest of Lodge Hill, or Dicul's hill, 275 feet just above the village. The southern third of the parish is downland, rising steeply to the Beacon. There is an extensive common at the north end of the parish, with St George's Retreat, a convent of the Sisters of St Augustine, and a sanatorium, in the north-east angle. Near the northern end of the common is Jacob's Post, the remains of an ancient gibbet. The Pound is situated just to the south-west of the railway bridge, and adjacent are the studios once owned by the Guild of St Joseph and St Dominic, the Roman Catholic Community of Dominican Tertiaries engaged in various crafts. The subject property consists of a Grade II listed studio, outbuilding, and dedicated chicken house...

The candles flicker on the bedside table. Margaret brushes the old woman's long white hair, dries her watery eyes. 'That's it,' Margaret says. 'You're feeling better now, aren't you?' You watch the two of them with longing. You might have had a future with Margaret and her ailing mother-in-law. You could have been the Good Samaritan instead of Kevin.

'So,' Margaret says, 'it just so happens that you were outside our door?' Dona Matarazzo has stopped coughing. She sips from her mug, and the two of them wait for your reply.

You stare at your soggy tea leaves. *Gardener's Question Time* saves you.

'*We're simply encouraging everyone to keep track of any strange insect activity. Write down your observations, send them in by email, text, or tweet. It's all part of our general awareness plan with the British Trust for Ornithology. The question all of us are asking is, are these changes in plant life due to the reductions in native birds?'*

'You don't have to answer,' Margaret says, smiling a little. 'It's only Mama who was frightened.' She gets up, leans Dona Matarazzo carefully against the pillows, takes the mug from her hands. The old woman's eyes have started to close.

'Her cough sounds awful.'

'She's been this way ever since Carlo died.'

'Have you had her checked out? I'm not sure this damp is good for her.'

Margaret looks up sharply. 'What would you have me do?'

'What about Italy?'

'She's got no one there. Everyone's dead or moved away. Her husband passed a long time ago. So she's here, where I can keep her safe. It's not every night that she gets frightened half to death by strangers opening our door.'

'I heard voices. I thought you were in trouble—'

'You're a crap liar.' Leaning over, Margaret blows out the candle on the bedside table. 'Maybe Kev's right. Maybe you are some kind of spy.'

'You don't know how it is. You think Americans *like* traipsing around? Hunting down the vestiges of their heritage when they have enough problems at home? The English emigrants would never have left if they'd known what was going to happen.'

Margaret puts on her raincoat and comes to the table. 'I was only teasing, John. Relax.'

'They couldn't have anticipated the consequences…'

'I want to smoke a fag. And then I want to sleep.'

She reaches for the pack of cigarettes on the table, and

you are momentarily caught by the warning photo – a grainy ultrasound of a little pinched creature fighting for life. You want to tell Margaret that you'd rather be this nicotine baby than a man who feels dead each morning you wake up, dead as you drive to work, and dead when you park on the top floor of the garage, ride the elevator down into the forest of cubicles, and voluntarily become encircled by them, fifty hours a week.

Margaret takes the pack from the table, and the baby disappears into her palm. 'Have you found anything else of your grandfather's – besides that book?'

'Not yet.'

'I know where he lived.' She shakes out a cigarette and searches her pockets for matches. Over on the bed, Dona Matarazzo has started to snore.

'Where?'

'An old artist's studio, not far from here.'

'How did you find out?'

'Because I'm trying to buy it. Kev's helping.' She walks around with an unlit cigarette, blowing out the candles. The room turns wispy with smoke. She saves the candle on the table – fat and white, half melted on a saucer. 'There are a number of studios out there, and he's down as a former owner.'

You glance at the file on the table. 'Out on the Common?'

'The title search is in the pizza shop. I'll show you tomorrow if you promise to be nice.' She comes toward you, slips her hand around the back of your neck. 'You've got so much hurt inside. Take off your coat. I'll be right back.'

The door opens and closes. For a while you watch the wax drip down the candle into the saucer. Over on the bed, Dona

Matarazzo is still snoring. And then you see it – a partition to the side of the room, blocking off what might be a cot.

When Margaret returns from her smoke, she doesn't speak. She is calmer, her movements languid, almost defeated. She takes the candle from the table and disappears behind the partition.

For a moment you sit in the dark and listen to Dona Matarazzo's snores. Then you get up, walk slowly toward the partition, and peer around the side. Margaret lies on top of the cot, in her pajama bottoms and T-shirt, her hands behind her head.

You sit at the foot of the cot. On her nightstand, there's a photograph of the two of them, Margaret and Carlo, at the oven inside the pizza shop.

'How did he die?'

She sighs. The candle flame crackles in the wax. 'He'd been depressed. Being over here, mostly. I don't know. We had an argument – he had big plans, Carlo, and this isn't a big place. The next day he was gone.'

'Gone where?'

'No sign of him, almost a week. I was frantic, nobody in his family had heard a thing. There was an inquest because he had been having problems with depression. He'd admitted…that he didn't want to live. A few days later they found some of his things in the river, his wallet and shoes. His wedding ring. Everyone said he'd drowned himself.'

'Is he still…?'

Margaret shakes her head. 'They never found him. He is gone.'

'I'm sorry,' you tell her, and this time you mean it, to the degree that you're capable.

'It's been a long time,' she says, 'and I'm tired of being sorry.' She curls a leg around your hips. When you lean over to kiss her, her mouth tastes like cigarettes and wine. She keeps her eyes averted, as if there's another man beside you, a man that isn't dead.

She strips off your clothes until you're down to your underwear. It's happening – and you simply step to the side of yourself, in the place she has created for you, the place Carlo used to occupy. She moves hastily, perhaps afraid of changing her mind. When she runs her hands across your chest you can feel her wedding ring bump against your skin.

You get under the covers. Margaret lies beside you, waiting. Her body is ready but it's the mole you're after.

There it is, the dark spot under her chin, the only home that's truly yours. You put your fingers to it. You stroke the mole as you enter her and imagine that you're laying claim to her innermost secret passages. The whole time you make love, burrowing into her, you imagine that you are working your way slowly into your past, and her past, back to the time before the two of you were born. You burrow past her parents, and her parents' parents, down the tunnel through the spiraling genetic chain. What power, what glory there is, burrowing into her mole. It is because you didn't go straight home that you have achieved this moment. It is because you roamed a little further, just as Dicul the Saxon would have done.

Afterward, you lie beside her in the cot. There's barely room for one, but it doesn't matter because you are happy now, no matter how uncomfortable it is. You press your back against the cold wall and smile in the dark.

Margaret raises herself up in bed. In the flickering can-
dlelight, her eyes are rimmed with tears. 'I have to ask you
to go. Mama's an early riser, you see.'

'Of course…'

You search for your clothes. Your shirt is damp from the
cold as you pull it on. By the time you've dressed, Margaret
has turned back on her side, the blankets tight around her
neck.

You blow out the candle, make your way to the door in
the dark, let yourself out. There are no more lights scattered
along Boddington's Lane. Ditchling sleeps soundly – not
even the birds are awake.

6

You trudge up the carpeted staircase, passing the framed pictures of the racehorses, the locked doors, the empty rooms. It's almost three in the morning, and you have entered the insomniac's no-man's-land between night and morning.

There is no telling what this will mean, what happened tonight with Margaret. Does the fact that she slept with you mean that she actually *likes* you?

You must admit that it is the idea of an Englishwoman that appeals to you as much as Margaret herself. Margaret, in turn, seems more interested in the idea of an American than you as a person. Isn't this enough – to fulfill each other's fantasies? Margaret carries the uncanny familiarity of a long-lost family member, a reunited cousin. You'd like to slip under the bedsheets and dream of her mole. But right now you dread sleep even more than you dread being sleepless. Nightmares become truly frightening when you open the door and find Eric Gill at your desk.

'You've been gone a while,' he says.

You close the door quickly. 'How – how did you get in here?'

Eric Gill's reading *Scorper*. With his eyeglasses, he almost looks professorial. 'Frankly, I'm surprised. The best artists show more discipline. You can't stay out all night and neglect your work.'

'Did Sheila let you in?'

'I think she thought I was you. The sketchbook, probably. I might ask to have another key made…'

You take off your coat and hang it on the hook. 'I'm trying to build a reputation here. The last thing I need is you ruining my relationship with my landlady.'

Eric studies you over his eyeglasses. He puts *Scorper* back on the shelf. 'It's high time you heard some advice about how to conduct yourself in this country.'

'I beat everyone at Quiz Night.'

'That's exactly what I'm talking about. You have a tendency to boast. At least *pretend* to be modest.'

'I prefer to speak openly. I don't put on an air of false politeness.' You sit on the edge of the bed and take off your shoes and socks. 'Let yourself out quietly, please. I've had a long day, and I have to get up early for breakfast.'

'Artists don't think of eating. Not with unfinished work. They find the lack of sleep restful, and hunger nourishing.'

'Let me be. Please.'

He goes to the curtains and places his nose in the gap. 'While you've been shagging Margaret, I've been doing research for our book.'

'Don't be so coarse.'

'Sorry, I forgot about your delicate sensibilities. You think one night will make a difference to a woman like that? You need to prove yourself further.'

'Later.'

'That's right. You're on holiday, after all. Soon you'll be back in sunny California…'

'I don't want to go back. Not without accomplishing something.'

'I'll make you a deal. You do pen-and-ink drawings for the bootscrapers – give each one a bit of personality, of course – and I'll consider using one or two in the book.'

You want to hug him. It's your first commission. But you're too tired to even stand. 'Thanks, Eric. I'll start first thing tomorrow.'

He turns, eyebrows raised in his typically austere manner. 'To-morrow? To-*morrow*? Thanks to your American-sized boasting about our book, we don't *have* until tomorrow – the others will beat us to the bootscrapers. Beat us to our share of the Lottery fund.'

'But it's the middle of the night. I'm at my wits' end.'

Eric winks. 'Nothing like a little mental fragility to aid artistic excellence. Now get out there and locate those bootscrapers. After your breakfast, you'll find me at church. I want to see you there, along with your preliminary sketches.'

'You think you can just throw down a deadline like that?' It galls you, the way he stands at your curtains, casually telling you what to do. 'Get away from that window! I paid for that spot.' He dances to the side as you lunge at him, and you bang your shin on the dresser. The pain shoots up your leg, and fragments of light spin around your head.

There are now two of him – Eric Gill, and his identical twin, standing on either side of your teapot.

'Get away from that teapot. And don't you dare lay claim to my teacups!'

'We don't care a jot for your teacups,' the Eric Gills say, in stereo.

Ex-girlfriends and Eric Gills, they're all the same. As soon as you think you've rid yourself of them, they return and multiply. The Eric Gills keep lingering beside your teapot, tormenting you with its sentimental importance. You reach for one of their coat sleeves and miss. You snatch at the twin, and he spins away. They retreat into the corner of the room, arm in arm, staring at you over their eyeglasses like a couple of drunk professors.

'Fine. Stay there all night for all I care.' You take off your clothes as indifferently as you can, though it's strange to be undressing in front of two men. Getting into bed, you switch off the light and try to ignore their gleaming eyes.

'Too slow, isn't he?'

'He's got to be faster than that if he wants to get the better of Kevin.'

They're keeping their voices down – at least *trying* to be considerate – but it's not easy to sleep with Eric Gills in your bedroom. They're trying to give you the illusion that you're at peace in bed, but you can practically hear them laughing under their breath, sharing secret jokes. They're muttering something about your pointy knees. They aren't the kinds of knees, the Eric Gills say, one typically finds on artists. They are the knees of charlatans, chameleons, Americans.

It's no use, the Eric Gills have won, so you switch on the lamp. You've become frustrated and teary-eyed, but your handkerchief is there on the nightstand, right where you left it. Unfold the cool cloth, press the fabric to your eyes. Thank goodness for white cotton and a delicate fringe.

Get out of bed. That's it, stretch out your hanky – a sign of truce for the twins.

'I'll do it,' you tell them, 'I'll go and sketch the bootscrapers.'

But as you make your way to the corner, there's nothing there but moonlight and dust. After rousting you from bed, the Eric Gills have gone.

The newer housing estates, past the Village Hall on the outskirts of town, offer nothing notable near the doors. They have been built to accommodate automobiles, back when nobody cared about the horse muck a man might accumulate on the soles of his shoes. Among these newer houses one looms higher than the rest, a gaudy edifice behind a steel fence at the end of a private drive, with satellite TV dishes littering the roof.

It's not until you come back down North End Road, down into the older part of town along the lanes, that you find what you're looking for. The bootscrapers emerge out of the darkness at the bottoms of doors, like shy nocturnal animals. Eric was right – it's best to work at night. You can sneak up and sketch them under the moonlight.

After just an hour you've finished three – just studies, but a start. They're on the small side, little foot soldiers of old black iron, huddling on the edges of your sketchbook as if embarrassed to be prototypes. But you reassure them, the more you nurture their shapes and shade them in. Within your sketchbook they radiate an almost menacing beauty.

Outside the Village Hall, you find a rare specimen hiding in the shadows. You don't know how you missed him during Quiz Night. He's a grand, double-sized bootscraper standing guard outside the entrance – a bootscraper made for a pair of gentlemen, two brothers or friends, walking arm-in-arm into a gathering of Ditchlings. Above the parallel scraping bars, the ironwork has been outfitted with ornate filigrees and an eagle with a snake in its talons.

SCORPER

You are tempted to raise your shoe, to test it out. But you mustn't get carried away this early, not when you've got work to do.

Sketchpad out, you stand at a respectful distance and begin with the eagle and its snake. You draw the twin boot holders in the shape of Roman arches. The light filtering down from above makes the boot holes look inviting. One could say that you've improved this bootscraper in your rendering of it.

The image is too much and you cannot help it – you step forward, address the bootscraper with the deference afforded nobility, lift your shoe, and drag the sole tenderly over the parallel bar. Oh! The history of this venerable object sends a shiver up your leg. How many ancient Ditchlings have cleaned the shit from their shoes on this very piece of iron?

The book is taking shape. You keep walking, searching the doorways, adding every bootscraper you find. Eric was right – the Ditchlings have neglected their unsung history. They've let the weeds grow around some of their more interesting specimens. They've allowed iron to rust, crossbars to break. One family has even used their poor bootscraper to chain up a dirty bicycle.

Back on the High Street, you stop outside a two-story Victorian house with a white fence. There must be five or six bedrooms upstairs, each equipped with thick curtains. Rose bushes surround the front garden. Yet there is nothing of note by the door, nor the handrail of the staircase. How could such a grand house function without a bootscraper? You are about to keep moving when you notice her – a slender maiden at the bottom of the front wall, overlooking

131

the grass. She is alone and forgotten. The builder placed her away from the door, perhaps to allow visitors to approach the door along the grass, but in doing so he relegated this poor creature to obscurity. She probably hasn't been noticed in years.

You sit on the pavement, open your sketchbook, and try to capture the bootscraper's sadness. It doesn't take too much imagination. You know what it's like to stare day and night at a desolate landscape.

This aging dowager has acquired a certain dignity from carrying a lifetime of pain. For years, people scraped their soles across her midsection to rid themselves of their stray clumps of grass and horse manure. Now that the roads are paved and the horses have been swapped for cars, she's been deemed obsolete. You know how it is. You've worked for years on print publications and seen them change overnight into cheap electronic ephemera. There are lessons to be learned from her forbearance.

The bootscraper remains at her post, ready to bear more. Her restraint is typically British – here I am, she says quietly, I may be an antiquated relic of a forgotten age, but I can still perform without complaint. Even as those young roses bloom around me, even as my master hosts his garden parties with frolicking guests, I won't make the faintest cry for attention.

The sun peeks over the horizon as the bootscraper takes shape within your sketchbook. What if your Village Hall foot soldier could catch sight of this pretty little number? What would he think of his neglected cousin? Maybe he's a statesman, a poet and freethinker – maybe he once courted this particular bootscraper. She was a lover of literature in the days before emancipation, and she caught his eye at the annual gooseberry fair.

Allow me, he would have said, taking her parallel bar in his, *allow me to tell you of the men whose boots I've had the pleasure of scraping – Edward Eggleston the cartwright, James Tennant the financier, even Lord Ditchling himself, who paused on his way into the Village Hall to admire my eagle and serpent. His perfumed soles were perfectly clean, but he dragged them across my back just the same.* And the slender young thing would have stared wide-eyed as he recounted his brushes with fame. When was the last time she offered her midsection to a passing boot?

The sun isn't fully over the horizon when her owner appears. He's a middle-aged gentleman, emerging from his two-story house in a terry-cloth robe and slippers. His fresh milk waits on the top step. He's got a wireless device in one hand, and he's reading something on the screen. His other hand, plump and pink, reaches for the bottle.

He sees you and stops. You sit quietly, holding your breath.

'Don't mind me,' you call out from the pavement, waving your pencil. 'I'm a visiting artist.'

You can't blame him for being surprised. The way he's still bending down for his milk, his hairy calf exposed, his house framed by rose bushes, gives you an idea. It's the title for your book: *Victorian Bootscrapers and their Modern Owners.*

'Can you hold that position a little longer? With that electronic device in your hand visible...'

The man just stares. He's complying, maybe confused. You've almost finished the hairy calf when he abruptly takes the milk inside and locks the door.

A little later the front curtains twitch. You can picture him inside watching you as he clutches his milk. Doesn't he know that your mental image will suffice? You sketch the master as he appeared to you, hair flattened on one side of his head and sticking straight up on the other. Underneath him his bootscraper takes shape, unobtrusively guarding her patch of grass.

A few finishing touches, some shading for perspective. As the sapling grows into an oak, spreading branches over its broadening trunk, you will labor steadily on the pavement, adding flourishes and contrasting details to your bootscraper until your drawing is complete. You were born with a desperate need to make sense of the great straining tugs of your heart – and even if you're doomed to express yourself badly, even if the masses laugh at your sentimental attachment to all things English, all things quaint and outmoded, you will never again apologize for your impulse to depict this country's glory years.

Tuck your sketchbook under your arm and get to your feet. Occasionally a man knows when he's finished something important. You can practically hear them at the launch, the book-buying Ditchlings. They will lean over their copies, bending their heads as they turn the pages, murmuring their admiration in low tones. On the flyleaf will appear an advance review:

> 'In this slim but handsome volume of bootscrapers, the American artist John Cull demonstrates an uncanny understanding of these unheralded staples of Victorian life.'

But in a well-regarded literary review, another critic will counter in studied opposition: 'How earnest are Mr Cull's depictions? We must ask ourselves: does his "foot soldier" really have our best interests in mind? Is the "lady bootscraper of the manor" truly demure? Or has she been slyly, perhaps sarcastically represented by the American in order to conceal her true identity as a gossip, the street furniture equivalent of one of Henry James's aunts – an unmarried spinster who provokes duels by spreading lies?'

Yet another critic will opine, in a morally brave departure from this historically limited binary approach to literary criticism: 'We must allow that Mr Cull has captured a thoroughly *modern* England in his depiction of our rural village life. With an outsider's broad perspective, he is simply more aware of England than the English themselves. Resist the easy, outmoded accusations of "bad faith". Put away the knives. This American exhibits a fresh boldness of vision: one we should celebrate, not vilify.'

You skip along the pavement as the debate flashes before your eyes. There is no question about it: you are an artist at last. You are about to inhabit the 'I' that you've concealed for too long – the 'I' belonging to your true inner voice. So what if nobody outside Ditchling will appreciate your work? No longer will you be afraid to announce yourself to the cultural gatekeepers. Never again will you pander to the aesthetically neutering influence of the masses and their salaried academic mouthpieces.

The sketchbook under your arm, everything awaits your artistic interpretation – the spire, the churchyard, the High Street, the post office and the little shop selling postcards. Margaret, asleep on Boddington's Lane, her face turned to the partition – perhaps she too wants you to sketch her, in the early hours before she rises.

The pavement ends, the road narrows under an overpass.

You jump into the road and walk between the high walls. When the horn blares, you barely have time to press your back to the wall. It's a Land Rover, clattering and banging toward you. There is no place to escape. You drop the sketchbook and tremble as the machine bears down. It's a newer model, painted forest green, with mud fashionably splattered across the lower panels. The driver doesn't bother to slow down. The wheels roll over the open pages of the sketchbook, the driver looks on and laughs – Kevin, in his fishing hat.

You unpeel yourself from the wall, pick up the book. The pages are torn and blackened. Across the road, in the crown of an oak, there is a flutter of wings – three or four, maybe half-a-dozen finches. They come darting out of the branches and zip through the air above your head.

Do it, do it, do it!
Get Kevin back, Cull.
He's going to do it, do it, do it. It's time to take him out!

Yes indeed, you tell the finches, it is time. You are the remedy Ditchling needs. Kev, with his dimpled chin, his uploaded videos of himself on his phone, his leg cocked without a kick – such a man has no respect for art. What would Dicul do to someone who ran him down in the middle of the street?

The finches have flown to a cottage across the street. Two pensioners stand outside, a woman in a cardigan watching from the top step as her husband fills a bird feeder hanging from a holly tree.

It is time for you to declare it, once and for all: I am prepared to act now, little finches. I am someone else entirely.

136

I am no longer John Cull of America, but John Cull of England. For my letter of reference, Eric Gill of Ditchling will be my advocate and endorser, my cultural attaché. And for my first official act, I will kill.

The pensioners will be the first witnesses to your new-found self. Go on. Cross the street, approach their garden gate. Speak up, make your presence known. 'Morning! You have a minute? That Land Rover – I'm sure you noticed it barreling down the High Street?'

The man joins his wife on the top step. He holds the bag of seed in his hands, and in response to your obvious anger, he cranes his powdery white neck under the collar of his checked shirt. A faint moustache tickles the top of his ancient lips.

Beside him, his wife smiles benignly in her skirt, cardigan, and heavy brown shoes. The door of the cottage has been painted green to denote their tenant status. They have unapologetically signed on to the village color scheme, adopted the long-standing social conditions. The pensioners do not answer you. They do not wish to be a party to your grievance. They simply take you in, the visiting alien.

'The driver's a maniac. Look, he's ruined my work. It's a miracle I'm still alive!'

The woman continues to smile. 'We've certainly been lucky with birds this morning,' she says.

'They like that particular seed,' her husband says, looking down at his shoes.

Your voice trembles. 'I thought your parish council was supposed to keep watch on public rights of way. Well, what are they doing about it?'

The man rolls up his bag of seed. 'Much better than it was. They've put in traffic calming measures.'

'*Traffic calming measures?*' The phrase sounds Orwellian, oxymoronic. 'But these traffic calming measures are hardly working, are they?'

'The bollards have been of some benefit,' the woman says. 'A man was knocked off his bike a few years back.'

She leaves the front step and crosses the grass. She moves slowly with what looks like a bad hip. Under the bird feeder, she stops and watches the finches dart and flutter. 'Lovely creatures, these are.'

'We haven't seen the like of them in some time,' her husband says. 'The bills are shorter but the twitter is just as sharp.' His watery eyes are placid, his gaze calm. His gentle manner makes you self-conscious about your rage – and anyway, who are you to lecture him on the safety of his own village?

'They do like this seed,' his wife says.

The husband squeezes the bag. His hands are controlled and powerful and speak to you with each squeeze of the fingers.

We keep steady.

We choose our battles.

Cull is calm now, along with the traffic – he won't lose control of his hands.

Soon breakfast will be served – you must eat, stay stable, conduct yourself as a gentleman. It's a Sunday, after all. You must go to church.

'Traffic calming measures,' you say, taking your leave.

The man nods. 'They've been of some benefit.'

This morning, while certain men float their feathered hooks over a pond of defenceless fish, you will visit a worshipful place of crisp white robes and gentility. The enervated must be given their measure of calm, the overworked granted peace.

You go downstairs to the breakfast room. The walls are creamy white, with vaulted ceilings and crown moldings. On the walls are etchings of country cottages, photos of the South Downs, a welcoming cross-stitch of a psalm in a wooden frame:

> The Lord is my shepherd, I shall not want;
> He makes me lie down in green pastures.

Your place at the window has been arranged – a table set for one, with cutlery and cloth napkin, salt and pepper, cup and saucer. Go on, go over to the padded chair. Sit down and have a look at your laminated placemat. It's from the Ditchling Museum, of course, with its photos of the church and churchyard. You will be eating your eggs on top of Ditchling's graves.

The curtains are open so that you may watch the High Street while you have your breakfast. The High Street, in turn, can watch you having your breakfast. You sit with your hands folded on your lap and wait.

There are sounds of pots and pans clattering behind the door of the adjoining kitchen.

Time passes. Surely Sheila will come out soon. But you hear a radio being switched on, plates placed on a table, clinking knives and forks. There is something else that concerns you – the smell of toast and fried bacon. Bobby and Sheila are eating their breakfast.

A few Ditchlings walk by. A man walking his dog sees you at the window, and he glances instinctively at the place where your plate would be, if you had one. A couple of middle-aged women out for a stroll do the same – they see you and pause, glance at your table – and you are forced to keep your hands folded on top of the placemat, while smiling at an area in front of your face, doing your best to appear content.

On the windowsill there is a collection of porcelain dogs. They are polished and gleaming in the sunlight. The little white dogs are positioned so that their little porcelain dog heads face you at the table with their hungry eyes. There's a terrier, a border collie, a Dalmatian, a greyhound, a bulldog, and a German shepherd. There's a poodle standing by himself. A St Bernard has a little barrel around his neck, together with a silver key. Then there's a Great Dane, a sheepdog, and a squat dachshund with long ears and tiny little porcelain legs.

The cloth pad on your chair is tied down with little strings, and as you stare at the porcelain dogs you untie these strings in your impatience. The moments pass until you cannot take it any longer. As loudly as you dare, you cough twice.

On the other side of the door, Sheila and Bobby stop eating. You can hear the legs of a chair scrape across wood. The radio is turned down.

You must look away so that you do not appear to be waiting impatiently for your meal. You reach for the tiny terrier and stroke its little porcelain head.

'You've got your eye on my darlings!'

As the door swings shut behind her, Sheila stands across the room, chewing up her breakfast. She's wearing an apron over her print dress, her hair in ringlets. 'They say children give you a sense of being needed and those are my little darlings, those dogs. Just me and them, most nights. Bobby's not much company, fixed to his telly...'

She comes toward you and finishes what's left in her mouth. Her legs are strong and stocky. She is descended from a tribe of Iron Age bog people, an ancient race occasionally found buried in peat, perfectly preserved, their hands clutching Roman coins.

'The Labrador's on order...'

She plants her heels at your table, and you cannot help continuing to admire the power in her legs. Yes, her tribe would have come to England from northwest Jutland – you can tell by her short, squat calves, her truncated torso and broad shoulders. On her head she would have worn a skin cap fastened to her chin with a hide thong. Her family would have moved with a herd of antelope. You've seen the migration patterns, the swooping drift of beasts and Iron Age man. Sheila would have camped in the huts above the marshes and fens. It would have been cold for her, during winter, and she would have worn leggings bound to her calves with woolen strings.

'Ready for church today, Mr Cull?'

'Please nudge me if I happen to nod off.'

Her eyes flicker with delight. 'No sleep again? I've got myself an artist upstairs.'

'Am I still in time for breakfast?'

'Of course you are, luv.' She's got a notepad in her hand, and she opens it. 'Room number?'

'Sorry?'

'Your room number,' she says, 'for your breakfast order.'

'I believe it's room number one?'

She hands you a laminated menu. There are two options – full English, or eggs on toast. 'What will you have, then?'

'Full English, please.'

'Granary or white bread?'

'Granary.'

'Eggs scrambled, fried, or poached?'

'Fried.'

'That's the way I like them.' She gives you a lipsticky smile. 'Bobby makes them runny.'

'That's fine.'

The door opens. 'What's he want, then?' Bobby says, poking his head and shoulders into the dining room. His hair is combed, and he's wearing an apron over his shirt and tie.

Sheila shoots him a glance. 'I'll be back in a moment.'

'I'd like to get his food started, if you don't mind. Then there's the washing up to do, isn't there?'

'There's plenty of time.'

'Not at this rate. What's he want?'

'You want to take a look at yourself,' Sheila says, turning her back to him. 'Going to church with that scowl on your face.'

'I go to church for one straight and simple reason – to pay tribute to the Lord.'

'I do, too.'

'You go to be seen.'

Sheila lets out a long hiss. 'He's having full English with granary. Fried eggs, runny.'

The door swings shut. Sheila remains at your table, breathing in rapid gusts. 'Coffee or tea?'

'Coffee, please.'

She strides over to a sideboard against the wall. She whips a tablecloth from a row of cereal boxes. There's also a bowl of fruit, an assortment of jam packets, and a plastic squirt bottle of Marmite.

'Help yourself to the cereals and things. We leave for church at a quarter 'til. You've plenty of time to enjoy your breakfast.'

'Thank you.'

She stays at the sideboard, back turned. Her voice drops almost to a whisper. 'We never thought you'd come.'

'This morning?'

'When you made the booking. Surely he'll cancel, I says to Bobby. He'll do a no-show. Nobody from California has stayed with us before, you see. Even when you showed up I didn't think you was real. And there you are, Mr Cull, sat at our breakfast table for all of Ditchling to notice. Makes me chuffed. Bobby, too, though he don't show it. We'll be a special heritage site for tourism at this rate.'

You get up out of your chair. 'I'll just have a bite to eat…'

She turns. 'Those drawings you've done – I saw them, tidying your room. I'm going to mend your sketchbook while you're here. I heard what Kev did. He's got a vicious streak, he has. He's best avoided.'

'Did he really know Margaret's husband?'

'Well – Kev introduced them. Poor Carlo. To be fair, I don't know what was in her head, marrying an Italian. I suppose Kev and Carlo met at Cambridge University.'

'Kevin went to Cambridge?'

'He did. How he passed, I can't imagine.'

'Your universities really are in decline.'

'They've always been full of tossers. Kev never worked a day in his life – and they made him Managing Director of the Bone Ash Works! Must be nice, having your dad on the Board.' Sheila hisses through her teeth. 'You seen that house of his, on the private drive at the top of the High Street?'

'The one with the fence? The satellite dishes?'

'That's soap dispenser profits, that is. Still, he'll never get that Angling Club he's after. Now don't look so glum, Mr Cull. I'll patch up your book for you. I'll mend the pages he drove over. You won't know the difference.'

'You don't have to do that.'

'Not at all. We want you to enjoy yourself in Ditchling.'

'I like it so far.'

'Really?'

'Really I do.'

Sheila smiles. 'Help yourself to the cereals and things,' she says. 'I'll just get your coffee.' She pats her hair and heads into the kitchen.

You hurry to the sideboard, pour some cereal into a bowl, unpeel a banana. Kevin – a Cambridge graduate? You try to find the justice in it, then remember Bush went to Yale.

On the wall, a framed photo shows a young boy and girl on a horse. The boy is holding the reins, and behind him the girl grins at the camera with the back of his shirt in her clenched fist. You recognize those faces – they're Bobby and Sheila's. The horse is not looking at the camera. Its head is lowered, as if it's ashamed.

You go back to your table, slice the banana into your

cereal. As the Ditchlings pass, you sit up straight with your napkin folded on your knee, your elbows off the table.

Sheila comes out of the kitchen with a plate and a pot of coffee. You move your cereal aside so that she's got room to put the plate down – two fried eggs, bacon and sausage, tomato and mushrooms, black pudding and buttered granary toast.

'I hope it suits,' Sheila says.

You pick up your knife and fork and head straight for the eggs. 'It looks wonderful. I've been hungry.'

Sheila lingers at your table. 'Look at you! You've got your fork the right way round. Not like a shovel.'

'My parents taught me to eat like this.'

'That egg runny enough?'

'Yes – perfect.'

'Bobby gets them nice and runny, I'll give him that. He's good with eggs.'

'He looks like a fine cook.'

'People slag off Americans, don't they? Stupid. Don't know their own geography. Loud. You're not like that.'

The egg drips down the side of your fork. 'Thanks.'

'No culture. Arrogant and lazy. Fat. But you don't have to answer for your ancestors, do you?' She comes closer to your table. 'I've got a question, Mr Cull.'

You put down your fork. 'Yes?'

'If you don't mind.'

'Not at all.'

'Since you work in the advertisements and everything.' She glances at your plate. 'Go ahead and eat – don't let your food get cold.'

'That's all right. Did you have a question?'

She tears a page from her notepad and places it beside your plate. 'It's the wording I'm after, Mr Cull. Before it goes on the notice board.'

You pour yourself a cup of coffee and sit forward. The ad marches across the page in black ink:

ROAD KILL DESIRED. IF YOU HAVE ANY UNWANTED BIRD BONES (NOT PHEASANT OR CHICKEN OR DUCK) OR IF YOU HAVE SPOTTED A SORRY DEAD BIRD (NOT BADLY SQUASHED), PLEASE DELIVER TO SHEILA SWIFT AT THE B&B. I AM IN NEED OF SKELETONS FOR SOUP.

'Skeletons? In soup?'

'A family recipe, Mr Cull.'

'I see.' The egg yolk is hardening against the toast. 'Well, the wording seems fine.'

Sheila smiles. 'Do you really think so?'

'It gets your point across.'

'Not many birds about these days. I used to get my moorhens from the pond, right after they laid their eggs. Bleed and gut 'em, grind the skeletons into paste. These days the little lovelies have all but disappeared. I've got hardly any bones at all.'

You stare at your plate. The pool of orange yolk has congealed with the sausage. 'What time did you say church was?'

'Quarter to.' Sheila checks her watch. 'My goodness – I should be getting ready! Now don't worry about being a Billy-No-Mates,' she says, leaning over your table to adjust the porcelain bulldog. 'You'll sit with us, Mr Cull, right in our pew.'

'All right.'

'We've seen all kinds at church over the years. As a rule they're friendly enough. We've got a new vicar, too – a *woman*.'

You sip your coffee. 'Oh?' The cold black pudding and wizened mushrooms, the tomato surrounded by hardened yolk – it could be an English breakfast replica in a museum.

'I'm not of the mind that we're ready for that sort of thing, Mr Cull. Lucy's been a member of the church for years, but it's hardly traditional having a woman vicar, is it? Bobby, of course – he approved of her straight away.'

Your hunger has become a cold iron rod that runs the length of your forehead, down your chest and stomach, straight into your shoes. 'Change doesn't necessarily threaten the best traditions, if I may say so.'

'What?'

'The Priory used to dominate village life, right through the Middle Ages. The monks would have encouraged decorations and paintings – then, in the mid-sixteenth century, your Priories closed. Thomas Cromwell whitewashing the murals, the Tudors, the fierce battles fought over whether or not vicars had to bow their heads at the name of Jesus. Female ordination is just the latest skirmish, if you don't mind me saying.'

'Goodness gracious!' Sheila says, holding her hand to her mouth. 'I can't wait for you to come to church. Now we do like to get there a bit early, just to say hello to the others. There isn't any time to waste, I'm afraid – go on, Mr Cull. Go and get ready.' She reaches for your plate. 'Plenty left here for Miss Manners, I see.'

Bobby and Sheila walk on either side of you across the High Street. You tower over them like an overgrown child.

It's time for your appointment with Eric Gill, but you don't have your sketches. As you reach the pavement in front of the church, you see him. He's coming toward you, just ahead. He's wearing his four-cornered paper hat, over-coat, stockings and sandals. He takes you in with one glance, in particular your empty hands, and walks right by. He acts like he doesn't know you.

'Wait, come back – I'll have the bootscrapers done soon!'

'Here,' Sheila says, taking your arm. 'I told you I'd mend your sketchbook.'

He could have at least waved. You see Eric Gill in his true colors now, a man who greets you one day with a smile, and the next a cold shoulder. The bells ring for service. They are real bell-ringers, live Ditchlings, clanging up in the belfry. The time has come to worship, the heathens must be shaken from the hills.

'That tower's thirteenth century,' Bobby says, guiding you toward the gate.

Others are heading to church in front of you – elderly descendents of Bog people with handbags and coats. You walk in step with them. They could be your people. The ancient Culls could have been clothed in wolf fur or deer hides, buried near the dewponds along the Downs. Build them a neb, a ness, a megalith. And Kevin's tribe – where are they?

Gong. He won't kill.
Gong. He will.
Gong, he won't. Gong, he will.

'Mr Cull? Are you coming?'

At the church gate you hesitate. Socrates – son of a stone-mason – would stand still for hours, listening for his *daimon* inner voice. Even on a Sunday, you can't stop thinking of what you'll do to Kevin.

Gong, he'll scorp.
Gong, he'll shake.
Gong, he's an American – he'd better bow and
scrape.

You wish you could silence your voices. Supposedly people who hear opposing thoughts are unstable – yet if your mind *weren't* divided, how could you use your rational self to appeal to its irrational sibling? If a man weren't at odds with himself, he would only say what he thought and think what he said. There would be nothing distinguishing him from a simpleton, a robot. Sheila guides you through the gate, up path toward the church. Yes, you depend on your internal divisions and subdivisions, just as England depends on its agencies and cities and towns, its villages and hamlets, its multiplicity of components and departments, to maintain its veneer of unity.

Bobby holds up your left, Sheila your right. Bobby's tie bobs against his stomach as he walks. You can smell your bacon on his breath. The three of you reach a tree, and you must separate to pass. Bobby hangs back, lets you and Sheila go forward, then quickens his pace to catch up. It is this gesture that endears you to him.

The dead roll under your feet in their grassy mounds and burial chambers. The stone headstones advance in rows and columns. You hang back – it's happening again. The voices of the dead have grown stronger. How can you stop blood draining from your face?

'Mr Cull?'

You break away from Sheila and Bobby and wind your way through the graves. There is one in particular that calls to you the loudest. You know the one. It's got your name on it, after all, scorped into the lichen.

'Where on Earth's he going?'

'John! John Cull!'

They call after you, like your parents once did. You sprint past the church and hear their voices all the way to your grave.

7

E ric Gill has taken off his overcoat. In his roughly hewn sculptor's smock, stockings, and sandals he appears to you as he always does, when you are too depleted to believe in yourself. You're on your back, out in the churchyard. He hovers above you with his arms outstretched and his beard crackling with electric energy.

'The bootscrapers taught you to see details, John. It's what your grandfather did, when he trained as an apprentice. Now that you know how to sketch the ordinary objects with an eye for detail, you must move from the inanimate to the living. As you do, keep one thing in mind – depict everything you see with love.'

'Love?' You look to the left and the right and see only graves.

'Love! All living creatures are evidence of God's love. Learn to see and treat people with Christian love, even when they seem to hate you. *Especially* when they hate you. Then you will depict everyone with love...' His voice trails away. He floats higher and disappears, leaving only dusty particles in his wake.

You blink and sit forward on your grave with the spike in your hand. In the milk-white sky, the sun is small and red – a devil's face. You lurch forward, slash the air.

'Oi! It's only me. You've been having a little nap, luv. A little dream. Put that away.'

Make-up and yellow ringlets obscure the devil's face. The face becomes Sheila's, with the sun behind like an angel's halo. 'Get up, now,' she says, 'still time to find an open pew. Now we'll just catch our breath...'

Her hands grasp your elbows. You plant your feet on the ground and rise toward her breasts. 'You're running a fever – sweating.' She puts the back of her hand against your forehead. 'You mustn't run off like that. Gave us a fright.'

Surely you are allowed to perspire, given the circumstances. You are standing above a grave with your name on it. Your birthdate has been added, but the date of death is blank. You point to it, hoping Sheila will notice the name.

'Goodness me, you've blood on your hands!'

'Probably from my spike.' On your palms are scratches and gouges.

'And on your forehead where you must have wiped them. Never mind. Turn to me.' Sheila licks her thumb, wipes your forehead clean. 'There, all sorted.'

She leads you from your grave. The morning is misty – the little devil sun's wearing a shroud. The sky has lowered over Ditchling like a coffin lid. You will be trapped with the dirt and grass, the blowflies in your eyeholes, the worms and mice. Under the barrier hedge, little heads peer out at you – birds hiding in their nests, playing dead in the damp.

'Look at those Nosy Parkers,' Sheila says. 'They'd watch their own reflections.'

On the footpath, the churchgoers have gathered. They're watching Sheila walk you over the burial mounds. Bobby's there. And Malcolm Ketteridge-Wilson, leaning on his cane beside his wife Jilly. You have caused a minor commotion, it seems. One woman is watching you and texting. Notes from the underground, sent into the Ditchling ether.

Down one grave, up and over the next. The church on its raised ground is a forbidding sight. It feels like you're walking toward a skyscraper.

Gong, gong. Gong, gong.

Up in the conical belfry, the campanologists are back at it, pulling their ropes like nooses. Down below, the woman on the path is still operating her infernal electronic mobile communicator.

'I can't go inside, Sheila. I have to meet someone.'

'You still on about Eric Gill, lovey?'

'I'm not fit for Ditchling, I'm not prepared...' You stop and grasp Sheila's shoulders. 'Wait, did you say "Eric Gill"? Did you see him?'

'You've been talking in your sleep. I hear you every night, you know. Come on, the others are waiting.'

'Tell me what you've heard. Please!'

'Nothing to worry about.' The wind blows the yellow ringlets across her face. 'In Ditchling, Eric Gill's everywhere.'

'My bootscrapers are ruined.'

'I told you I'd mend them. Come along, time for Eucharist.'

Sheila takes you squelching over the remaining mounds. Seeing you approach, the churchgoers disperse. Under your feet lie the dead whose headstones fell away – the graveyard veterans, the long-termers, the lifers. Your English Mummy will protect you from them. Maybe your American parents adopted you shortly after you were born, and Sheila and Bobby are your true biological parents. Your American parents – your adopted parents, that is – discussed your English roots to the point of compulsion. It is slightly suspicious, now that you think of it, that they couldn't give it a rest. There was no real evidence to back up their claims, just stories handed down over the generations – discussions over dinner, arguments over breakfast, compromises over lunch about this great-grandmother from Devon or that great-grandfather from Yorkshire, one of whom might have been an earl and another a duke, maybe even an orphan.

Mummy guides your feet onto the stone path. The others have gone inside, but Bobby's waiting just ahead, outside the church door. It's the first time you've seen him out in the square light of day, with his dimensions defined. He leans against the doorframe in an old gray suit and tie, like a forgotten dusty statue.

'Here's our American,' Sheila says. She brushes the grass from the back of your shirt.

Bobby stands up straight, hands in his pockets, eyeglasses smudged. 'What happened to him?'

'He wanted to clean a gravestone,' she says, speaking of you in third person, past tense – as if you belonged to history, as if you were no longer alive to object. 'Natural enough.' Sheila opens the door. 'Welcome to St Margaret's, Mr Cull. Be sure to notice those columns on the south aisle. Built by monks from Lewes, they say.'

Bobby hurries to your side. 'And look at those funny heads under the arches, carved in chalk...'

There is a powerful smell of damp stone. It's as if all the headstones, out in the churchyard, have walked inside with you. As your eyes adjust to the dim light, you find a red carpet at your feet, leading to the altar. Another carpet leads to a nearby alcove with a couple lying side by side in effigy. A brass plaque above the alcove reads, POLLARD SANCTUARY.

'Welcome to St Margaret's. Welcome to St Margaret's.'

Two churchwardens greet you – Lawrence Savage and the woman from the museum. They hand you a hymnal and a prayer book. You hadn't noticed it before, but the museum woman's pregnant. She blinks at you under the fringe of her dark hair, trimmed evenly along her eyebrows.

'Our American lodger,' Sheila says, reclaiming your elbow.

'I'm Larry,' the grocer says. He nods to the woman from the museum. 'My sister, Grace.'

'Be sure to notice the oak screens in our chapel,' Grace says.

'Carved by one of Eric Gill's craftsmen,' Larry says. He looks up at you and grins. 'Your American won Quiz Night, Sheila. I bet Kev didn't like to hear that.'

'The male corn bunting can't always claim the highest perch,' Sheila says. Grace puts her hand to her mouth and suppresses a smile.

'Hello there, Bobby,' Larry says. 'You behaving?'

'Only just.'

'I'll be keeping an eye on you during the service – making sure you stay awake.'

You wander over to the carved oak screens in front of the chapel and obediently admire the craftsmanship. Soon your surrogate parents usher you down the nave, and the congregants turn in their pews. It's too dark to be sure about their faces, but you can practically hear them muttering.

Brother and sister have finally produced a child.
The way of most creatures, the natural thing.
Frankenstein, that one is.

Sheila slides into a pew near the front. Bobby stays on his feet, waiting for you to slide in after her. Then he takes the end, lowering his heavy frame and straightening his gray jacket over his stomach. The two of them huddle close on either side, squeeze in tight. Bodily warmth takes the chill away. The little devilish sun beams splinters of light through the stained-glass windows.

The organist starts to play. Bobby opens up your hymnal, points out the page. Here comes 'O for a Closer Walk with God', by W. Cowper.

Back on your feet to sing – and from the wings of the church a choir emerges, men in white robes, women in blue. They file toward the altar, take their places in the choir stalls, finish the hymn along with the congregation. Larry and Grace have changed into robes and joined them. The Quizmaster is up there, too, moustache combed. And as the sun shifts, casting blues and greens across the whitewashed walls, the vicar appears.

She is a tall and handsome woman, a scarcely converted pagan princess. Her long red hair cascades down her back. At the pulpit she raises her hands, and the sleeves of her robe slide down her wrists.

'Grace, mercy and peace from God our Father, and the Lord Jesus Christ.'

Her voice is deep and clear, with the saucy lilt of a songstress. Bobby sits up a little straighter. He takes off his eyeglasses, rubs the smudges clean.

'O Lord, open our lips—'

'—and our mouths shall proclaim your praise.'

Ah, what a joy it is to submit to this woman of the cloth, to bray and bleat in good company. You fumble for the *Parish*

Beacon in your hymnal and find her name: Reverend Lucy Burgoyne-Hancock.

'We have come together in the name of Christ—'

'—Lord God we have sinned against you,' Bobby replies, cheerfully. 'Wash away our wrongdoing and cleanse us…'

Reverend Lucy! How unholy, how profane to find her so *attractive*, yet how can you help yourself? And how different is it from America, filing into the evangelical megachurches, titillated by the silver-haired, white-teethed car salesman ministers, with their smoky voices and perfumed hair? Here in humble Ditchling you've joined Reverend Lucy's ragged band of believers in England's age of atheism. She leads you through the exchange, talking down to you with her double-barreled surname as you reply in the meek voice of your ancestors, the single-syllabled Culls, daring to make furtive eye contact, ready at a moment's notice to prostrate yourself. There is a rope hanging above her shoulder – a bell pull rising to the belfry, made of interwoven blue and yellow ropes. Reverend Lucy has the physique of an acrobat. Maybe she'll grasp the bell pull, push off from the pulpit in her heels, and swing over the pews in her billowing robe to offer up private glimpses.

In the *Parish Beacon* you search the names – there's a Richard Burgoyne-Hancock listed in the choir.

'Is she married?' you whisper to Bobby.

Bobby nods toward the nearest choir stall, where the Quizmaster stands. 'Her brother Dick,' Bobby whispers back.

'Renew a right spirit,' Sheila intones, 'restore us to the joy of your salvation…'

'Set our hearts on fire with love for you,' Bobby says, 'now and for ever. Amen.'

Reverend Lucy turns her back with her arms raised.

'It's time for the prophecy,' someone in the next pew whispers.

'Yes. Time for the prophecy,' Bobby says. And Sheila nods.

Reverend Lucy walks to the altar. She removes a silk cloth from the table, and when she turns around she's holding an enormous hand.

The congregants stand, and you automatically join them. Reverend Lucy raises the hand high above her head. It's made of intertwined tree branches and dried flowers, with little stuffed birds perched in the gaps between the fingers.

'Sussex!' Reverend Lucy says.

Everyone replies, in unison, 'Where we are free.'

'Ditchling!'

'Where the hand of God protects his brothers and sisters.'

'How does God protect us?' Reverend Lucy asks, raising the hand higher.

'The wood. The trees, the trees.'

Bobby and Sheila repeat the words to each other, their prayer books at their sides. 'The wood. The trees, the trees.'

'I'd like to invite the children to come up.'

From the pews the youngsters come scrambling forward. Reverend Lucy sets down the hand beside her, smoothes her robe, and sits gracefully on the carpet. The children sprawl at her feet.

'Who would like to speak this morning?'

One of the younger boys raises his hand.

'All right, Sam,' Reverend Lucy says. 'Why do we care about trees?'

'Because they're big.'

'That's right. Trees *are* big! God's way of protecting us from harm. And what is it that trees hold in abundance?'

Sam puts his fingers to his mouth. 'Tigers,' he says. 'Tigers and tiger tails.'

Laughter rises from the pews. The boy's mother, in the front pew, shakes her head with embarrassment.

'Not tigers, no,' Reverend Lucy says, smiling. 'Nor tiger tails. Anyone else?'

'Birds,' a young girl in a dress says, standing up at the reverend's feet. 'Trees have birds. I can recite the prophecy.'

'Go on, then, Sophie.'

'Ditchling is ruled by God's brothers and sisters. A stranger will threaten this bloodline – you shall know him by the disappearance of birds in the sky.' Sophie hesitates a moment, staring at her shoes. She wanders over to the hand and sits beside it.

'Very good start, Sophie. But you've forgotten the final line. The reason why we have the hand to remind us.'

'Whoever buries the hand of the stranger rules the rest.'

'Thank you, Sophie. Good.' Reverend Lucy speaks over the heads of the children to address the congregation. 'Sussex is the last place in England for us to be truly free. And the trees in Sussex are signs of God's love and protection.

'Now I know a great number of you are excited by the announcement of the UK Heritage Lottery Fund,' Reverend Lucy continues, 'and the opportunity it brings to draw attention to the national treasure that is Ditchling. But with outside attention comes the possibility of intervention. When strangers come, they sometimes try to tell us how to do things, don't they? How to worship, how to behave. When we're not careful, they chop down our trees, build motorways we don't need, tell us what to say in church.' She looks back to the children. 'Birds know this instinctively, don't they? And our native birds have been disappearing lately. We're duty-bound to put out food and hope for the best, but what else can we do?'

One of the older girls raises her hand. 'Feed them some more.'

'Play songs they like,' a boy says.

'Kill the nasty things that threaten them,' says another boy.

'Goodness me!' Reverend Lucy says. 'What a lot of brave young voices we have in church today.'

'They're birds of habits, those finches,' Malcolm says, standing in his pew. 'We simply can't see their habitats threatened any further – or invaded by outside species.' He sits back down, and some of the congregants nod in agreement.

'The prophecy is about preservation,' a voice in the back says.

'The preservation of identity,' says another.

'In the past,' Reverend Lucy says, 'our prophecy has been interpreted literally, and at other times symbolically. It falls on the people of Ditchling, and not anyone else, to determine its unfolding.'

'Strange American,' a man behind you whispers, 'someone's going to get his hand cut off if he's not careful.'

You turn. It's Kevin, sitting with Dona Matarazzo. You turn back round, but you can feel his eyes boring into your skull.

Sheila wheels in the pew. 'He's *not* a stranger,' she whispers. 'Not to us.'

'You'll take his money, you mean,' Kevin whispers back. 'Put him by the window like one of your porcelain dogs.'

'The bounty of Ditchling,' Reverend Lucy announces. She stands up with the hand and tilts it toward the carpet. Out of the birds' mouths tumble individual pieces of candy. Shrieking, the children scoop them up.

Your breathing becomes shallow and quick. The children run back to their pews as the organist begins the next hymn. You stand along with the congregation and sing, and you try to make sense of it all. Reverend Lucy takes the tree hand back to the altar, covers it with the cloth – and after the hymn Kevin slides out of his pew. In the aisle he glares at you. He straightens his corduroy jacket and walks to the lectern opposite the pulpit. Reverend Lucy, perched on a chair, follows him with a smile. In the program you find him: *Reader Kevin Pollard.*

"'Moses spoke to the people, saying 'When you have come into the land that the Lord your God is giving you as an inheritance to possess…'"'

The top of your scalp burns red hot. Seeing 'Kev' up at the lectern is altogether too much. This hypocrite and bully, this driver of Land Rovers, may be more evil than you imagined.

"'You possess it, and settle in it. You shall take some of the first of all the fruit…the fruit of the ground…'"'

'Kev' isn't merely a brute. He's cultivated a multi-faceted streak of guile, weaseling his way into Dona Matarazzo's good graces through his false displays of religiosity. His reading finished, he leaves the lectern and walks past you, head high like a modern-day Tartuffe. The couple in effigy was called Pollard – and this is the history you must contend with, the Ditchling lineage, the depth of social privilege.

'Let us pray,' Reverend Lucy says.

It is important not to give in to anger. Don't be afraid of the Ditchlings' pagan ways and strange customs. *Study the people with love,* Eric Gill said. Should you judge a man just because his parents named him Kevin? Mock him as he reads from Deuteronomy? Kevin went to Cambridge University. His father invented England's first automatic soap dispenser.

Suddenly ashamed, your overlarge hands pressed between your thighs, you stare dumbly in front of you and remember your smallness before God. The padded kneeler is waiting. Flip it over.

'Our Father, who art in heaven...'

Fold your hands, repeat the Lord's Prayer until you've cleansed your sins. It is an honest purge: the tears are streaming. When you're finished, the service is over and everyone's gone. Only Bobby and Sheila are left, and they're watching you from the pew.

'Blimey,' Bobby says.

'I told you Americans were religious,' Sheila says. She leans over you as you wipe your eyes dry. 'You wouldn't want to join us at the pub, would you, Mr Cull? It's pretty lively, Sunday afternoons.'

Cardboard beer mats stuck to the wall, brass rails and curved walls like the hull of a ship, people chatting at beer-soaked tables – this is how Sunday afternoons are meant to be spent. You sit between Bobby and Sheila under a round porthole window with a pint in your hand.

Sheila's enjoying her white wine spritzer. 'Something festive,' she'd asked as you bought the round. Bobby's 'on ale', and with each sip he slumps a little further into his chair. Their friend Brenda appeared. She asked for 'a spritzer like Sheila's' and she sits across the table from you with her back to the radiator.

The pub is busy, all the tables full. There's a fire going, but the crackling flames are muffled by conversation. The three crossword men are at their stools, their backs to the pub. A group of young drinkers stand behind them, crowding around the beer taps – men in white tennis shoes and tight jeans, women paying them only slight attention. This group has been drinking all day, it seems. Their faces are loosely knitted, manic, slightly insane. 'My missus wouldn't let me come out last night,' one of the men says, though he looks no older than twenty. One of the women is Rhiannon from *Animals in Distress*. She's talking without stopping, her pint spilling over the edge of the glass.

Brenda keeps staring at you, as if trying to figure out how to paint your nose. Luckily you've brought *Scorper*, and you sneak in a page whenever you can. You've got to learn about Ditchling as fast as possible.

Working with Mr Gill meant working with a man who worshipped God. He would speak of William Morris and John Ruskin; he would speak of architecture and he would speak with equal passion of lettering. But his favourite subject was the Holy Spirit and the kind of art that reflected this Spirit.

It was known that Mr Gill's father was a preacher, a reputable man in a voluminous black gown. Mr Gill's grandfather was a Congregational minister, as was his brother. He had deep and pious feelings for his family. It is true that he had a reputation that we dared not enquire too closely about, regarding his beloved sister—

'Our Christian scholar,' Sheila says to Brenda. She points her spritzer at you. 'An artist, too.'

Brenda smiles shyly. Since you have been referred to so openly, you can't exactly keep reading. You fix your eyes directly in front of you, as if adopting the expression of a 'Christian scholar'. Over by the bar, one of Rhiannon's friends is pinching a pimple on her bare shoulder.

'We never had any scholars in the family,' Sheila says. 'Did we, Bobby?'

Bobby stares out the porthole. 'Uncle Jack liked books.' During the ensuing silence you return to *Scorper*.

'I was, in a not too inaccurate manner of speaking, "mad on lettering"' Mr Gill once told me.

It was assumed Mr Gill had been in love with his daughters after he named his font Joanna. And all those woodcuts I scorped of nude Petra. It is not for me to judge. A man is judged by his work and by the glory found unto it. Mr Gill's work was the work of God delivered. 'The senses are a kind of reason,' Mr Gill would often quote, after St Thomas Aquinas. And by this Mr Gill and Mr Aquinas must have meant that we can argue about the logic of a thing, but only tastes, touch, smells, sounds and sights are the means to knowledge—

Brenda is making little cooing noises at you. 'Coo, coo,' she says, waving her little pinky. 'Coo, coo.'

Perhaps this is a local greeting. 'Coo, coo', you reply, but a gurgle behind you makes you turn and come face-to-face with a baby. It is draped over a shoulder, its mouth bubbling with white froth. Before you can move, the baby blasts you with its milky vomit, soiling the pages of *Scorper*. You cry out and wipe yourself off.

The baby has also started to cry. 'What's happened?' the mother says, turning around. Spittle dribbles down her baby's mouth – and she glares at you, as if you caused her child to be sick.

Sheila comes to your rescue, fetching napkins, dabbing at your shirt and the pages of your book. You move a little further away from the mother. Malcolm Ketteridge-Wilson appears, tapping over with his walking stick.

'Your American fell asleep on his way to church this morning. On a grave, no less.'

'My name's John,' you tell him. 'Not *the American*.'

'Oho!' Malcolm says. 'Someone's touchy.' He taps his stick on the wooden floor.

Rhiannon and her friend come closer, together with a wisp of a man in turquoise trousers and a tight-fitting T-shirt. You put a bookmark in *Scorper*. You examine your shirt splattered with digested breast milk. Margaret invited you to the pizza shop today – but you cannot go now, especially if Kevin will be escorting Dona Matarazzo along Boddington's Lane.

'Out on the piss last night, was he? Drunk?'

'You've had your share of nights on the tiles, Malcolm. I dare say you've slept on a grave or two…'

The pub darkens, the walls close in. Brenda and Rhiannon are watching you. Malcolm's wife Jilly comes through the front door, and the conversation at your table turns back to America.

'…we spent a lovely holiday in Atlanta, didn't we, Malc? Back in '78. Never seen so many black people in all my life.'

'My brother and I did Colorado. Then we did the Grand Canyon, Las Vegas…'

'What do you mean you "did" Colorado? I think you mean you *went* there, luv…'

'They say there's nothing to see between the coasts…'

The drink, the warm fire, the conviviality – gradually, as you look around The Lantern with something approaching familiarity, you start to hope, to allow yourself the delusion of all Americans: you are connected to people, you are more than just a tourist.

They crowd around – Shoulder Pimple, White Sneakers, Rhiannon, Turquoise Trousers. Bobby and Sheila sit a little closer, beaming proudly. Would they have taken such interest if you were German, or French, or Chinese? You Americans are like dying elephants searching for your burial grounds. The elders circle with their sympathetic trunks, taking pity, throwing you bones.

'Lovely people, the Yanks…'

'Without them we'd have had difficulties in the war…'

'We're too complacent by half. They're miles beyond us…'

'Mind you, it's not all roses over there, is it?' Malcolm says to Jilly 'Our granddaughter's in care – poor little girl's got spina bloody bifada – she wouldn't quite make it in the U-S-of-A in that condition, would she?'

Jilly pulls nervously at her fingers. 'From what I understand, their health care system is shocking.'

'No class culture in America – that's because there's no culture in America!'

'Shockingly ignorant, the people. A full forty per cent voted for that Mormon in the last election. And how many have passports? No offense, Mr Cull.'

'He's *tall*, isn't he? Look at those hands. Not as tall as the blacks, of course.'

'Nobody doubts the Yanks' contribution in the war. But I know one thing – we wouldn't be sitting here if it weren't for the carrier pigeon. We'd be in a beer garden speaking German.'

'Now they've got a black man in the White House. A *black* man, in the *White* House!'

This comment – from Malcolm – goes too far. 'I have to defend my country,' you say, 'from this thinly veiled bigotry. I must extol the virtues of immigration. Surely England's historical institutions – literary, political, horticultural, architectural, legal – surely within these traditions there is room to own up, once and for all, to the negative aspects of your colonialist past? And in this owning up, isn't there a stronger nation, unafraid to embrace a multicultural future? After all, multiple cultures are in your past! *Spaniel* is a Spanish word. *Duck* is Dutch. *Church* is German, and even your English breakfast tea is Asian! Don't you all know this?'

There is a silence after you're finished. Maybe the silence means nobody cares.

'Where do you live in America?' Rhiannon asks. Someone tells her it's Los Angeles. She squeezes past Bobby, leaving Turquoise Trousers to stand on his own, texting of course, beside the porthole.

'What's it like in LA?' Rhiannon asks. Her eyes are hungry for faraway places.

Sit right down, you want to say, and I'll tell you what you want to hear about California, the land of olives and figs, the land of wine. Palm trees, fresh oranges, clean beaches and sunshine, every day of the year. Instead you tell her the truth. 'If you looked at my apartment building, you'd see hundreds of windows like TV screens. I choke in the smog.'

'Do you go to Hollywood?'

'Why would I? There's no TV behind my curtains, just books.'

'He's old-fashioned,' Brenda says.

'In America, when you get used to a taco stand, or a park, or even a city block, you look up and it's gone.'

Rhiannon studies your dirty shirt, streaked with grave-yard muck. 'England's supposedly becoming more like America.'

The pub reaches its equilibrium It is a sanctuary for people to commiserate, to huddle and grieve about the world's inevitably advancing commercialized inhumanity. Then the door opens, and Kevin comes inside. Nervous glances shoot to his face and yours.

'Keep quiet now,' Bobby whispers.

A collective gloom falls over your little group. Kevin heads for the bar, and in an instant it feels as if all the Ditchlings are being punished for interacting with you. You can practically hear everyone privately recalling your skirmishes – the pizza shop, the pond, the confrontation in front of the B&B. You cannot take it any longer. You get up from the table.

'Wait – what are you doing?' Sheila says. She grabs your wrist.

'Going to the bar.'

'Leave him, Mr Cull. At least for now. I've seen that look on Kev's face before. It's busy on Sundays – he might not have been able to find a parking spot.'

'Kev likes to drive his Land Rover,' Jilly whispers.

'She's right,' Malcolm says softly, leaning toward you on his stick.

'Let him be,' Brenda says into her spritzer.

You sit back down. A deeper silence descends, the silence of defeat. The handheld devices and phones come out of pockets and handbags. Suddenly everyone is absorbed by their own tiny digital screens. And in this private absorption they are drawing attention to your public predicament. Kevin is volatile and tempestuous while you should remain an appeaser, a coward.

'Yes, you're better off staying here where it's safe,' Rhiannon says. Then, out of nowhere, she grins.

The grin forces you to stand back up. 'I don't care what anyone says, I'm going to the bar. Anyone need a drink?'

Bobby and Sheila look away, as do the Ketteridge-Wilsons. Brenda keeps her eyes on her spritzer. Even Rhiannon pretends not to have heard. Bobby angles his knees sideways and allows you to pass. You sense everyone watching you walk the wooden floorboards. The pub has fallen completely silent as you make your way between the crowded tables, past the mother and her expectorating baby, toward the Ditchlings standing at the bar.

You reach the vicinity of Kevin's shoulder. Paul Tanner is serving someone, and the man himself, the volatile Pollard, is leaning forward with his elbows on the bar, waiting to order. You gather up your nerve to approach this inexplicably tempestuous creature who creates masculinity challenges for you everywhere he goes. He is thick about the loins and limbs, like the Green Knight. You must be like Gawain, too courageous, too foolish, perhaps, to be called brave. Meanwhile the crossword men, their pencils momentarily at rest, are actually speaking.

'I can't see the clues. It's my specs – they keep sliding.'

'You ought to get some nose pads.'

'He's only looking for sympathy.'

'Nose pads don't work. My specs slide just the same.'

'It's only sympathy he's after, I'm telling you.'

'I'm not. I can't see the clues. I can't read.'

'I told you I'll bring in fresh nose pads. And I'll have a look at your arms.'

'My arms? What's wrong with my arms?'

'On your specs. The screws are probably loose. I've got a tool I'll bring in tomorrow.'

'I thought it was his eyes.'

'You need nose pads. And a good solid tightening of your arms. What did they say at your assessment?'

'That I had a recognized condition.'

'He's always got some condition. Yesterday it was his neck.'

'My neck did bother me yesterday. How can you do the crossword if you can't bend your neck?'

Kevin finally notices you behind him. He turns to face you, and the crossword men fall silent. You smile and try to find the right words. Kevin's aggrieved expression, with his hard, dull eyes momentarily inflamed, is almost pitiable.

Perhaps something went wrong after he walked Dona Matarazzo home – the same something that goes wrong every time Margaret sends him off too early for his liking.

'Hi there, Kevin.'

'What the fuck do you want?' he says, standing taller.

'I want to be friends. If there's anything I've done to cause offense—'

'Get away from me.'

'Maybe it's a cultural misunderstanding.'

'Get away or I'll thump you.'

'Hiya, Kev,' Paul Tanner says, coming over. 'Pint of Stella?'

Kevin nods, his back to the barman. He has the eyes of a hunter fixed on his prey.

'I'm trying to ask your forgiveness. If I've done anything wrong, I mean.'

'Get the fuck away.'

'I will if you want me to. But – I love you, Kevin.'

And now, inside the dreadful silence that follows, the mausoleum silence of the Ditchlings turning in your direction, it is your only hope that time will somehow reverse itself. The pub feels small and cramped, like a fighting cage with just you and Kevin inside – and how can it be, at this moment, that you *do* love him, just as Eric Gill advised? How can it be that Kevin's yellow eyes, still bearing the frustration from parking his Land Rover, reveal a poignant sadness? For the first time, you almost understand why Margaret is with him – why, after all, he is worthy of sympathy. Green Knight, you want to say, brave, tormented upholder of the chivalric code, can't we adversaries lower our axes and be friends?

But Kevin is wincing, as if he's been struck. His fist comes forward quickly, and the next thing you know you're on the ground with your mouth on fire. You squirm on the wood among the Ditchlings' shoes. There's a gap in the floorboards near your face, and as you peer into the bowels of The Lantern, down at the kegs of beer in the cellar, there are raised voices over your body.

More shoes come closer to your head. Somebody is panting. A tongue slides along your lips and into your mouth. It's a foul tongue, slimy and long, the breath horribly rank. The springer spaniel looms above you, licking up your blood.

8

I served Eric Gill not only because I found his lettering and sculpture to my liking but because his ideas
were not wanting, and his words conjoined with his
work. He believed that the best artists collaborate with
God.

I realise now that he was a radical philosopher, a
Christian revolutionary. It is no coincidence that Mr Gill
chose to live and work in Sussex: it has thickly wooded
slopes, secret villages, and stiles that lead visitors to
stinging nettle fields and impenetrable ancient oak and
beech. Mr Gill was fond of saying that Sussex was the
last southern county to accept Christianity.

Yes, I joined his Guild. As a scorper and apprentice
engraver no other occupation seemed as worthy to me.
Maybe I thought they were grand at the time, some
of the activities that now I look back at with shame,
but when I think of our little society of radical Roman
Catholics, I still feel bound by our common faith. Some
of Mr Gill's sayings are as fresh to me now as when he
uttered them.

'Art abides entirely in the mind. Yes, and the idea of a
drainpipe must be as clearly in the mind as the idea of
a painting.' And, 'All things are evidence of love. A pair
of scissors, no less than a cathedral or a symphony.'

The most famous of my master's sayings gave me courage to create my own work. I sometimes say it to my own little children, who one day with God's blessing will be my own apprentices, as their children will be apprentices in turn: 'The artist is not a special kind of man, but every man is a special kind of artist.'

Upstairs in your room, curtains drawn, you lie in bed with your grandfather's book. It is best to take things easy, to digest his disclosures over the course of your stay.

You have been in bed all day, as you were the whole of Monday. Sheila has been bringing up your meals. She knocks lightly, then retreats to afford you a measure of peace. You haven't even bothered getting properly dressed. For the first time since you arrived, you've been getting sleep.

Perhaps it's because the curtains give you a sense of protection. They enclose you behind a veil, especially when you draw the outer fabric tight over the outer translucent curtain. Behind this double veil you've recovered somewhat. You have almost convinced yourself that your experiences in Ditchling have been minor versions of 'holiday dramas' you occasionally see in the newspapers – a visitor finds romance and local intrigue, uncovers a crime, and escapes at the last minute to make it home alive. Here in Ditchling the potential crime seems to be one of tradition, and you no longer know what 'home' consists of.

It was yesterday, just before noon, when something disturbing happened.

'I know you're up there!' a woman screamed below your window. 'My son – he's up there!'

There was no doubt it was Eve – but you made the fateful

error of getting out of bed. You parted curtains from the side, taking care not to expose your nose, while protecting your swollen upper lip from the cold.

It was Eve all right, standing on the pavement in a nightgown and slippers. She stared up at your window with her hands clasped. 'Come home, David.'

'I'm not David,' you said.

'I see you up there. Why are they keeping you from me?'

A car pulled up beside her, and Brian jumped out. He glanced up at your window, then collected his mother.

'Don't tell them!' Eve shouted. 'Don't tell them you've spent time in America...'

On the High Street a couple of Ditchlings chatted away while Brian guided his mother into the car, as if nothing strange was happening. That was when you noticed the white van parked next to your car. There was a picture of a wading crane painted on the panel beside the company name:

A.J. TAYLOR
SUPERIOR QUALITY BIRDFEED

You withdrew from the curtains. You made yourself a cup of tea, paced the floor. All afternoon you returned, and returned, and returned – and returned to the window, only to find the van in exactly the same place, parked just behind your car in front of the jeweler's. At sunset you retreated to bed, only to hear the engine roar to life.

The van had remained on the shoulder of the road for four and one-quarter hours. Serious questions loomed: Why did A.J. Taylor park by your car? Why did he stay so long? And who was buying so much birdseed?

The questions plagued you all evening. You drew the covers to your nose and fell asleep to the sounds of Bobby and Sheila's TV rising up through the floorboards. Then, this morning, something else happened.

The doorbell rang early, just after sunrise. You hurried to the window, sneaking to the side of the lace outer curtain, making sure to keep the heavy fabric almost completely drawn. Malcolm Ketteridge-Wilson was down on the pavement. He had a package in his hand, in brown butcher paper. He glanced up at your window.

You withdrew from the curtain. Down below, you could hear Sheila open the door. You returned to the curtain. Stray phrases lofted up to your window.

'...the right size?'

'Biggest they had.'

'...if he doesn't agree to wear them...'

'Have Bobby show him how to put them on...'

Malcolm handed her the package and descended the steps. He walked up the High Street, tapping his walking stick on the pavement. You returned to bed and tried to process your hideous fears, your dispositional anxiety and obsessive forebodings, which seemed to be taking form in Ditchling, and in the Ditchlings themselves.

The possibility of a conspiracy has become stronger. Because there *are* birds under the hedges, sparrows and swallows in the sky, geese honking toward the pond, goldfinches swarming to feeders in holly trees when they are supposedly starving. And an enormous white van, filled entirely with seed, stays for four and a quarter hours, like a petroleum tanker pumping into the wells of a filling station? And now, stranger – what should you do? By missing your appointment with Margaret you lost the opportunity to learn about your grandfather, to see the document she alluded to. It is possible, of course, to visit her in the Pizza Shop, but Kevin has kept you from venturing down Boddington's Lane.

Go on, get up. Make yourself a cup of tea. Back to bed with *Scorper*.

Mr Gill was not content with war memorials and gravestones. Even at the height of this enterprise, when all the apprentices were engraving and lettering with gladness and industry, and met each commission on time, Mr Gill would say that we had to strive harder to inspire reverence. By that he meant the reverence of God.

It is why we all posed for him. We went into his private studios. At first the posing was considered a privilege. Then it became a duty for the sake of the holiness of his drawings and sculptures.

Mr Gill was called many things because of his erotic depictions of Biblical figures. He would not have called them 'eroticisms' but 'celebrations'. He published books on many of his ideas. They concerned the proper way to dress, and to wear clothes in the manner that he wore them. *Clothes* was one such book. And, *Trousers and The Most Precious Ornament*.

'His ideas only serve men,' one of the apprentices complained. She was a young engraver, and the only woman allowed in certain areas of the workshops. It was known that Mr Gill asked her to take measurements of his penis both 'down' and 'up' and to record these variations over the course of many days.

177

There are footsteps on the stairs. You place *Scorper* on the bed and cover it with a pillow. Soon there's a knock on your door.

'Mr Cull?'

'Yes?'

'Bobby and I are popping down to Brighton for an evening. Taking in a film.'

'All right. Have a good time!'

'Help yourself to the cheese board I've left outside your door. And there's soup as well.'

'Thank you, Sheila.'

There is a shifting, a shuffling, outside the door. She has not gone directly downstairs. There is a second, lighter knock. 'Mr Cull?'

'Yes?'

'Don't let what happened at the pub bother you, luv.'

You look at the closed door and reply as honestly as you can. 'I'm trying not to.'

'He's got a *temper*, that's all. I wouldn't tell him you love him again.'

'No.'

'You've been warned, Paul Tanner says.'

'Warned? At the pub?'

'Not banned. Warned. He and Kev are friends, you see. Fledgling members of that angling club they're trying to get off the ground. Paul will let you drink there if you don't cause trouble. People here are decent sorts, all around.'

'I know they are.'

'I wouldn't let what happened keep you from enjoying your stay.' Sheila paused. 'But you won't confront Kevin again, will you?'

'Confront him? No – no, I won't.'

'Not before it's time. That's sorted, then. See you later!'

There is something familiar about this room – perhaps the trace of a memory, passed down from one generation to the next, inside your DNA. Did your grandfather visit this house? Did he run his fingers along the molding, or stare out the window and daydream? Here in your bedroom, with your cup of tea and a book, you have finally joined the long line of Ditchling Culls, a chain of inheritance that bound you here, even while in Los Angeles. An ill-fitting place to be raised an Anglophile, the City of Angels. It doesn't matter – the Culls have probably always been alien.

Not before it's time, Sheila said. There are larger forces at work, people both living and dead who have conspired to bring you here to fulfill your predestined role. Meanwhile it is best to keep your mind clear of declarative voices. That's it, sip your tea, do not approach Kevin, not ever, express your Christian love at a safe distance. Remember you're here to find out about your grandfather, to gather the scraps of information that might guide you toward an appreciation of your circumstances in general and your current predicament in particular.

The way you hold your teacup annoys you. Your finger doesn't fit into the loop. Consequently you must take the handle between thumb and forefinger, but the affected way in which your pinky hangs in the air makes you look ridiculous, even to yourself. You have no choice but to hold the cup in your palm, like a can of beer. At the window you part the curtains – and across the street, in the flat above the jeweler's, you can see a face above an easel, the glint of a paintbrush.

You are hungry, but apparently it is necessary to close the curtains in order to eat in private. Your lip is still puffy, and one of your front teeth feels loose. You must be careful as you chew. Outside your door, the tray is waiting – take it to your desk.

Sheila's left a nice cheeseboard. There's a good strong Cheddar, a wedge of Stilton and a big chunk of Camembert, along with oatcakes, olives, and a portion of homemade pickle in a white porcelain pot. Her chicken soup is delicious – you had it last night as well – not too salty, with a rich fragrant broth. You sit at the little wooden desk to eat.

There are occasional bones. They don't bother you much – you take them out as you find them and line them up to the side of the bowl. Soon you have a small collection.

Bird bones wanted, Sheila wrote.

You take one and hold it out – by all accounts a thin white bone like any other, with a fragment of tendon on the end.

Down you go, past the framed racehorses. Their eyes track you from one landing to the next.

> *Look at Cull creep.*
> *He's up to something.*
> *What would Sheila think?*

Something has changed, and you can't quite place it. For a moment you hesitate in the entryway – then you realize it's the whole house that's changed because the TV isn't on and it's completely silent.

In the dining room, beyond the empty tables, a lamp has been left on beside the window. This must be where Sheila sits at night, at the breakfast table with her porcelain dogs, the curtains pulled shut.

The dogs' white ceramic faces watch you creep to the kitchen. You have every reason to believe the door will be locked, but it swings open as if expecting your arrival. You put your hand in and feel along the wall for the switch, ducking as you come inside.

The light flickers on. It is a spotless kitchen. Tea towels hang over a stainless-steel sink. On the counter there's a rack of drying dishes. There's a folding table and two chairs, a small TV on top of a stack of cookbooks. The linoleum floors are swept and mopped.

On top of the oven, two large vats stand on the burners. You listen for footsteps and lift the lids. The first vat is empty. It's been cleaned and placed back on the hob, perhaps after Sheila brought you the last of the soup. It's hard to make out what's in the second vat – a cloudy, lumpy mixture with a cloying smell of sugar. On the counter a recipe is wedged between two cookbooks. Sheila's making marmalade.

The cupboards, the contents of the fridge, the washing machine under the sink – nothing seems out of the ordinary, nothing to justify an investigation. It is paranoia, no doubt, fueled by Ditchling. You're about to leave when you notice, against the wall, a small black feather. On closer examination, the wall has the faint outline of a door embedded into the plaster. A small keyhole has been painted white.

You search the kitchen drawers. There's cutlery, table-cloths, napkins, a drawer filled entirely with wooden spoons, a utility drawer with batteries, electric wire and small tools. Here you find a ring of keys.

You listen again to the silent house, as if conspiring with it as you plan your next move. The house reassures you that Bobby and Sheila are still in Brighton at the movies, and they won't be back for some time.

None of the keys fits the small keyhole. You return them to the drawer when you have an epiphany, and you rush out of the kitchen into the dining room, straight for the porcelain dogs and the silver key dangling from the St Bernard's little white neck.

Back in the kitchen, the key fits. The lock turns, the door swings open, and from the bright light of the kitchen you can see the outline of a single, white, incandescent bulb. There is a damp avian smell, and in the back of the larder are moving shadows.

You pull the string on the light bulb. Dozens of headless birds hang from the ceiling, their shapes dark and dusty, like leaves of tobacco. The birds hang upside down on hooks between their rear claws. There are crows and sparrows, pigeons and doves. There's a bird that looks like it was a duck. The one closest to you is a fat moorhen with its head still on, the red and yellow beak pointing at the floor, the tiny black eyes reflecting shock.

There are cages against the left wall full of decomposing bird heads. Earthenware jars line the shelves, individually labeled: *Beaks and nostrils. Front claws. Feet, morning meals.* A cardboard box is labeled, *Dressing-Up Outfits.* Does Sheila enjoy dressing up here in the larder? Hopefully this is simply a storage decision.

Near the light bulb a long winding coil, twisted like a double helix of DNA, is coated with dead flies. These flies, together with the black eyes of the moorhen, tell you that your so-called paranoia – a paranoia that you'd suspected was wholly irrational – has been justified. You've known for some time that you've been given to flights of fancy and momentary hallucinations, but it seems your paranoid defenses were in fact safeguards against a reality more horrific than you'd thought. In short, *you have not been paranoid enough* to protect yourself from Ditchling.

You thought you could come down here and incorporate Sussex into your consciousness? The eyes of the moorhen tell you otherwise. *You have been incorporated into our collective consciousness*, the bird tells you. The more you look into its eyes, and the more you study the dead flies twisting on the sticky double helix, the more you realize that you will never, ever, be free of Sussex. You could board the fastest spaceship and take off, out above this island and into the atmosphere, and as you kept traveling further into space, way down in Ditchling there would be your psychic carcass, permanently embedded.

Against the right wall there are blue plastic tubs with white powder inside, together with a blue industrial strength barrel. You lift the lid, and inside there is a chemical solution that smells like formaldehyde. A small wooden stool, similar to the ones used by shepherds, sits beside a circular grinding stone and a marble rolling pin.

Lock the bedroom door, turn out the light. Get under the covers, pull your blankets to your nose. Has she been poisoning you this whole time – turning you into a bird? She's only making stock for soup, you tell yourself, nothing to be alarmed about. And yet the scale of her operation seems a tad excessive. How much soup stock does a person need?

You imagine you are back in California, on a beach under the palm trees, waves lapping at your feet. Sailboats in the distance glide across the water. How foolish, all those tourists who visit damp England! How tranquil it is on the sandy beach...

Jolting forward, you realize you've left the kitchen light on. Your eyes fixed on the shadowy outline of your door, you curse your stupidity. Soon Bobby and Sheila will return from their night out, only to discover their kitchen's been invaded.

The American's seen all me birds. I shouldn't have hung the key on the dog.
It's your own bloody fault, asking him to look over that posting. Fancy him snooping round our kitchen! I've got half a mind to straighten him out.
Hush now – he'll hear us!

Maybe it's not too late. You could run downstairs and switch off the light – but what if they came home and caught you? How could you get past them and up to your room? In the silence you lie under the covers, terrified, resigned to your fate. You cannot leave the bed, and you cannot go to sleep.

There's the front door, footsteps at the bottom of the landing, a muffled shout. There is no mistaking it. A man is coming. There are heavy boots clomping up the stairs, a throaty wheeze outside your door. Lie still in the dark – pretend to be asleep!

You've been a bad boy. The boots are not going anywhere, and this wheezing person is loaded with rage. Quivering in bed, you stifle the urge to scream out, to give yourself up, to plead for mercy. Shadows shift at the edge of the carpet, under the light of the landing. The story of the Sandman echoes in your head – your mother told it to you every night as a child.

The Sandman attacks all the naughty boys who do not shut their eyes and go to sleep. He will throw sand in your eyes if you're not careful. He throws naughty children into his sack, carries them to the moon as food for his children. The little Sandman children have crooked beaks like owls, and they will peck out your eyes.

Yes, the Sandman is out there waiting, on the other side of your door, his fists full of sand. The ends of his boots are angled at the gap under the door, as if his toes can sense you. It's Sheila's fault – she lured Bobby away and left you a trail to her bone-grinding activities. She wants you to lose your mind so she can cut off your hand for soup.

The Sandman will do her dirty work. The tales your parents told you were true, and now you know why – they knew, one day, you'd need to protect yourself in a place like Ditchling.

The Sandman wheezes outside your door. Each passing minute brings you closer to screaming. Soon he will be breaking in, kicking you with his boots, taking you to the moon and feeding your eyeballs to his owl children in their nests. What if the birds of Ditchling are being fattened with the hands and eyeballs of tourists?

9

In the morning you wake to a smell of perfume. For a moment you lie on your back, eyes closed, until you realize – someone is in the room with you.

You have a hunch it's Sheila – you hear sniffling beside you, possibly coming from the chair beside your bed – but rather than let on that you know she's there, you turn onto your side with your back to her and pretend to be asleep. Someone has cleaned during the night – there are fresh cups and saucers on the tea tray. Your dirty towels have been replaced with clean towels on the radiator. Even your robe has been taken from the floor, which means you've got no clothes in reach.

'Sleep well, lovey?'

You sit up and pull the duvet up over your chest. Unfortunately this means your bare feet are exposed – and you cannot help feeling embarrassed at the sight of them, hanging off the end of the bed. Sheila is sitting in your chair, legs apart, elbows on her knees. She's still wearing the dress from last night, the one she wore to the movies. Her rouge is smeared, her mascara smudged.

'You've been talking in your sleep again.'

'What…what was I saying?'

She sighs. 'A lot of nonsense, to be fair. Giving yourself nightmares, you must have done. That's what happens when people poke round my kitchen.'

'I didn't mean to be nosy.'

'Didn't you?' Sheila shifts in her chair, picks a bit of lint from her dress. 'I thought you liked my soup.'

You keep your eyes straight ahead. She's laundered your underwear and folded them, lengthwise, beside your socks. 'I do like it.'

'It must have been a shock, finding those birds. But I wouldn't have broth so tasty otherwise. You understand that.'

'Of course.'

'Larks' tongues were a delicacy, once upon a time. Wheatears got gathered up by the farmers and sold in our Saturday market. It's only the EU, and the regulations that's in the way of it all.'

'I understand. Still, there were so many ...'

'Don't believe everything you hear about the bird short-ages. Food prices have gone sky high. And the young birds sometimes fall from their nests, don't they? Bird bones – they're free, aren't they?'

'You don't have to explain. I found a bone in my soup, that's all. So I went down to the kitchen to see what kind it was. I was concerned by what I found – because of the recent bird disappearances ...'

'That's nothing to do with *me*. Some of the species – that's down to global warming. There aren't as many caterpillars on the oak tree leaves. Malcolm would tell you about that. About how all the ospreys and falcons, because of that ... is it DDT? It gets inside their bodies, this chemical does. And because the falcons are on the top of the food chain it goes straight down to the smaller birds. *That's* why they're dying, Mr Cull. And then there's all the domestic cats in this country. They don't help matters, do they?'

'I don't know. I'm not blaming you or anything. But when I saw those birds in your larder—'

'You took the key from my St Bernard, didn't you? It's no use looking out the window, Mr Cull, I can see the truth of it on your face. Bobby was in a right fit. I had to calm him down.'

'I'm sorry.'

'That's all I wanted to hear, an apology. We're Christians and we're forgiving. Bobby was set to give you a bollocking. Whenever he has too much to drink—'

'Was he really very angry?'

'He's a softy, really. Still, you'll want to apologize to him all the same.' She pats your shoulder, leaves her moist palm on your skin. 'I'm glad that you admitted what you've done. Your poor feet! They must be cold down there, hanging off the edge of the mattress.'

Sheila gets up. Taking the bottom of the duvet, she pulls it over your feet. You sink down into the bed, so that the duvet covers your chest again. 'Have you been here all night, Sheila?'

'You've been feeling poorly, luv. Running a fever and thrashing about. I nearly called the doctor's. Now – on your way to Margaret's, drop by the lounge and speak to Bobby about what you did. He'll be watching his baseball.'

'On my way to Margaret's?'

She turns with her hands on her hips, and her mascara-smudged face looms above you as it catches the daylight. 'Don't take the piss! She's got something of your grandfather's, you told me last night. You said you're going round to see her today – remember?'

'Oh, yes.' This gives you an excuse to be rid of her. 'I'm

running late.' You spot your robe on your door, hanging on a hook. 'You must excuse me – I'd better get up.'

'All right, then,' she says, waiting at the foot of your bed.

'I don't have any clothes on.'

'It's not as if I haven't seen a naked man before, is it?'

'I really don't know.'

'Bobby walks around all the time with his willy out.' Sheila lets out a loud cackle. 'Now *that's* taking the piss!' She walks over to the door. 'You missed breakfast again, but I can make you a sandwich and a nice cup of tea if you'd like.'

'I'll grab something at Sprinkles, thanks. Oh – Sheila?'

'Yes.'

'Malcolm and Jilly. Are they brother and sister?'

Sheila snorts. 'They act like it, don't they? No, they're very traditional, from Yorkshire. Moved down to Sussex to retire.'

'Close friends of yours?'

'Well – Malcolm used to be.' Sheila takes your robe and brings it over to you in bed.

She lingers a moment, staring down at you. 'The new-comers always fight me. They soon find out who's in charge.' The white belt of the robe dangles over your face. 'People are always fighting with me. Fighting over Eric Gill and how he should be remembered in the museum. Beer gardens and angling clubs? Parking petitions at the parish council? Ditchling's always been a place for families, Mr Cull. God's brothers and sisters. Whoever buries the hand of the stranger rules the rest.' She drops the robe on your bed. 'Bobby would love a bit of baseball chat if you can manage it, Mr Cull. You have no idea how long he's been waiting for an American.'

'I'll do my best.'

'That's a dear. And I'll get your bootscrapers sorted, just as I promised. I'm well handy with the Sellotape.'

In my first year of posing for Mr Gill in Ditchling Common the winter was a frightfully cold one. I would scorp the wood one day and pose the next. All the male apprentices would argue among ourselves about who was the real model for his nudes. Mr Gill allowed you to be clothed for a few minutes in between sketches but as soon as he set to work on what he called 'the most beauteous human form, without the restriction of clothing' we would remove our shirts and trousers and feel the cold immediately return to our bodies. We posed sometimes for hours. Though a fire was kept up I remember on one occasion that the water in my cup on the mantelpiece became frozen. I always consider the bad cough I acquired, which lasted for months thereafter, a result of these sessions.

Mr Gill was an exceptionally hard worker. Of my experiences in his studio a few are more memorable than others. They had to do with his family members who served as models. The woodcuts that resulted from these days in his studios are judged by art critics and theologians to be prototypes of spiritual enlightenment, but I would think that the celestial bodies judging these artistic achievements might be taken aback by the relatives that provided him inspiration.

Mr Gill's daughters were artists in their own right and often were found bending willow boughs to form decorations. The hand of God guided their art, which inspired some of our number to give up our hands in marriage to them. The women would hang apples from the boughs and create a recreation of Eden. They wrote calligraphy and were exceptional weavers. Many from Sussex and beyond came to study us as we worked, and the Guild grew in proportion to the attention it received.

Soon the plan arose that I might go to America and thus take with me the training I had acquired across the Atlantic and pursue my fortunes there. Then it was that I met my wife Jane. She had long caught my eye as her face was lovely to behold, and she and I were blessed with a son and soon thereafter a daughter. I had always lived in Sussex, always known only the ways of Sussex, and so it became reasonable to conclude I would forever live in Sussex until the day of my burial, whereupon my children would take up scorping and continue the great circle of those who belong to the countryside.

In the same way that aimless cutting and digging on bits of wood can lead nowhere, so in life can we spend years without direction, trifling about, only to realise when it is too late that we need God to guide us. Mr Gill began to command more money for his drawings and engravings. People from the village and beyond came to have their umbrella handles carved. Others asked for handbills, programme notices and trade cards for which they wanted especial fonts. Later Mr Gill's sculptures were chosen to stand in museums and ornament a number of important buildings in London, even if

Mr Reith did insist on reducing the size of the penises outside Broadcasting House. The BBC were quite content to use his Gill Sans font for their typeface. Mr Gill would go on to design the Stations of the Cross in Westminster.

Some of his sculptures might have caused offence, but Mr Gill always said that the holiness of the human form eclipsed its interpretation. 'Even pornographic photographs are generally photographs of things very good in themselves,' he said. In Ditchling Common our stonemasonry and headstone lettering proceeded apace. We kept animals. We rose early, prayed before our crucifix and held Catholic Mass.

Everyone in the Guild lived together. There was a small group who produced weaving, others pottery. We established a printing press, designed pamphlets, and published books. There were children everywhere and it was a joyous time. With each year we had almost forgotten our planned journey to America.

It was at this time that Father O'Neill, who traced his ancestry back many generations in Ditchling, moved into Mr and Mrs Gill's house to share their residence. He became the priest for the Guild. One night Father O'Neill became very drunk and spoke of an ancient prophecy which concerned Ditchling. Its interpretation augured the eventual break-up of the Guild. Father O'Neill claimed the prophecy had existed long before England was a country and possibly dated to the Romans.

The prophecy was short and I remember it exactly. The wording of it Father O'Neill pronounced very carefully, leaning forward in his chair with his finger in the sky, as if it were scripture:

The place known as 'Ditchling' is ruled by God's brothers and sisters.

A stranger will threaten this bloodline — you shall know him by the disappearance of birds in the sky.

Whoever buries the hand of the stranger rules the rest.

The next morning when questioned about his prophecy Father O'Neill at first denied speaking of it. When questioned again, he again denied his memory of the words he'd uttered the night before. Finally, after being given bacon and eggs, and generous helpings of shortbread, he admitted that the prophecy dated from pagan times. He said 'brothers and sisters' was probably a euphemism referring to communal living. A close community of artists producing godly works, he said, had always been essential to life. He did grant that others favoured a more literal interpretation.

There followed the unfortunate circumstances that brought about the dissolution of the Guild. We had a Dutch engraver working with us who had great command of the English language but nonetheless was mocked in town because of his pronunciation. One day he simply disappeared, and he was never heard from again. A little later, one of our weavers fell out with a family from Ditchling town. This family's daughter had taken up with our weaver, who originated from Iceland, and when this Icelander proposed to marry her, there followed a decline in the number of waterfowl. This poor Icelander was blamed, and soon after he too disappeared. Some said he was killed in the very pen where we kept our chickens and his body fed to our pigs in the night.

The police were called but did not sufficiently investigate the matter. For a time there were displays of pride, even celebration, in some of the more unpleasant members of the town, including pig noises made by a man called Pollard. Allegedly this family, along with one or two others, had been granted dispensations by apostate priests allowing them to couple within forbidden degrees of relation.

The fact that Ditchling is not accessible by rail should not have excused the poor police investigation, as some in the village have claimed. When the villagers went so far as to hire a 'bird expert' to corroborate the disappearance of waterfowl, the situation reached an intolerable point, especially when this expert published a pamphlet on his 'findings' and sold it at the post office. Outsiders, this man argued, had arrived with their foreign cats and strange smells, which had a negative effect on our local birds.

When I protested about these findings on purely scientific grounds, I was called a bird hater, a stranger lover, and worse. 'Why can't you have locals do your scorping?' the villagers asked. 'Why do immigrants take these jobs?' Mr Gill removed himself. 'Art is our focus', he kept repeating. But eventually even Mr Gill could not avoid involvement in the scandal. His family activities were exposed and ridiculed, especially the romantic love he professed for his own sister, leading to his removal to Wales. From what I understand, his last words in Ditchling were something to the effect of, 'This matter will haunt you all,' which many interpreted as a curse.

It was under this cloud of murderous suspicion that the Guild fragmented permanently. My wife and I, along with our children, decided to put into action our earlier plan to leave for America, and we travelled to New York and eventually California under the guidance of God on 5 February, 1939, where I continue to create small pieces of artwork.

As I write this account, the question for me still is – where did the prophecy come from, and why was it responsible for my leaving home, in effect becoming a stranger to my own self? Why? Is it only because I did not have a sister to marry, or that I did not befriend the most powerful brothers and sisters? I have since followed the goings-on in Ditchling, and I have noted with some irony that it is the villagers who have kept our Guild's work in the public eye. One day a museum about us may even be built.

In closing I confess I cannot help feeling homesick for Ditchling. Despite the circumstances of my departure, and my growing affection for America, I cannot stop hoping to return.

Stand up, put *Scorper* back on the shelf. Close the curtains tightly so Brenda can't paint you in this compromised light. As you stand there in your room, staring at your clothes folded by Sheila, you cannot shake the sensation that everyone in Ditchling knows what you are about to do.

Slip on your shoes, leave the room and pass the framed racehorses on the stairs. The sound of baseball on TV grows louder. You make your way forward and peer into the lounge. Bobby's on the sofa in a Los Angeles Dodgers cap with a bag of crisps in his hand. You rap on the frosted glass.

'Who's playing?'

'Dodgers versus Cardinals,' he says. 'I'd have thought you could tell by the uniforms.'

You wait by the door. The lounge makes you slightly nauseous and smells of sweaty feet. The wallpaper is dark, the curtains drawn. The coffee table and end tables are scattered with old newspapers and magazines.

'You never liked baseball?' Bobby says. 'Not even as a boy?'

'I played in Little League.'

'I would've liked that.'

'Maybe you should have been raised in the States.'

He shrugs, still staring at the screen. 'You're on your way to see Margaret, I expect.'

'That's right.'

'Mind that you don't miss breakfast again.'

'Sorry. I slept late.'

'Mum told me.' Bobby still doesn't take his eyes off the TV. 'I've always called Sheila Mum, you see. She calls me Dad, sometimes.'

'That's...sweet.'

'If you don't like it here I can always drive you to the chalk pit.'

'What chalk pit?'

'Not a real chalk pit. The Chalk Pit Inn, just outside the village.'

'I like it here, Bobby.'

'Mum makes a good soup.'

'Listen, Bobby, I want to say sorry for entering the kitchen—'

'Ball two,' Bobby says. On screen, the pitcher goes into his windup and throws wide.

The batter steps away from the plate. He spits on the dirt, taps the bottom of his shoe with his bat, stares down the pitcher. 'Come on, Dodgers,' Bobby says.

The pitcher bends forward with his elbow on his knee. He stares down the plate, gets the sign from his catcher. Bobby leans in as well. He pretends to throw and watches the ball all the way into the catcher's mitt. 'Strike.' He glances at you by the door. 'A bit low, but still a strike.'

'That was a nice pitch, all right.'

'Now it's two balls and two strikes.'

The batter steps away from the plate, taps the bottom of his shoes. The pitcher puts his elbow on his knee, gets the sign from his catcher. The tedium is excruciating, and slowly you inch away.

'Here the pitch comes,' Bobby says.

'I should be getting going…'

'Don't worry about the kitchen, then,' Bobby calls after you. 'You can make it up to me by acting like a man.'

On the top step of the B&B, you survey the High Street. It's a windy afternoon – the cold catches your neck and stings your tender upper lip.

'Hi, John!'

Across the street Brenda waves. She's carrying an easel.

She unlocks the door to the flat above the jeweler's, and as the door closes behind her, you wave back.

Hold out your hand. Turn it around, wiggle your fingers, see your flesh as Brenda might. For the first time it strikes you that you have dimensions, here in England. Your thoughts have substance, your body is composed of living matter. After all, you're not just a blob taking shape at the end of someone's paintbrush.

Act like a man – your time on Earth expands, along with your place in it, so that you are no longer a you but a he, not a momentary visitor to Ditchling but a part of its history. There is a grave in the churchyard with your name on it. A man such as yourself, a man named John Cull – a part of England's past with his future still in front of him – might take this opportunity to assert himself and leave behind the limitations of an imperative present. Such a man might stand up taller before the curtain-eyes. He might even convert.

> *Something metaphysical is occurring here on the High Street.*
> *It's happened before, and it will happen again.*
> *Cull's being contextualized and historicized, everyone –*
> *right now, right this minute.*

Yes, contextualized and historicized, curtain-eyes, and if this John Cull who converts to a he can position himself properly against future critics, he might characterize himself for once, thereby escaping all the pedants who want to retroactively psychoanalyze his behavior, herme-neutically interpret his artistic tendencies, and reductively deconstruct his work as the necessary product of external forces.

He won't escape.
He can resort to all the literary jargon he wants, he'll always
be under our immediate curtain-eyed scrutiny.
He's thinking hard on that top step — let's see what he
does next.

The events of the past week came back to John Cull in a
flash – yet something had changed. He had finally become
the subject of his own creation. And why *wouldn't* he? Bobby
and Sheila had referred to him in the third person, past
tense, even in his presence. They had practically encouraged this transformation. If you were on your way to meet
your lover – if John Cull, say, had been on his way to meet
her – wouldn't he, recognizing the importance of the
moment, start to feel differently? Didn't pianists playing
the fugues of Bach wander into deep musical black holes,
never to return the same?

All his life, he had been suffering insults about his
domed forehead and awkward gait, his stooped shoulders
and overlarge ears – but what if he was no longer content
to be on the receiving end of these pointed index fingers?
A man such as this would no longer stoop. He would speak
his mind and defend himself against dark forces. At every
opportunity he would show the Ditchlings his noble side,
revealing dimensions that spoke to his innermost dreams.

On the top step of the B&B, John Cull became baptized
by the cold wind off the South Downs, howling with the
sound of trumpets. Sketching bootscrapers might have
helped him observe the details of things, as Eric Gill suggested – now it was time to move to the next artistic plateau,
the world of his heart.

Dressing this morning, perhaps unconsciously anticipating his rebirth, he had chosen his finest silk shirt, a red one with a broad collar, to accompany his corduroys and dress shoes. Now he needed a hat – something striking to demonstrate his new goals. He also needed another sketchbook, preferably with powdery white pages, scalloped edges, and a durable cover to protect his work from heathens in Land Rovers. But before all of this, he would have a sausage roll.

Cull barreled down the steps. He set out up the High Street, weaving in and out of the Ditchlings. They had their coats pulled tight and their heads lowered, but he could hear them gossip as he passed. The best critics would see the threads of these early years in his art.

So Margaret became his muse.
She changed the trajectory of his career – a fact established
by contemporary scholars.
Students of John Cull's work will observe the intertextual
connection between the bootscrapers and his poems –
'The Shape of the Sussex Downs', for example, and his lyric
confessional, 'I am the American of Ditchling'.

Yes, Cull fancied as he approached Sprinkles, from now on he would openly proclaim his goals instead of apologizing for them. The bell jingled brightly as he came inside, as if announcing his freedom and movement. He tried to stand tall, he tried not to stoop and shirk from the Ditchlings' gaze – but unless he wanted to hit his head on the doorframe, he had to duck. The displays of muffins and cakes and teapots were in his way as usual, and he had to hold his elbows close to his sides to avoid hitting them. As the Ditchlings turned to him with their silent stares, he had to look away unless he wanted to rudely stare back. And as he made his way to the counter to order, unless he wanted to bang into the little dollhouse chairs, he had to proceed slowly and carefully, to mind his step.

Against the walls, the watercolors of the South Downs had been moved aside to make room for an exhibition of Eric Gill reproductions. There were nudes both slender and plump, nudes reclining on letters, nudes shooting bows and arrows from heraldic plants, nude lovers entwined in various angles of copulation.

Cull tried not to stare. But as he glanced at the pictures he was caught, as it were, by two elderly women eating cake. Their mild, almost indifferent expressions indicated that they were proud to be perfectly comfortable with this explicit display of Fabian pornography around them as they ate – so why couldn't he play the part of a well-adjusted young American, on his way to the counter to order a sausage roll?

At the register, a young couple was discussing a small painting propped against the plastic case of croissants.

'Funny,' the man said to his girlfriend.

'"Frankenstein Holding a Teacup",' she replied, reading the title of the work, and she laughed.

The picture was a bald caricature of Cull himself, garishly splashed with bright colors and broad brushstrokes. A terrifyingly tall man with a domed forehead and protruding ears stood framed by the window, hunched forward in a robe, peering out of his curtains, a small teacup in his enormous palm.

Cull felt his face redden. He tried to regard the painting as if he were just another customer waiting to order.

'It's a common enough error,' he said, 'calling the creature Frankenstein. The title should be "Frankenstein's Monster Holding a Teacup".'

The couple looked at Cull. Then they looked quickly back at the painting, and this act was so furtively executed, so delicately and politely disguised, that he could bear the discomfort no longer. He left the queue and made his way outside.

The bell rang as Cull came into *Animals in Distress*. Luckily he was the only customer. In these more exclusive establishments he would shop unencumbered by the intrusions of curious onlookers. Rhiannon stood behind the counter.

'A fine afternoon,' he said to her. 'There's a colder wind. Dare I say, an *ominous* wind.'

'Haven't seen you in a while.'

'I've been keeping to myself.'

'Kev got the better of you the other day, didn't he?' She grinned. 'He's got the upper hand.'

'For the moment.'

'I warned you not to go near him.'

'Your ironical warnings, Rhiannon, come across like invitations – but I suppose you know that. At any rate I am back on my feet, as you can see.'

Cull sorted through some knick-knacks on the counter, thrown together in a cardboard box – buttons, odd pieces of cutlery, commemorative coins. 'I'm looking for a hat,' he said at last.

'Got plenty of those. They come in all the time.'

'Yes, I should think the hat wearers of the world are always giving up their heads to the weevils and the worms.'

Rhiannon giggled. She was a raw and lascivious woman.

The red streak in her hair was brushed straight up, straighter than usual, in a kind of exclamation point. She brought him over to the hat rack against the wall, where various possibilities hung on hooks – a trilby, an assortment of flat caps, a beret. There was even a black bowler. None of them suited Cull's purposes. He wanted to show Kevin he meant business.

'Anything else?'

'I just got another box of donations. Come on.'

Rhiannon took him to the back of the shop, where the unsorted merchandise had collected on the other side of the curtain. She dug into a box and held up a wide leather belt, followed by a handful of ties. 'I thought for sure there was a hat here…'

'I want that one,' Cull said, pointing to an article flung in the corner. The hat was from a grander, unbridled time. It would allow him to be more unguarded, and it would conceal the majority of his overlarge ears, protect his head, and provide air holes to hear with.

'This old boxing helmet?' Rhiannon said. She went over and picked it up. 'Are you going to a costume party?'

'No. Everyday use.'

'What – you're going to wear it round the village?' She snorted. 'God, can't wait to see *that*.'

She helped Cull put it on. She pulled the leather over his head, tightened the chinstrap, and stepped back, her eyes widening. Cull looked around. His head felt prepared for anything. The leather even made his scalp warm.

'I'll give it a good polish,' she said, hurrying into a back room. 'So it's nice and shiny.'

She applied the polish and rubbed down the leather,

buffeting his head this way and that. 'This hat will allow me to sublimate my poetic impulses,' Cull said. 'I will be respectful of the classics while pioneering new forms. And the ear holes will allow modern voices to penetrate my occasionally antiquated thoughts.'

'I'll let you have it for a fiver,' Rhiannon said.

She led him over to the mirror. The hat made his head look small and fierce, like a copper-topped bullet.

'Now you're a fighter,' she said.

'I've never been in a real fight,' Cull said sadly.

'Don't worry. You'll get one soon, wearing this.'

'The only hat I've seen Kevin wear is that fly-fishing hat.'

'You'll want to stay on your toes,' she said, dancing round him and giving him a few jabs. 'Right up until the moment you strike. Go on. Give it a go.'

In the mirror he shadow-boxed and tried out some uppercuts.

Rhiannon clapped. 'You'll thrash him.'

Cull followed her to the till. He was sweating from all the activity, and from the heat of his head. He paid in front of a poster of undernourished cats. Rhiannon walked him out and watched from the door as he made his way down the High Street.

Passing Sprinkles he spotted Larry and Grace. Larry was in his greengrocer's apron, Grace in her museum shirt. They were holding hands and having coffee under an Eric Gill woodcut of a nude, her breasts pressed into her lover's face.

And what was strange, after all, about a brother and sister having a coffee, enjoying a break in their day? Shouldn't siblings be allowed to hold hands? Noticing him at the window, Larry and Grace looked up – soon, others in the café turned around, until everyone was staring. Only now, their stares didn't upset Cull any longer. It was them – the people of Ditchling – who had created him.

He'd forgotten to buy a sketchbook. He also needed something to write with. It would be best to fetch his spike – if he felt inspired, he could find a blank gravestone. Back he went, up the steps to the B&B and through the front door.

Inside the lounge, Bobby was still watching baseball. Sheila stood in the dining room, at a table near the door, bent over the torn bootscrapers. 'It might not be possible,' she said, shaking her tape and scissors at Kevin's tire marks, 'to get your work back to new. But I'm trying...'

Sheila's eyes were red-rimmed. The wayward child had kept her up all night, and she'd cooked and cleaned all day. 'Please don't worry about it, Mum,' Cull said.

'Bobby,' she said, staring at Cull in the helmet. 'Look – look what he's wearing.'

Bobby sat forward on the sofa. Seeing Cull in the boxing helmet, his hands flew up his throat, as if tickling his neck with glee.

The strange way the two of them behaved made Cull run straight upstairs. At the desk, he fetched the spike, and he waited at the door. How was he going to get by them? He snuck back down and found them there, waiting at the door. Sheila was holding the package wrapped in brown butcher paper, the one Malcolm Ketteridge-Wilson had brought.

'Be quick about it,' Sheila muttered. She gave Bobby the package and slipped into the dining room.

'Come in, Mr Cull,' Bobby said, holding open the door

to the lounge. 'Sit down.' Cull went inside and perched on the edge of the sofa. Bobby moved aside the magazines and empty crisp packages and sat beside him. He placed the package on his knee.

'We're glad you're finally getting serious about Kev,' Bobby said. 'We're proud of you.'

'It's just a hat.'

'No. It's more than just a hat, Mr Cull. You and I both know that.' Bobby switched off the TV, but he turned and continued speaking to the blank screen. 'He's starting to get ideas about his position here. His power over other people. It always starts with a planning permission application, or a parking space – where does it lead?'

Cull spoke to the TV as well. 'A man simply cannot endure continuous displays of malice. Especially when that malice is unjustified. You become paranoid – I became paranoid – and if you're already born with a paranoid disposition, then your paranoia becomes outright fear. Maybe I need to do something. Maybe a man needs to act before he is attacked again—'

Bobby patted his knee. 'I understand.'

'Did Kevin have something to do with Carlo's disappearance?'

'There's been all sorts of rumors.' Bobby unwrapped the brown butcher paper and held up a set of brass knuckles. 'Slide'em on, son. Make sure they fit.'

Bobby took Cull's hand and slid the brass knuckles around his right palm. 'Perfect,' he said, tightening Cull's hand into a fist. 'Straight to the jaw, got it? Then follow it right quick with another, down in his kidneys. Kev shouldn't give us any trouble after that.'

Even in his boxing helmet, carrying brass knuckles and a spike, the old fear struck Cull as he started for Boddington's Lane. What if Margaret no longer cared a whit for him? England was technically part of Europe, after all – the sexually liberated continent. One 'shag' as they called it, could hardly claim a woman's heart.

'I am John Cull of Ditchling,' he told himself as he walked the cobblestones. The sun was setting, the lane was growing dark. 'Margaret loves me, sort of – or she wouldn't have slept with me.'

His feet betrayed him. He turned and headed to the churchyard. The gravestones waited like a long-suffering audience. There they stood in the rain, scattered under the lime trees. Tourists went to Italy for its food and wine, Greece for its beaches – but those who visited England came for misery. Cull saw the truth of it now more than ever before. Misery permeated British life. It was in the old women waiting for buses that never came, in the crumbling walls of the houses and the sputtering radiators inside. The people of England suffered under a constant cloud – misery settled into pews of churches and drinkers in pubs, and in the mornings it found exaggerated smiles of underpaid workers forced by their employers to undergo Americanized customer service training. The nation moaned and moaned and moaned – a collective grievance that entered the lungs and stayed, until the condition became hereditary.

He wandered the path toward the gravestones. He would have to demonstrate to Margaret his own willingness for misery, at least in the beginning, as a sort of courtship ritual.

Some loves were born out of innocence, others out of convenience. Their love would stem from a desire to experience pain. At first they would compete against each other, exposing their raw wounds, but she would win because of her dead husband and failing pizza shop. He would moan as best as he could, then capitulate to play the role of her consoler, her wound-licker.

Among the graves, Cull began to have the sensation of being watched. He turned and saw the young girl from the pub, walking toward him from behind the nearby gravestones. Her blonde hair was dripping from the rain, and she was panting.

'Are you all right?'

'I run from school,' she said, catching her breath. 'I always do. The others get picked up by their parents...'

'You should get off that grass. Your shoes are soaking wet.'

The girl stayed where she was. 'I like your hat.'

Cull smiled. In the same way that he had a kinship with animals, he felt comfortable in the company of children. He unbuckled his chinstrap. The leather helmet had shrunk in the rain, and his head steamed as he took it off.

'Here you go,' he said, holding the hat out. It carried a smell of death and dead animals, and the girl kept her distance.

'Did it hurt when Kev hit you?'

Cull touched his lip. 'Yes.'

'Dad likes him. But I think he's a horrid man.'

'You're supposed to try and see the best in people. Maybe he just had a bad day.'

She balled her hands into fists. 'You'll hit him back next time.'

Cull nodded. He put the helmet back on his head and

tightened the chinstrap. He looked up, over the horizon, to the storm clouds collecting over Dicul's hill. 'My first priority is love – just love, all by itself. I'll protect myself from attacks, but I'll try not to antagonize him.'

'You weren't banned, Mr Cull.'

'Still, it wouldn't be right to go looking…'

Cull lost his train of thought. He stared at the muddy grass, suddenly embarrassed. He felt something small and cold slip inside his palm. It was the girl's hand.

'She's in the pizza shop,' the girl said. 'Alone.'

'Margaret?'

The girl nodded. 'I saw her just now.'

'How sad,' Cull said, 'that she doesn't have any customers. Why don't more people eat pizza in Ditchling?'

They stood looking out over the churchyard, and in their joint melancholy it seemed they shared a spark of happiness. In the furthest rows at the top of the hill, the neglected headstones tilted toward the ground. His own grave was up there – how unfortunate it would be to die, and be buried.

The girl followed his gaze, her hand still in his palm.

'Go and find her,' she said.

He remembered how she'd directed him to the pizza shop on the day he arrived. She took her hand back and bolted down the path between the lime trees.

Cull grew tired, standing in the rain. It was a tiredness that made him feel much older than his thirty years. The great ones had become so by leaps and pirouettes, feats of uncommon mastery of their craft, while he was still trawling around churchyards, gazing submissively at the poets in graves who had already lived.

He wandered the rows and read between the lines of the epitaphs. *Struck down in front of the locals. Warned by the publican. A man the schoolgirls pitied.* Here in Ditchling, his only chance at redemption was art. And yet as he hung his leathery head, and the rain ran off his neck onto the soil, his first step had to be finding the woman who'd inspired him. He would leave it in his will to be with her forever, with strict instructions to have his ashes mixed with chalk, pasted into the lettering of her epitaph when she died.

He trudged down the path and through the hedgerow onto the High Street. He turned left and started up Boddington's Lane. The flint walls rose around him, with their letterboxes embedded into stone. He reached the turn in the lane before the pizza shop.

One by one, the lights in the houses turned on. He could hear his footsteps on the cobblestones. This was dangerous territory – he had been warned, after all, to steer clear. He stopped as he neared the pizza shop. Something had changed. Something was wrong.

The restaurant was dark. The lights were off, the door locked when he tried it. A hand-written note on the window simply said, *Closed until further notice.* Cull hesitated, wondering what had happened. Quite apart from spending time with Margaret, he'd been looking forward to some pizza. He thought the curtains were twitching, two doors down, over at the house she shared with Dona Matarazzo.

Did he dare knock? What if Margaret had taken Kevin home for tea and they were all inside, waiting for him? Cull strode to her door. A man had to have hope. After all, wasn't that what Americans were *for*? To set an example for the world – to overcome impossible social and economic obstacles, to break through cultural divides by sheer force of will. If he didn't pursue Margaret further, as he'd done at Quiz Night, he'd be a defeatist. A hand-wringer. A Brit.

He reached for the door and knocked. Soon he heard footsteps. The door opened, and Dona Matarazzo stood before him, lips pursed, long white hair brushed against her shoulders. Behind her, the candles were flickering.

'*Sangue di Dio!*'

'I am here to see Margaret.'

'What this hat?'

Cull stood taller and maintained his composure under the woman's sneers. 'I'll have you know that Lord Byron wore a hat in your country to much admiration. It had a buckle and a black feather, I believe – and the people of Genoa never dared to ridicule him.'

'Not here.' She started to close the door.

'Wait. Margaret said she had something of my grandfather's— '

'Not here. Not here!'

He peered inside. 'Can you tell me where she's gone?'

Dona Matarazzo pointed over the flint walls. '*Basta!* She away! To that commoner.'

Cull turned his earhole to her. 'The commoner? She's with Kevin?'

'The one she buys?'

'Ah, Ditchling Common. The studio?'

'Yes. The commoner!'

'Then I will go and catch my little bird.' A verse was coming, and Dona Matarazzo would be his audience. He felt for the chinstrap, gestured to the sky, and gave vent.

> Why are your ancestors
> dead, their voices
> not hoarse but scorched
> wisps of flame?
> What does it sound like to flutter
> in silence, my bird?

He might have delivered a second verse, even more inspired than the first, but Dona Matarazzo closed the door and turned the deadbolt.

In his leather helmet he jogged at an easy pace, shadow boxing. He passed horses by the side of the road.

'I'm coming for you, Margaret!'

Out in the country he could sing all he wanted. He could sing to the Downs and over the flinty ridge of the Weald.

He would sing the poetry of love. What was it about Margaret that appealed to him in particular? There was that mole, of course, but before the mole he had been struck in a more general way by her beauty. Was it her eyes – the way one of them was situated to the left of the other, equally spaced, on either side of her nose? Or was it the fact that she had two lips, one just above the other, to form a mouth?

> My love has two eyes,
> Two lips and a nose.
> Two lips —
> And a nose!

The road opened up. He left the last of the housing estates and saw a sign pointing to the Common. This was where people grazed their animals once upon a time, according to *Scorper*, without paying a duty to the Lord of the Manor. Eric Gill and his Guild had lived here, away from the prying eyes of the villagers, set up their chapel, their printing press and studios, their communal living quarters. A second sign for the studios pointed down a smaller road.

It was a darker road than the one he'd been on. The sun had set but the stars had not yet appeared, and in the dusk the nocturnal animals were hiding in their shrubs and caves and distant trees, preparing to emerge. The lights of the village disappeared behind him – and ahead lay only this deeper darkness.

He came to a stone bridge, with a white-capped river rushing below. If Margaret had ventured this far tonight, would she have come alone?

Cull crossed the bridge and found more horses in the next field. He stood by the fence and waited until they came to say hello. He had no food to offer the horses, nor any news they might be interested in. He wanted to ask them why there weren't as many birds in the sky, but the horses just stood there with the steam coming off their coats, nibbling at the wooden fence posts.

Now that he'd stopped running, he shivered. The rain had stopped and the night had grown colder, but he didn't mind because the discomfort would keep him alert. He had to arrange his thoughts. He had to calm his nerves. Sussex wasn't Los Angeles, with its gangs, carjackings, and drive-by shootings. So what was the source of this fear?

The road turned, and in the distance there was a light. He came closer and saw that the light belonged to a studio in the middle of a semicircle of buildings. He recognized this place

– there was a photo of it in the museum, and on the back flap of *Scorper*. There were about ten separate studios made of stone and timber, arranged around a dirt clearing. Someone had erected a chicken coop near some trees. A stone crucifix stood in the center of the clearing, and in front of the studio with the light on, Kevin had parked his Land Rover.

Cull kept in the shadows cast by the light. He hugged the darkened walls as he came nearer the door. There was a window without curtains and he might be able to peek in. He thought of how Rhiannon encouraged him, how Bobby had taught him how to punch with the brass knuckles. Hadn't Margaret practically invited him here? He was sweating so badly, his shirt collar sucked at his neck.

It had already been written – all of this. His brain was prefigured and this moment preconstructed. All he had to do was relinquish control, give up to the cosmic forces behind the eternal laws, or the eternal laws behind the cosmic forces. When he reached the door he tightened his chinstrap, flattened his back against the stone, and quickly swung around for a view inside. Kevin and Margarat were in there, and they were kissing.

Cull sank down to the ground, his back to the wall. He stared at his muddy shoes. He could feel the ants and worms in the damp soil, crawling and nibbling at his socks like needling thoughts, begging to slip inside his trouser legs and become members of his family.

He pulled his socks down and waited for the ants and worms. Kevin kissed her. In his grandfather's property, no less – Margaret had been sitting on the sofa with a glass of wine, and Kevin had stood above her, his back to the window, leaning down to kiss her before droning on. Cull could hear him now, though none of the words were distinct.

Why did Margaret *like* him? Because he went to Cambridge with Carlo? Before the melting ice separated the continents, before Ireland broke apart from Britain, there would have been Kev on the tundra, pushing his Neanderthal equivalent of a Land Rover, a clunky cart made of teeth, flint and shin bones. He would have mated and lumbered and grunted in the same droning voice, 13,000 years ago. Under his stone wheels he would have crushed rare sculptures and figurines. Sooner or later, the artists had to fight back.

Cull slipped on the brass knuckles. From his pocket he removed the spike. Slowly, he reached over and tried the door handle. As much as the Brits pontificated about ignorant Americans, Kevin had left the door unlocked.

Cull swung open the door. Margaret stood up from the sofa and cried out. Kevin wheeled. Seeing Cull armed and wearing a leather helmet, his face drained of blood.

There was a shout. Something struck Cull on the back of the head, and he stumbled. It was an umbrella.

'*Mannaggia!*'

Cull dropped the spike and held up his hands. Dona Matarazzo hit him again with the umbrella. 'Fall to ground,' she said, her hair flying as she kept hitting his head and shoulders. 'Fall to ground!'

Cull started to run, but Kevin tackled him. He fell face down on the stone floor and felt the man's heavy knee on the small of his back.

'He not stop breathing, this one,' Dona Matarazzo said, pointing the umbrella at him. 'So who the bird catcher now, and who the bird?'

10

Cull awoke shivering on a thin scattering of straw. His whole body felt bruised. Next to his head lay a couple of dead flies on their backs, staring up at the ceiling as if the end of the world had come.

He'd been thrown into the chicken house. They'd stripped off his clothes and left him in his underwear. They'd taken his boxing helmet.

The corrugated metal walls rattled in the wind. The chickens were perched on a wooden nest box against the wall, seemingly asleep. There were four of them – three brown, one white. A plastic feeder hung by a rope attached to the ceiling. He crawled over to it and saw that there were two partitions – one with food pellets, the other with murky water. Some food pellets had found their way into the water and were floating around bits of straw.

The house was drafty, and he kept shivering. He could see the dark sky through the narrow gaps between the wooden slats of the ceiling, enclosed by wire mesh. He got on his feet and immediately drew a sharp breath. Pain shot across the small of his back, where Kevin had dug in his knees.

There was a small door in the chicken house made of wood and wire mesh. It was just closed by a piece of twine on the outside. The door had a hole cut out of the frame designed for a hand. He untied the twine and opened the door, ducking to get out. It was even colder outside. A steady mist was falling, and the wind was blowing hard. The dirt run was enclosed by a perimeter fence. There was a second door, made of stronger wood, and this one was padlocked. The run was empty except for an old head of cabbage pecked to pieces. Through the wire fence he could see the dim outside light of Margaret's studio, across the clearing. The house was dark, the curtains drawn. The Land Rover was still there.

In his underwear he paced the run. He could take exactly eleven steps up and back. He told himself not to scream just yet. Still – could Margaret really be inside, knowing he was here?

The wire fencing wasn't the strongest – he could probably dig his way out. But he was cold and sore, his fingers numb. After a few minutes outside in the wind, he retreated back to the relative warmth of the chicken house.

He was thirsty, but he decided not to drink the water in the feeder. Instead he gathered up all the straw he could find on the ground, stole a few handfuls from the chickens, and made a small bed against the wall, in view of the door. Then he took the two dead flies outside. He pushed them through a hole in the fence, came back into the house, and tied the twine to fasten the door shut.

Curled up on his side in a tight ball, he could almost get comfortable – but the relentless cold, and the hard ground, kept sneaking up on him, shaking him violently awake, so that he remained in various stages of agony, even desperation, for hours. He wondered if Sheila and Bobby had sent out a search party. He rocked his way into snatches of sleep.

When light appeared through the roof, Cull kicked his legs and stood up. He moved quickly, as if he were suddenly late for a meeting.Thirsty, he reached for the feeder before stopping himself.

He must have been mistaken – there were only three chickens in the nest box, not four. There were two small brown ones and a large white Leghorn. They bobbed their heads and made nervous little clucks as he leaned toward them, allowing him to search the straw underneath for eggs to eat. They hadn't laid any.

He opened the door and poked his head out. The run was empty. He proceeded cautiously across the dirt, and in the daylight, he could see how small the enclosure was. He walked with his head down, occasionally kicking the cabbage out of his way with his bare feet. Walking back and forth in the chicken run, he felt he had entered a recovered memory seen from the perspective of the first captive animals.

After a few rounds he went to the fence and put his fingers through the holes. He imagined what the Common would have been like, hundreds of years ago, when the poorest people in the area lived here with their dogs and cats, their geese, their pigs. They would have lived in rough shelters of wattle and daub. Eric Gill and his Guild of engravers and stonemasons must have liked the remoteness of the Common. They could work in privacy and raise their families the way they wanted without the prying eyes of the villagers. You couldn't hear anything but the wind in the trees.

'Hello! Anyone up yet?' His voice was raspy, constricted from the cold. 'Margaret?'

Her studio was maybe twenty yards away. He counted a dozen in total, situated in a half circle around what looked like a medieval font and the stone crucifix. None of the other studios appeared occupied – some had windows broken or missing. A few had no doors at all.

'Hello! Is anyone there?'

Cull shook the fence hard. It wobbled, but the supports ran deeper into the ground than he thought. He walked over to the door and shook it in its frame, but the padlock held. He crossed the run and faced the nearby trees in the direction of the road. The bridge stood at the bottom of a long narrow track. There was nobody around, just horses.

The chickens ventured out to join him. A brown one headed straight to the cabbage and attacked it with vicious lunging rips of its beak. The big white Leghorn stayed by the fence. The other brown one came over to Cull and pecked at the dirt near his feet.

He was getting very cold in his underwear. The mist had stopped, but the wind was strong and turned his skin into rubbery goosebumps. He paced back and forth, flapping his arms to keep warm. Then he saw someone under the nearby trees.

It was Kevin, kneeling over something, half turned. Cull was almost happy to see him – he raised his arms and waved.

'Kevin! Hey!'

Kevin didn't reply. He had a hatchet – the blade gleamed. He brought the hatchet down then stood up and came toward the run with a brown chicken, hanging by its feet, a chicken that now had no head.

Cull glanced quickly at the other chickens. They didn't seem to notice that their friend had just been decapitated. He backed away as Kevin kept coming, the head balanced on the flat of the hatchet.

At the fence, Kevin stopped and flung the head in the air. It landed on top of the wire mesh that covered the enclosure, rolled, and came to a stop, face down. Blood dripped from its neck and onto the dirt. Kevin walked back to the studio.

The cold sun climbed in the sky. Soon smoke came from the chimney over at the studio. Cull could smell wood burning. Once or twice, in the distance, he thought he heard the sound of a car or a motorcycle, and he screamed.

Cross-legged beside the feeder, Cull appraised the murky water. The chickens watched him from their nest box against the wall.

'You regard me with a measure of distrust. I know what you're thinking – greedy Americans! But you might be happy to know that we have provided for you in the past. We haven't been eating potatoes and turnips for the last century, you know. We've been growing our military, expanding our farms.'

He held the feeder to his mouth. 'Now I'll just sample this punch…' He tilted it back and tried not to gag.

'Yes, we Americans continue this "special relationship" like a cat plays with its favorite brain-dead mouse, batting it back and forth, just to see how stupefied your British captors get without actually expiring. So don't worry. If Kevin gets *really* cruel, I'll call in the big guns.'

The chickens just stared. They had all come indoors after it had grown dark, a couple of hours ago. Cull had created a small pit in the corner where he pissed and shit.

'I'll leave the rest of that punch for you,' he told the

chickens. He forced down a handful of the cabbage and hoarded the rest under his straw. Against the wall he gathered the straw around his haunches and prepared for the long wait. He would escape tonight, he decided, using the plastic feeder to dig his way under the fence.

'John! John, are you there?'

Cull stood up. It was a woman's voice – Margaret's. He brushed the straw from his underwear, and untied the twine at the door, and peered out. She was standing outside the run with a torch, and she was alone.

She pointed the torch at him. 'Come and talk to me, John. It's all right – I'm not going to hurt you.'

He ducked back into the house. The chickens clucked and pleaded with him in their nests, as if to warn him of a trap.

'John! Come on out.'

He straightened his hair, came through the door, and made his way to the fence. Margaret was in her warm coat, zipped up to the neck. She had no smile for him, not even an expression of sympathy. They stood without speaking for a moment, as if they had other places to be. It would be best, Cull decided, to pretend he was perfectly happy and had everything he needed.

'How's the pizza shop?'

'I closed it for a few days.'

'Why?'

'The final paperwork came through on this property. I shut the restaurant so we could come out here and look it over.' She took her cigarettes out of her pocket. 'Why did you do it, John?'

'Do what?'

She shook out a cigarette out and lighted it. 'Why did you try and attack us?'

'I didn't attack anyone. I would never—'

'You had those brass knuckles. And that spike.'

'That was in case Kevin tried to attack *me*. You saw how he knocked my hat off in the street. He tried to run me over and punched me in the pub!'

'Where'd you get the brass knuckles?'

Cull shrugged. This was why she wanted to talk – to get information out of him. 'Nowhere in particular.'

She stared at him while she smoked. Her eyes had turned colder and harder, and she almost seemed to be enjoying his discomfort. He had to stamp his feet to keep warm.

'What about that thing you had on your head? What an intruder might wear. Mama wanted to break your arms, do you know that? They do that to intruders in Italy.'

'We're not *in* Italy. You invited me here – don't you remember?'

'Not in the middle of the night, John. Not armed to the teeth.'

'Call the police, then. Call them and report an instruder! I'm cold, Margaret. And hungry.'

'You don't ring the police for every little thing. Not out in the country.' Margaret fished in her pockets. 'You're hungry, are you?' She took something wrapped in tinfoil and pushed it through a hole in the fence. 'Take this,' she said.

'You're not going to let me out of here?'

'Kevin's not about to. And neither is Mama. I can't say that I blame them. Go on – take this if you're hungry.'

'What is it?'

'Leftovers.'

222

He grabbed the end of the foil package and pulled it through the hole. Inside was a roast drumstick. Over at the studio, the front light came on. The door opened, and Kevin came across the clearing, carrying the hatchet.

Cull stepped back from the fence. 'What's going on?'

'You'd better not move,' Margaret said. 'He won't hurt you if you don't make eye contact with him and don't speak.'

Cull kept his eyes on the dirt as Kevin's boots crunched along the gravel. He could hear the key turn in the padlock, and then Kevin walking by, into the little door to the chicken house. There was an awful commotion inside. He could hear the chickens squawking and flapping their wings. Then Cull heard Kevin pass by again, followed by the key in the padlock. When he looked up, Margaret was guiding Kevin's way with the torch, all the way to the trees. Kevin had taken another of the brown ones. The bird hung upside down by its feet.

'I need water,' he said.

'He promised to fill the feeder tomorrow if you behave yourself.'

'What do you mean, behave myself?'

'The last owner had CCTV installed. I wouldn't try to escape – Mama watches the monitor all night.' Margaret took a last drag of her cigarette. She rubbed the embers against the fence and dropped the butt through.

In Margaret's face Cull tried to find any trace of the love she showed him the other night. He tried to locate the mole. He must have been staring too closely because she turned away, self-conscious in front of him, even as he stood there half-naked.

'Look, I'm doing the best I can with him. You have to give him time to cool off. Stay out of trouble – build up his trust. Here,' she said, slipping something else through the hole. 'It's a photo of your grandfather. I found it inside the file on the house.'

Cull took it. 'Please. I'll go back to the B&B, Margaret. I won't press charges.'

'It's not up to me, I'm afraid.'

'What does Kevin have on you? Has he threatened you or something?'

Margaret kept the torch aimed into the trees. Kevin was kneeling in the same spot as yesterday, the chicken in his grip. He raised the hatchet.

'I didn't want to mention this before,' Cull whispered. 'Some people at Quiz Night – they said Kevin had something to do with your husband's disappearance.'

Margaret shook her head. 'Kev and Carlo were best friends.'

'People said—'

'People talk a lot of nonsense in Ditchling. It doesn't mean anything – you should know that by now.'

'But how you can be *friends* with this man?'

'Kev's all right. He's always been a bit overprotective.' She tracked him with the torch as he came out of the trees.

'How long have you been involved with him?'

'All my life, I suppose. He's my brother.'

Kevin reached the edge of the fence. He held the decapitated chicken by its feet, and in his other hand he carried the bloody head, balanced on the flat of the hatchet. He flung the head on the roof, where it rolled and came to a rest against the other one.

As he leaned over the chickens' nest box, Cull could see fear in their flat red eyes. Brother and sister! There was panic in those eyes, terror, even a plea for help. Could it be true that Kevin and Margaret were already sleeping together? The faces of the chickens flushed and their lips foamed white. The British Isles are appalling, their white chicken lips mouthed. No wonder Darwin became religious.

Only two birds left – and who was next? The house was dark, the feeder dry. The wind rattled the corrugated iron walls and blew through the holes in the mesh roof. Cull leaned further into the nest box and spoke as calmly as he could, though his voice trembled and betrayed his fear.

'It's all right. They can't help being brother and sister...'

He turned and scanned the rafters for CCTV cameras. 'No, we're safe in here. The cameras are outside. We don't have to fear technology, not in the enclosure. Nobody will know what we're doing. Nobody will overhear.'

The chickens made low clucking noises, as if reassured. He fed them slivers of cabbage. He took the brown chicken's neck and squeezed. 'We're hybrids,' he said.

There wasn't anything to it, he just wanted to know what it felt like. Such a thin neck! The chicken pecked until he let go. He reached for the Leghorn, but she flapped her wings.

'Forgive me. Lonely, that's all. Distraught! Still, I shouldn't have used force, shouldn't have taken liberties. You like John Donne? "License my roving hands. And let them go, before, behind, between, above, below..."'

He reached for the brown one again. It was no use – the

chicken didn't understand that he only wanted to hold someone. He ambled over to the corner and peed into the pit. He kicked some dirt over it and sunk to the ground, gathering the straw around him. He squinted at his grand-father's photo, but it was too dark to see, and he tucked it under the straw. *Shoot us an email,* his parents told him before he left, forgetting how much he hated the phrase. *Let us know what you've found.* They didn't want to know. Not really.

'Let me tell you a story, my chickens. It is with consider-able difficulty that I remember the original era of my being. The events of that period appear confused and indistinct...'

He spoke softly but clearly, his legs under the straw. Anyone listening would have heard the voice of an American inside the chicken house, recalling passages of *Frankenstein* to pass the time, occasionally stopping to sob.

'I was born a poor, helpless, miserable wretch – I crawled the earth staring at the ground. When it was bright I looked directly at the sun, burned my eyes, learned not to repeat the same mistake. I gazed with wonder at the moon and the stars, hunted for berries. An American, wild and ungovern-able, ill-mannered and loud...'

The chickens kept silent, apparently entranced by his bastardization.

'I needed guidance, someone who spoke better English. Alas, my creators wouldn't speak to me in my early years. They treated me as they would an idiot – because as a young child I was unable to articulate any meaningful sounds, and they mistook my babble for lack of thought. One day, still young, I discovered a book. A simple book on horses. Or dogs, I can't remember which. I learned how to associate letters with sounds, matched words with thoughts. I read more books, and as I grew older and went to school, I learned about science and mathematics and law. I longed to visit the island where my ancestors were from. But no matter how much I excelled in America, there was still a gulf between my understanding of the world and the sophistication of my English ancestors. I still felt inferior...'

The chickens were wheezing and clucking in their nest box. They were unaware that they were mortal and started to snore. For hours Cull rocked in his bed, talking to forget the cold.

'Shudder-drug. Cawp. Yawp. Cawl. Murmuration of starlings, murder of crows, cull of gulls...'

Broken light fell across the scattering of straw. He reached for the photograph of his grandfather. It was a black-and-white photo, taken from a distance, of a young man in tweed standing against one of the studios. He leaned against the doorframe, tall, arms crossed, neither smiling nor frowning, a man confident without being cocky, utterly normal – at least, not abnormal. The eyes were intelligent, with a nose between them. The ears weren't too large.

'He was a fine apprentice,' a voice said. 'My best scorper.'

Cull looked up. Eric Gill was in the chicken house, sadly regarding the dirt floor and empty feeder. 'Look where you've found yourself now,' he said.

'I'm in a pinch,' Cull said. He stood up and brushed away the straw. He put the photo of his grandfather back under his makeshift bed.

'No beer to hand. Not even a cup of tea?'

'I'm afraid not.'

Eric sighed. 'Ah, the Common. A good place to pray, and to work in peace. Brings back memories of my dog. Ah, well.

I didn't come all this way for the amenities, or to walk down memory lane – I came to wish you farewell.'

'Farewell?' Cull hurried to the door, to block his friend's way out. 'Don't leave – I've been so alone.'

'It's only farewell for now.'

'Where are you going?'

'It's not me that's going anywhere – it's you. What I recommend in the short term, if you don't mind me saying, is to dig.'

'Dig out?'

'Dig for the strangers' hands. You need proof for Margaret. Your grandfather wrote about it, didn't he? The Pollards were a nasty family – they have a history. Some people said those hands were here in the chicken house.'

'But what if Kevin catches me?'

Eric stood on his tiptoes and clutched the American's shoulders. 'Be brave. It's a difficult place to live, Sussex.'

There were footsteps outside – boots crunching in gravel. The chickens stirred in their little holes. Cull's grandfather called out from the photo on the ground.

Hello, Mr Gill. Sorry to see you mixed up in all of this.

Kevin's coming – he's nearing the door.

Sorry to interrupt, Mr Gill, but my grandson's in trouble.

'Quite all right, my old friend,' Eric said. 'This American is a good man. He's learned how to see people with love. Now it's time for him to show a bit of courage. Good luck,' he said, ducking under the chicken house door. 'See you soon!'

'Wait!' Cull said, but Eric had already gone.

His mouth dry, Cull hurried to the door and peered

through the mesh. Eric Gill floated above the perimeter fence with his robe billowing in the wind. Down on the ground Kevin came into the run, a bucket in one hand and the hatchet in the other.

The chickens started squawking and flapping their wings. Cull ran back and forth inside the house. He couldn't help being frantic. His mouth foamed and frothed and little fearful garbling sounds came out of the back of his throat. Everything was collapsing around him – and yet in his fevered state, he started to form a plan.

Kevin's face appeared at the door. 'I'm coming in! Stay back, or I'll chop you down in three seconds flat.'

Cull hoisted himself onto the nest box. He sat in one of the empty nests with his legs dangling over the frame as Kevin came inside.

'That's good. Stay right there where you belong.'

It was the first time Kevin had spoken to him in days. It gave Cull hope. Maybe Margaret was right, maybe Kevin *was* calming down, now that he knew what to expect. Weren't people with anger issues just damaged souls in need of reassurance? Hadn't he frightened Kevin, sneaking up to the studio in the middle of the night?

Kevin took the bucket over to the feeder. Cull felt his mouth water as he watched the water splash over the partition. Kevin had also brought a loaf of bread, which he tore into pieces and scattered across the floor. Food! Cull resisted the urge to jump out of his nest and eat it straight off the ground.

'You lay any eggs last night?'

Kevin came over to the nest box with the hatchet. Cull couldn't help it – he started shivering with fear. He lowered his eyes and kept his mouth shut, even as the two chickens beside him shook their rose combs and flapped their wings.

The dimpled chin, the smell of cologne – Kevin was coming closer, searching the straw under Cull's legs.

'Nothing – no eggs at all. That means I'll have to eat you.'

Kevin reached for Cull's neck and laughed when he flinched. 'What a soft wanker.' He rested the hatchet on Cull's bare shoulder, the blade pointing at his neck. It had dried blood on it.

'Those brass knuckles. Who gave 'em to you?'

Cull didn't reply. His knees trembled as Kevin leaned in. There wasn't time to move – Kevin brought the blade right under his chin, so that the metal cut into the skin. 'I'll only ask you once more.'

'Bobby,' Cull said. 'It was Bobby who gave them to me.'

'Fucking Swifts. That's what I thought. When I'm in charge of the parish council they'll never get their heritage status.' He lowered the blade and patted Cull's shoulder. 'Margaret's going into town later. Leaving you here with me.'

'I won't be any trouble,' Cull said.

'I heard you've been asking what happened to my old friend Carlo.'

Cull shook his head. 'No, I was just—'

'You'll find out tonight. We'll have a little tour of the company, a little field trip to the incinerator. Ever want to see how bone ash gets made?'

Kevin withdrew the hatchet and seized the brown chicken. It was over in a moment – the bird was taken from the nest without even pecking back. Then Kevin ducked through the door, leaving only the Leghorn behind.

Cull sat in his nest until he heard the padlock. Then

he climbed out, gulped some water, and ate half the bread as slowly as he could, making each mouthful count. He collected the other half of the bread and hid it under his straw. The Leghorn was watching him. Hiding food from a chicken made him ashamed. He took the bread back out and scattered it on the ground.

After a while he ventured out into the run. Now there were three brown chicken heads on top of the roof, three pairs of red eyes looking at him as he paced. He walked from one end of the run to the next, and the Leghorn followed close behind. He had almost grown accustomed to being outside in his underwear. He had almost grown used to the cold. As he looked over at the empty studios, there seemed to be people inside – men in spectacles, smoking pipes, bearded men bent over woodcuts and gravestones.

Carlo disappeared, Margaret had said – but had every part of his body? Cull watched her door and waited.

The CCTV camera, mounted above Margaret's door, pointed at the run. Cull paced a few more lengths, then slowed down as if tired. Then he returned to the house and closed the door.

Once inside, he tore a plank of wood from the nest box. He used it like a shovel and tore into the ground. He was looking for the Dutchman, or the Icelander, or Margaret's husband – any poor foreigner who'd had the misfortune of falling in love with a Ditchling sister. He dug methodically along the corrugated walls, filling each hole back in with the dirt he removed from the next one. When he grew tired he drank the water from the feeder and had a bite of bread.

The sun rose over the wooden roof, and still he kept digging. Then the plank hit something covered by loose dirt. It was an old cardboard box, moldy and torn, labeled faintly but still legible: DITCHLING BONE ASH WORKS.

Cull crawled to the door. The studio was still quiet, the clearing empty. He returned to the box, and when he opened it, the smell was like nothing he'd encountered before. It made him step back. He approached the box a second time with his arm crooked over his mouth.

Inside, there was a hand. It was much bigger than a normal hand, hacked at the wrist and almost black. The flesh was blistered, the fingers puffy, the nails burned off. Carlo's? There was nothing else in the box except white ash. Bone ash – it went into products like glue, fine china, pottery. He sat there thinking a moment, then picked up the wooden plank once more. *Whoever buries the hand of the stranger rules the rest.* There would be others here, talismans from the prophecy.

The ground loosened, the deeper he dug. The soil became dark and moist, intermixed with wet clay. The floor of the house rose up around him as he sank slowly into the earth. At one point the hole caved in, and no matter how many times he packed the soil, it kept collapsing. He climbed out, took the nest box completely apart, plank by plank, and used the wood as wall supports.

The Leghorn stood at the side of the hole and watched him with her blinking red eyes. She hoped the hole meant escape.

'I won't abandon you,' Cull told her. His forehead and back were coated with sweat, palms covered with blisters. The chicken bobbed her head and urged him on. He kept digging, and each time he looked up, the Leghorn rose higher, until it seemed she gazed down at him from the top of the roof.

At last he struck something, a hard metal object in the soil – he leaned down, brushed away the dirt, and found what looked like the lid of a rectangular metal box. He dug around it, lifted it out. The box was heavy, and he had to use two hands to hoist it over the side of the hole. The lid was rusty and didn't appear to have been opened in some time.

'Is it an ossuary, Little Leghorn?'

The chicken watched as he banged the metal sides of the box to loosen the lid. It came open with a puff of stale air.

The box was full of hands, all of them reduced to bone. Cull took them out, one after the other. There were nine of them, all right hands of men, judging from the size. He wondered if Kevin had ever tried to find this ossuary box, with its worn metal the color of dust. A few of the hands had names on them, typed on labels attached to the fingers. The names apparently didn't identify the victims, but the captors. A few said *Pollard*, others *Swift*.

Cull looked at the chicken, and the chicken looked at the door. There was a voice calling to him outside.

'John? You awake?'

'Margaret,' Cull whispered. 'What should I say?' The Leghorn just clucked softly, her little voice wobbly with fear.

'Come on out, John!'

He looked at the hands arranged on the ground. 'What for?'

'I'm heading off now. Picking up some things from the shop...'

Cull climbed out of the hole. The state of the chicken house didn't matter now – soon Kevin would see the holes he'd dug, and the broken nest box, and he and the Leghorn would be done for.

'Wait,' he called. 'I'm coming out!'

He piled the hands into the ossuary and came out through the door. It wasn't until he'd come all the way to the fence that he realized he was covered with dirt.

'Don't tell me you've been digging your way out,' Margaret whispered. She had her coat on and car keys in her hand. 'You're lucky Kevin's in the bath. Hurry up, clean yourself off. If he catches you – what's *that*?'

Cull placed the ossuary on the ground. He reached in and withdrew the blackened hand. Margaret stepped back in disgust. He was relieved – it meant she hadn't known.

'I think this is Carlo's.'

He showed her the smaller cardboard box it had come from, with its logo from the Bone Ash Works. Then he tilted the ossuary so that she could see the bones inside.

'These are strangers, murdered in Ditchling. In your grief you were blind to the truth. Your brother killed your husband, Margaret – so he could have you for a wife!'

Margaret stared at the bones and shrieked. She turned and ran across the clearing, and when she came back out of the studio she had Kevin, dripping wet from his bath, wearing tracksuit bottoms and no shoes. He was carrying the hatchet. Dona Matarazzo followed.

Cull held the ossuary to his chest like a shield. The Leghorn sprinted back and forth along the length of the run, squawking, flashing her bright yellow legs and flapping her wings, as if to warn all the chickens in the world to get away.

Margaret was yanking Kevin's arm, pulling him sideways and pushing him forward. Her eyes ran with tears. 'Ring the police, Kev! Go on, ring them! If you don't, I will!'

Kevin shoved her aside. He fumbled with the key in the padlock.

'It's the prophecy, Margaret,' Cull said, through the fence. 'Your brother killed Carlo in his factory.'

'What's he on about?' Margaret cried. She ran at her brother and swung with her fists. 'Where did he get that box?'

Kevin shoved her, and she fell. His hair still had shampoo in it. He entered the run, hatchet raised. Dona Matarazzo came right up to the fence to watch.

'It's the prophecy,' Cull said. 'Doesn't anyone see?' He knew he was going to have to fight in order to avoid his fate.

For a moment they stood at a distance. Then Kevin charged, swinging the hatchet. Cull blocked the first blow, but the pain of the blade ripping into his flesh made him cry out. Kevin came at him again, but Cull dodged and punched, catching Kevin in the ear.

Margaret screamed at them to stop. The Leghorn, flapping her wings, ran over and pecked at the tops of Kevin's feet. He howled in pain and stumbled. This was Cull's opportunity, and he took it – he heaved the box of hands at Kevin's head, slipped out of the run, and made it to the clearing.

He gained the trees and had the bridge in sight. His right wrist throbbed, but he didn't want to look at it, not until he was clear. Each time he checked over his shoulder, Dona Matarazzo was still coming toward him in her nightgown with her white hair flowing behind her. She ran faster than he thought – and then Cull realized he was losing strength.

He crossed the bridge and made it onto the main road. Finally, the old woman turned back. Cull kept jogging until Ditchling came into view. He still had two miles to go.

He listened for the Land Rover. If necessary, he planned to jump into the fields and run, but there was no sound of an engine. Now that he had time to look, he raised his arm. The sight made him nauseous.

His right hand dangled from his wrist. The hatchet had broken the bone almost completely, chopping through the tendons and exposing the nerves to the cold air. Blood streaked down his elbow and onto the road.

Up in the sky, a flock of geese was flying in a vee toward the nature reserve. Their little beaks were moving, but they were strangely silent. The only sound Cull could hear was a rushing in his ears. He took a step and stumbled. A new kind of panic set in, worse than it had been in the roost. He needed to stop the bleeding – in minutes, maybe seconds, or he might die.

He needed a tourniquet. The road was empty, and there were only pebbles and twigs along the fence. On the other side of the fence, the fields held only grass and the occasional horse. With the Land Rover, he could get to a hospital in time.

The next thing he knew he was running back toward the Common, his arm high in the air. He crossed the bridge and made his way down the opposite bank. He waded into the stream, placed his arm in the icy water, and tried not to look at the jagged flesh swirling like seaweed around his wrist.

Under the bridge he saw that someone had built a kids' camp made of wood, partly eroded from the passage of time and heavy rain. Cull waded up to it. There were some old clothes strewn around. He washed out a shirt and tied it tight around his wrist, then he built a stronger tourniquet near his elbow from some old trousers. He sat in the water, kept his breathing steady, and tried to stay calm.

He thought of Margaret and the Leghorn. What if they were in trouble? The little bubbles in the current shouted at him as they floated by.

There's Cull, slumped in our stream.
Has he really given up?
He needs to find a weapon if he wants to earn a place in the churchyard.

Cull splashed water on his face until the bubbles went silent. He stood up and kicked at a crossbeam. The plank was strong, the nails held. He kicked again until a piece of wood broke free, with the nails sticking out of the end. As he waded to the bank he found something bobbing in the water – a stainless-steel mixing bowl, battered by its travel downstream. The bowl fit over his right hand and served as a shield.

He made his way out of the stream. He crept through the trees toward the clearing until he had the studios and the chicken coop in view.

Kevin was out in the run. He was clearing the nest box and straw out of the chicken house. Everything else was as before – the parked Land Rover, the lights on with the curtains drawn, the smoke rising from the chimney. Kevin would put the ossuary back and fill the holes back in, perhaps move them somewhere else – and who would know the difference? Who would be next?

Cull kept low in the trees, circling the run from above. Margaret emerged from the studio in her coat, carrying a suitcase to the back of the Land Rover. Was she done with him at last? Cull snuck down to the coop from the lower trees, down to the bloodstained flat stump where Kevin had decapitated the chickens. The door to the run stood open, the padlock hung on the latch.

Kevin went into the chicken house and came back out with the plastic feeder. The poor little Leghorn stood at the edge of the fence. She looked up at Cull in the trees, her comb wobbling and her beak open as if beseeching him with John Donne like a battle cry:

> O my America! My new-found-land,
> My kingdom, safeliest when with one man mann'd
> My Mine of precious stones, My Empery,
> How blest am I in this discovering thee!

Cull raised his weapon and shield. 'To enter in these bonds, is to be free,' he answered. 'Then where my hand is set, my seal shall be!'

He charged the run. Kevin saw him and dropped the feeder. He stepped back, his face a mixture of confusion and fear. 'Margaret!' he yelled. 'Help!'

Cull came through the door, swinging the plank. On the first swing he caught Kevin on the side of his head. The nails went into his ear, and the plank stayed. Kevin wobbled on his feet. He caught Cull in a bear hug. The Leghorn flapped over once more, pecking at Kevin's ankles. Together they brought him down to the dirt.

Margaret ran to the fence, followed by Dona Matarazzo.

'Stay back!' Cull told them. He knelt on Kevin's arms and turned the plank in his ear. 'Tell Margaret to give me the car keys.'

'Not the Land Rover!'

Cull twisted the plank until the nails turned. 'Tell her!'

Kevin squirmed and kicked. 'I warned you about him,' he yelled at Margaret. 'For God's sake, do what he says!'

11

For four days, the Leghorn slept at the foot of the bed in the cage Sheila purchased from *Animals in Distress*. The cage came equipped with a feeder and water nozzle. Each morning, Sheila changed the straw. 'Bobby puts up a fuss about this,' she told Cull, 'but brothers always come round. Chickens are God's creatures too.'

Cull spent most of his waking hours in his room, recuperating, watching the sky through the open curtains. He didn't remember everything from the past few days, but he had a clear memory of the frantic drive to the A&E in Brighton, with Margaret in the passenger seat and Kevin squirming in the back.

Everyone called it a masterful operation by the team of hand surgeons. The bones were reset, the major nerves fused. The icy water of the stream, coupled with the speed with which he'd made it to the hospital, were key factors in the surgery's success. Cull couldn't stop thinking the hand looked strange. His fingers, protruding from the end of the cast, seemed much shorter than normal. The doctor said it was because they'd been deprived of blood for hours. If the bones and nerves healed, and he performed his rehabilitation exercises, 'the hand' had a chance of complete recovery.

Right after coming out of surgery, Cull had awoken with a fright. Still groggy, but clear-eyed enough to recognize faces, he saw Kevin looming above his bed in a hospital gown, a bandage covering his ear. Cull had cried out, and Margaret swiftly appeared to lead Kevin away.

In his panic, he'd lost consciousness. When he'd awoken, Sheila sat by his side. There was nothing to worry about, she assured him – Kevin had been moved to another ward and was under investigation in connection with Carlo's murder, along with three counts of animal cruelty. If Cull signed the forms she had with her, he would be authorizing the police to search his room, to examine anything they deemed relevant, to proceed with all lines of inquiry. They'd already made a 'preliminary' visit to Ditchling, and to the Common, she said.

Cull signed. Other forms passed in front of him, retro-actively authorizing his consent for anesthetic, the operation itself, and any transplanted tissues needed. Sheila had read aloud most of this paperwork, and because of the stultifying sedatives he'd signed without paying much attention. He seemed to remember the phrase 'bone and skin of recently deceased', and, on another form, the term 'bootscraper sketch'. This last phrase had caused him alarm, but when he'd asked Sheila for clarification, she said he must have been mistaken. He was cleared to leave the hospital, and she'd driven him back to Ditchling.

He was due back at work in a couple of days. With his hand in a cast, it was possible he could return to his job as scheduled, to continue his recovery in Los Angeles. But now, only one night before his flight home, nobody from the police had called yet. Nobody had asked for his state-ment, or taken him out to the Common, or even updated him on the status of the investigation.

Even more suspiciously, Bobby and Sheila had started to refer to his 'holiday out among the chickens'. They raised their eyebrows, even openly laughed, whenever he insisted he'd been kept under lock and key.

'What about those hands I found?' Cull had asked Bobby, the first day after he'd returned to the B&B. 'Did the police confiscate all the evidence?'

His landlord was in the lounge as usual, watching baseball, a packet of crisps at his side and the remote in his lap. 'That's nothing to do with me', Bobby said.

Cull rolled up his shirtsleeve. He held out his cast as proof, even tried to wiggle his motionless, discolored fingers. 'Is anyone going to answer for this? My hand was practically chopped off, Bobby. I could have bled to death!'

'You're saying that's my fault, are you?'

'You gave me those brass knuckles.'

Bobby grunted. 'I heard that didn't take long, you telling Kevin where you got them.'

'He had a hatchet to my neck.'

'Those brass knuckles were a gift, the better you might protect yourself. Now I've got to watch out, don't I? In case Kev uses 'em on me.'

'You could explain that to the police.'

'What, so they can charge me, or fine me or something? They've already come out here for a chat, Mr Cull. Nosed their way into each and every room of my house.'

'Good.'

'Good? What would *you* do next, take me to court?'

'Can't you at least help me move the investigation forward? Tell them I'm not making all of this up?'

Bobby didn't respond to that. The police, as it turned

out, were equally tight-lipped. Finally, after hours of pestering them on the phone, Cull was told the investigation had been suspended. 'Damage was done on both sides,' the detective said. Any appeals had to be submitted in writing.

It took nerve to leave the B&B and return to the High Street. When he did, the Ditchlings practically ignored him. At Savage Greengrocer's and Sprinkles Café, he was treated as if he didn't exist.

One afternoon he went into The Lantern for a pint. Nobody at the tables looked at him – not the crossword men, not even Malcolm and Jilly Ketteridge-Wilson. Paul Tanner took his money without a word. Then, when he started back to his armchair with his pint, one of the crossword men muttered, 'He might need a hand with that.'

'Don't give him a handle glass, whatever you do,' another said.

'Only hand-crafted ales served in Ditchling,' the last one chimed in.

'What do you mean by all of this?' Cull said, whirling. 'You want to repeat that to my face?'

Behind the bar Paul Tanner placed his elbows on the beer mat, his Dorito nose glistening. 'That's enough out of you. The village hasn't been the same since you arrived. Everyone knows what you did to Kev.'

Cull held up his cast. 'What about what he did to *me*? Look – I can barely move these fingers!' He tried to move his fingers, but they wouldn't budge. The crossword men didn't bother turning around.

'Finish the drink you've paid for and move on,' Paul Tanner said. 'You've cost me too much as it is.'

'I've cost you? How?'

One of the crossword men turned in his stool, eyeglasses smudged, a pencil tucked behind each ear. 'What – you didn't know?'

'No.'

'Leave it,' Paul Tanner said, and the crossword man turned back around.

'What do you mean – I've cost you?'

Cull waited at the bar. Nobody looked at him, nobody spoke. He took his beer to the armchair, silently fuming. After he'd finished, he left the pub and wandered over to the churchyard.

It was nearly dark. He roamed the graves, braving the cold wind as it slipped around the dead painters and poets, the sculptors and soldiers. *Remember that you are Englishmen,* one of the epitaphs quoted Cecil Rhodes, *and have therefore won first prize in the lottery of life.* Beside the grave Cull stood sadly, staring down at the letters. He wanted a grave rubbing of that. If only he could get in there, into the letters themselves, into his past, forever. He reached his hand toward the stone. There was a click and a whirr, a faint electronic hum coming from the church.

He searched the eaves and found it – a CCTV camera panning toward him, training its blinking eye. Cull could feel the lens zooming in. He hurried on, away from the front of the church, over the mounds toward the neglected graves at the back. He found his slab of stone. There was his name, his birthdate. Was this a practical joke? Someone had engraved the date of death, and it was tomorrow.

He reached down and felt the date. The numbers were superficially engraved. With another spike, or even a rock, he could get rid of that date, etch it into oblivion so that he could decide for himself when to die.

Cull searched the ground and when he turned, he noticed a couple on a nearby bench, under the branches of an overhanging tree. They were sitting in the shadows, holding hands, watching him. They were a large couple with bulky arms and shoulders that almost filled the bench. It was the Quizmaster and Reverend Lucy, guarding the grounds, including his own headstone, against people like himself.

The next morning at breakfast Sheila told him it was important, above all, to recuperate. 'The past is the past,' she said, after he'd finished what she called his 'last meal'. She brought him a fresh pot of coffee and stood next to his table by the window.

'Just concentrate on getting good and healthy, luv. When you get back to America, drop us a line. Let us know you're safe.'

'I think maybe I'll extend my stay. Make sure justice is done.'

Sheila stepped back from the table. 'What – stay here? But you've got to be back at work, I thought.'

'Kevin kidnapped me!'

'You did a bit of damage yourself, to be fair. Kev won't be hearing much out of that ear in future.'

'He was going to kill me.' Cull reached automatically for the milk with his right hand. He'd forgotten about his cast, and he clanged it into the coffee pot.

'There, there,' Sheila said, coming a little closer. 'I can tell you're frustrated. You're thinking of Margaret.'

He sighed. 'She hasn't once called, has she? Or even stopped by to check on me?'

'Afraid not, luv.'

'Even after I found those hands. Whose side is she on?'

'Margaret's *always* sided with her brother, when push comes to shove. That's as it should be. She knew she wouldn't have come into any soap dispenser money the way she was going. Not married to Carlo.'

Sheila placed a photo next to his coffee cup. It was of his grandfather. 'The police found this, out where you were living with the chickens – I made sure I got it from them, luv. Made sure it came to you.'

Cull glanced at his grandfather, a scorper in tweed, next to the Ditchling placemat.

'A handsome man, your granddad. But he *left* Ditchling, didn't he?'

'He did.'

'And Margaret's only just met you, Mr Cull. You can hardly expect…'

'Sheila,' he said, 'your name was attached to some of those hands. I told the police as much.'

Sheila hissed. 'Fancy you doing a thing like that. Everyone knows there were strange goings-on out there on the Common, once upon a time. Swifts have been in Ditchling donkeys' years.'

'What's happened to those hands I found – do you know?'

Sheila pretended not to hear. 'Yes, some strange goings-on, out there on the Common,' she repeated. 'Once upon a time.'

He sipped his coffee and studied her. Sheila was pulling nervously at her shirtsleeves. 'I'd like to stay on an extra few days,' he said.

'I'm afraid you can't, Mr Cull. We're all full up from tomorrow. Big group coming in.'

'A big group. Here?'

'Ramblers from London,' she said, looking away.

'You and Bobby have those hands yourselves, I suspect. Hidden them in your room.'

'Don't be silly.' Reaching across his table, she began adjusting the porcelain dogs, turning each of them so that their little white heads faced his chair. 'Lots of nonsense.'

'I'm not going to just forget this, you know.'

'Oh! You'll be heading straight for the lawyers, I expect.'

'Why do you say that?'

She shrugged. 'Americans like to sue.'

'I've never taken anyone to court. I *could* sue Kevin, if the police don't do anything about it.'

'There's self-defense to think of, Mr Cull.' She patted him on the shoulder. 'That's just it, self-defense. Besides, I should think it's too much to take on, involving the courts all the way across the Atlantic. All the way from Calif-orn-I-A.'

Cull glanced at his grandfather's mild face. 'I've never sued anyone,' he said again.

'Lawyers are more trouble than they're worth! They don't help you get better, do they? You'll be happy to know one thing – that grotty little pizza restaurant's shutting down at last. Kev's no longer churchwarden, either.'

'How did you hear that?'

'Reverend Lucy. She says those Pollards might have to make a donation if he wants to be considered again. I told her it's high time she gets a memorial plaque. I'll see to it myself, I will.'

'A plaque?'

'First female vicar in Ditchling!' She looked out of the window with a small smile. 'Yes, the Pollards will have to think twice before making a move like that again.'

'What kind of move?'

'Marriage, of course.' Sheila straightened the wedding ring on her finger so that the diamond caught the sunlight. 'The last couple in Ditchling to get the dispensation, Bobby and me. Married couples have a few advantages round here.'

She put her hands on her hips. 'Now stop your worrying. It's your last day in Ditchling before heading home! Go for a walk, visit the shops. Your flight's this evening, luv. You'll want to get there good and early.'

'I know.'

'And don't be fussed about that bird of yours, I'll take care of her. I'll extend your normal check-out until the afternoon, how about that? Go on, go and buy some souvenirs for your friends.'

Cull looked down at 'the hand'. His fingers had turned a shade of purple. 'Part of me does want to get back home.'

'Can't say that I blame you. Not normally such an eventful place, Ditchling.'

There was a scratching sound at the window. It was the spaniel from the pub, up on its hind legs. Sheila leaned over Cull's table, stuck out her tongue, and made a panting noise. 'Thirsty, girl?'

Cull sat back in his chair. Sheila kept leaning over his breakfast table, her breasts expanding in her blouse, the material stretching at the seams. She tapped on the window. 'Thirsty?' she said again.

'What a cute darling little dog. She comes round now

and then, looking for a bit of food and water. I don't think that drunk Tanner feeds her enough.'

The spaniel stayed up on her hind legs, her paws under the window, tail wagging. She had something in her mouth. It was long and fleshy, with exposed bone.

'What's that you've got?' Sheila said.

Cull put down his coffee. It was a finger. And it looked like his own.

Sheila raised her hand to her mouth. She gave Cull a quick look and ran to the door. 'She's been digging in the back garden!'

Cull got up from the table. He grew faint, and he stumbled. Bobby intercepted him from the kitchen.

'My hand,' he said, but Bobby helped him up to his room.

Cull made a cup of tea and tried to calm down. There was no point in fretting about his hand now. He fed the Leghorn leftover toast through the cage.

Between bites, she clucked with desperation – she wanted to be let out to walk around. The first night, he'd allowed her out, but she'd run frantically around the room and hidden under the bed. It had taken forever to coax her back into the cage.

The chicken was his only friend in England. Sheila had promised to keep her safe when he'd gone, feed and walk her, never kill her for soup – but Cull didn't trust her any longer.

'Only a few more hours,' he told the Leghorn as he gave her another bite of toast. 'Then we'll both be free.'

Taking home a few souvenirs wasn't such a bad idea. He'd get some postcards, maybe a couple of placemats for his parents. At the bottom of the stairs, Bobby was leaving the house at the same time. He was carrying an outfit on a hanger – a brown sculptor's smock, rope sandals and knee stockings. He also carried a four-cornered paper hat.

'What's all this?' Cull asked.

Bobby just blinked at him. 'What?'

'This! Your costume.'

'I don't believe I have to answer for myself. I wear what I like.'

Sheila leaned out of the lounge, a toothpick lodged in the corner of her mouth. 'Bobby's Eric Gill,' she said.

Bobby smirked. He put the hat on his head, shook a false beard out of his coat pocket, and picked the lint from its hair. 'The museum asked me to sit in the booth for a couple of days, carve a bit of wood. They're having some mechanical difficulties with the model.'

'We're hoping it'll turn into something permanent,' Sheila said.

Bobby snorted at her. He took a portable radio from behind the coat stand and headed out.

Cull wandered Ditchling in a daze. Inside his cast, his wrist throbbed with a dull ache. 'The hand', with its strangely short fingers, had turned numb.

He ventured up Boddington's Lane, but there was little warmth to the day, little light from the sun between the flint walls. The pizza shop was shuttered. The sign on the window still said, *Closed until further notice*. At Margaret's house the lights were off. A thin white curtain had been drawn over the window above the door.

He knocked, and he waited. For a long time he lingered on the cobblestones, plagued by loneliness. The village had changed – or had it returned to normal?

Back on the High Street, he passed more Ditchlings who ignored him. He ducked into *Animals in Distress*. Rhiannon sat at the counter with her head down, her thumbs working her phone.

Cull found the dog leads and searched for the smallest – a pink one, with little plastic diamonds encrusted around the collar. He browsed the stuffed toys, but they were all too big for a beak.

'Thanks for finding that cage,' he said while he paid. 'The Leghorn seems to like it.'

Rhiannon didn't look up. 'Please,' she said, 'I know you're trying to be nice, but don't come in again.'

Cull felt himself turn red. 'You mind if I ask why?'

Rhiannon glanced nervously at the door. 'A constable came the other day. Wanting to know about the boxing helmet.'

'But – that has nothing to do with you.'

'I wasn't supposed to have sold it, technically. I don't have a license to sell fighting equipment.'

'It was just an old boxing helmet.'

'This isn't America. There's regulations here.'

'What happened to that helmet?'

'The museum claimed it. They wanted it for display, and the constable agreed.'

'But it was mine!'

She shrugged. 'The police tend to be a bit twitchy when it comes to Ditchling.'

Cull reached for his wallet. He folded up all his remaining

cash, placed it inside the donation box, and continued up the High Street.

At Sprinkles, a woman was taping a flyer to the front window. There was a drawing on it, *his* drawing, enlarged and photocopied – the bootscraper in front of the B&B. There was also a photo of Sheila on the flyer, her face made up and her hair done in tight ringlets.

MEET THE AUTHOR!

Sheila Swift, author of the forthcoming
My Darling Ditchling Bootscrapers
Signed limited first edition prints.
Coffee and tea provided.

Cull struggled not to shout with rage. He remembered the word 'bootscraper' on the form he'd signed in the hospital.

'She's betrayed a number of us in the village,' said a voice behind him.

Cull turned. A middle-aged woman stood on the pavement with a man at her side. They were staring at the flyer as well.

'We couldn't get her to leave the trees on our road alone,' the man said. He took off his eyeglasses and cleaned the lenses with the bottom of his shirt. 'Spraying them, she was, with the latest chemicals.'

'Chemicals? But people *want* birds in their trees, don't they?'

The woman shook her head. 'Not since those sprayers came round. Sheila said it was only a temporary thing, that she had permission to control the worm infestation.'

'When was this?'

A curtain moved on the window above the café. The man took the woman's arm and led her away. As Cull stood on the pavement, he saw the curtains being drawn on all the surrounding houses. He could sense people hiding, placing their noses through the gaps, watching him walk to the Village Hall.

The double bootscraper with the eagle and snake greeted him. Cull lifted the sole of his shoe and hesitated – a notice had been posted onto the 'Announcements' board:

DITCHLING PARISH COUNCIL
announces its recent decisions.

Approvals: For contributions to the village, a Designated Heritage Site of Historical Importance has been awarded to Mrs Sheila Swift of Swift Cottage B&B, with all rights and privileges hereto. Title for this exclusive designation granted immediately and without delay.

The Council has also nominated a Chair of the English Heritage 'Streets for All' Campaign to Mr Robert Swift. Responsibilities to include redesignating road surfaces and pavements that clearly display double yellow lines. A Parking Space has been awarded to the Chair, in addition to usage of an electric buggie on the fourth Sunday of each month. Tourist coaches may appeal for use of parking: fees to be collected by Mrs Grace Savage.

Denials: Permission to establish a Ditchling Angling Club is hereby denied. The Planning Committee has also denied permission for a 'beer garden' behind the premises of The Lantern without an additional parking allocation. Planning

Permission also denied to Kevin and Margaret Pollard, Appellants, regarding a proposed extension of the Land known as 'The Studios', Ditchling Common.

Cull ducked under an oak tree and stood beneath the branches with his face towards the trunk. He didn't think anyone could see his expression there. How many spectators were watching Ditchling's rivals shamelessly square off over him? He walked back along the High Street. Some of the villagers stood out in their front gardens, pointing binoculars at the sky, their bird feeders full of seed.

Scaffolding had gone up outside the museum for the Heritage Lottery Fund refurbishments. Workers in hardhats stood outside smoking cigarettes, watching a man use an electric water blaster on the front wall. The museum had apparently stayed open for visitors. Cull made his way through the scaffolding and set in motion the bell above the door.

He passed the carousel of postcards and the paintings of the South Downs. There was a special on tea towels depicting Dicul's hill. On the shelves were books on Ditchling's history from the Stone Age to the twenty-first century. Books and pamphlets were dedicated to almost every conceivable object in Ditchling – chimney pots, sewage drains, door handles, fence posts, postboxes. Someone had written a book on how to write a local history book. Paul Tanner's *History of The Lantern* had been shelved beside Larry Savage's vegetarian cookbook. There was a crossword anthology co-written by the crossword men. Most of the books were published by vanity presses, with glossy front covers and cheap binding.

Cull thumbed through Malcolm Ketteridge-Wilson's

Controlling Your Local Bird Population. Inside, he outlined the exact techniques for attracting and repelling native birds with hedgerow management, hawk statuettes, pesticides, and the latest bird feed. Cull tossed the book back on the shelf. Then he saw his own name on the museum's copy of *Scorper.* The pages were practically sealed shut from sitting unopened for years. The book had the same vanity press imprint, the same cheap bookbinding materials. He'd been too proud to notice before.

Cull approached the gift shop counter. Seeing him, Grace Savage backed up. She retreated almost to the wall, protecting her pregnant tummy with her arm. Her monk's haircut had been recently trimmed just above the eyebrows.

'Please,' she said. 'I don't want any trouble.'

'Trouble?'

Her eyelid twitched, and she covered it with a hand-kerchief. 'You're not supposed to be here any longer.'

'I"ll tell you what I might do. I will burn all your books, one after the other. I will eat your tea towels and shit on your head. But first, I want to visit the museum again.'

He pushed through the turnstile. The museum was empty, and he entered the exhibits alone – the printing press letters in their sorting drawers, the engraving tools hanging on hooks, the headstones leaning on the darkened walls. Outside, the worker's sandblaster made a constant high-pitched whine.

Bobby sat in the distance, inside the Eric Gill booth. He'd changed into his outfit and sat on a stool in front of all the woodcuts. The glass door stood open, and the lights were on. He had his radio tuned to a baseball game.

'The rookie Jimmy Seales isn't expecting another curveball. Look

at him. Protecting the plate from the inside fastball. Veteran lefty Greg Slaughter looks for the sign, goes into the windup...'

Cull ducked behind the nearest partition. The exhibit he'd entered had rocks of different sizes and colors, various pieces of chalk, and an information placard:

> The upper chalk layer of forest beds in Sussex is made of almost pure calcium carbonate from the skeletons of small organisms that lived in a sea that covered much of the land almost 100 million years ago. Most chalk is made of single-celled algae called coccoliths which formed on the sea floor while dinosaurs roamed the Earth. See if you can distinguish coccolith from belemnite, ammonite and echnoid!

Cull put his face to the glass. One of the chalk samples was a white, pockmarked ball with an almost human face. Was this a Lord Coccolith, a Lady Belemnite, or another ancient member of Ditchling royalty?

'*...and he took another curveball. Stared at it. Protecting the inside of the plate...'*

Cull crept away from the gaze of the ancient chalk. Under the flickering fluorescent lights, he walked the flagstones. He passed exhibits of flint and bone – a hundred million years in a matter of footsteps. He moved among the shadows of spitstickers and engraving knives and scorpers.

Near the Eric Gill booth, someone had put up a temporary glass cabinet with his boxing helmet inside. The hat had been desecrated – there were feathers stuck to the leather and chicken wings extending out of the earholes.

Bobby sat on the stool inside the booth with his back to Cull. The mechanical Eric Gill slumped in the corner, facing Bobby in an identical smock and hat, motionless, dead, awaiting repairs. Cull crept closer, past the slabs of stone and the printing press that smelled of ink and creosote. Bobby had his legs kicked out in front of him and an open bag of crisps on his worktable. He might have been at home in his lounge.

Someone's phone rang – a workman's, outside. Suddenly Cull jumped forward in time, into England's current Dark Age of tweets and emails, blogs and e-readers, mobile texting devices, Eric Gill robots.

'Slaughter paces the infield. Goes to the rosin bag. Wipes his palms and retakes the mound…'

The phone outside kept ringing. The water-blaster stopped, and the museum went quiet except for the radio. Bobby got on his feet, his back to Cull. He bent forward on an imaginary mound, elbow on his knee, as if taking signs from the mechanical Eric Gill.

'Slaughter shakes off a fastball. He likes what he sees from his catcher. Goes into his windup…strike two! Another filthy pitch from the lefty.'

Bobby pumped his fist. His paper hat slipped off his head, and as he straightened it, he noticed Cull at the edge of the booth.

'Well – hello! You gave me a fright.'

Cull stepped over the rope cordon. Ducking, he poked his head inside. 'Mind if I come in?'

'Well—'

'I'm still just a tourist, learning about wood engraving. And you? Is this what Eric Gill whould be doing while on duty?'

Bobby turned to the model slumped in the corner. 'What

– him? He's got a blown fuse if you ask me. The electrician's looking at it next week.'

Cull came all the way inside the booth. Bobby moved out of his way, almost flattening himself against the glass. It was hot inside the enclosed space. Cull stepped past the woodcuts and engraving tools. At the mechanical Eric Gill, he fingered the putty on the neck. He lifted one of Gill's hands – some wiring had come out of the palm.

'You're not allowed to be in here, technically.'

Cull turned. Bobby hitched up his smock and scratched at the skin under his knee sock. 'Health and safety...'

'Sheila stole my bootscraper drawings,' Cull said.

Bobby looked away. 'Don't know anything about that.'

'What do you think of her title? *My Darling Ditchling Bootscrapers?*'

'What do *I* think?' Bobby backed up a little, toward the door. His mouth was quivering. 'I think it's time you cleared out of your room, Mr Cull. Take that chicken with you. Checkout's at eleven o'clock, you know.'

'Tell me where those hands are,' Cull said.

'What hands?'

'Tell me where you've hidden them.' He didn't feel like restraining himself any longer. It seemed somebody had invaded him – a violent stranger. He came at Bobby with his cast raised.

'Bloody hell,' Bobby said, glancing around for help. 'You've gone mental!'

There was a red button on the side of the booth that said, *Emergency Use Only*, and Bobby just managed to get to it before Cull had him in his grasp.

The fluorescent lights flashed throughout the museum.

The alarm sounded. By the time Grace Savage came running from the gift shop, followed by the workers in their hard-hats, Bobby was flat on his back in the booth, bleeding from the nose. Cull had him pinned. He knelt on his landlord's shoulders, his cast raised for a second strike, when he felt 'the hand' tearing from his wrist.

Cull opened his curtains wide, and the room filled with light. The little Leghorn stared out of her cage with eyes full of hope.

It took some work getting the collar over her comb. It was far too big for her neck, and he had to fasten it under her front legs and shoulders. The Leghorn nipped at Cull's fingers, smelling Bobby's blood.

'What a beauty you are,' Cull said, leading her out by the leash. She came clucking and prancing from her cage in the diamond-encrusted pink collar, waggling her earlobes and bobbing her head, just as she'd done during their days in the chicken run.

'Come on, Little Leghorn. We have to leave now. We have to hurry.' She kept pecking at the carpet and didn't listen. 'No need to pack our bags – we'll just go for a walk, and see where the road takes us.'

He led her out of the room and down the stairs. The collar obstructed her legs, and as she hopped from one step to the next she looked at the framed racehorses on the walls, as if for assistance. By the time Cull brought her outside and onto the High Street, she'd almost adapted.

The sun had come out. It was the first time the chicken had been outdoors in some time, and she looked like she was enjoying the fresh air. He'd wanted to walk her gradually, to acclimatize her to the surroundings, but the alarm was still sounding over at the museum.

A woman walking a dog came at them from the opposite direction. She had a Jack Russell, and the little beast lunged at the Leghorn and strained at its lead.

'I beg your pardon,' Cull said, stepping between the two animals.

The woman just stared. Her dog was barking and baring its teeth. The Jack Russell was about the same size as the Leghorn, but it was much more powerfully built, and the woman didn't even bother reining him in. The Leghorn frothed at the mouth in fear. She flapped her wings and tried to fly.

'You're a cruel people,' Cull told the woman. He picked up his chicken and held her close to his chest.

It seemed best to escape along the quiet lanes, up to the safety of Dicul's hill. After a lifetime in a cage, sensitive creatures needed to be eased into the perils of society. He carried her across the High Street and ignored the stares, the rude gestures, the laughter.

'This is what happens in England,' Cull reassured her. 'You get enticed by the language, the crumpets, the pastoral music. You feel temporarily at home – and then the nightmare begins.'

Once across the High Street he put the chicken back down and led her between the hedges toward Dicul's hill. It was pleasant to have a steady companion at last, an understanding ear.

'Don't take it personally,' he said. 'They don't always know they're being cruel.'

260

The path ended at an uprooted tree. They crossed the grass and joined the trail leading to the hill. It was damp going, and a little muddy. There were sheep in the distance and the Leghorn looked afraid.

'Want me to carry you again?'

He hoisted the chicken over the stiles and ran splashing with her across the dew ponds. She'd become accustomed to the collar and didn't squirm as much. Together they made their way to Dicul's mound, where the wind was blowing colder than before. Down in the distance, on the road, an ambulance was hurtling toward the museum with its siren on.

Once at the top, they could see the whole village – St Margaret's spire, the Tudor houses along the High Street, the pub and shops, the B&B. There were crows among the sheep in the nearby fields. Beyond the town lay the broad green ridge of the South Downs.

'Cluck, cluck,' said the chicken, bobbing her head.

'I see her,' Cull said.

Down at the stile they'd just crossed, Paul Tanner's little girl stood watching them, the spaniel at her side. She waved.

Cull held up his cast. The fingers had turned completely black, and two of the nails had fallen off. He was starting to feel faint again. He could smell honey blossoms and heather. He could hear the sound of running water. Where Ditchling had been, broad meadows and streams appeared. The stone lanes, the brick houses, the church and the shops, the hedges and enclosures all disintegrated, and in their place there opened up a wide expanse of downland and forest. He was looking into the future – where his spirit, in a different form, would return with the wind, rushing over the trees and down into meadow where the churchyard had been.

Cull blinked away his tears, and the picture was gone. The schoolgirl and her dog had left as well. Cull bundled up the Leghorn and pressed her to his chest. Together they stared up at the sky, where the sparrows swooped and darted like shooting stars. The sun disappeared, and gradually the sky turned black with descending shadows.

It was the birds. They flew over the village in wave after wave, as if released from an enormous aviary in heaven. There were sparrows and kites, moorhens and swallows, pheasants and mallards and geese, spotted flycatchers and goldfinches. The birds circled the steeple and settled into the trees and hedges.

The last of the sun reappeared in pinks and purples. The sound of birdsong rose from the trees. Cull turned away from this bittersweet music, and he wept onto his chicken. He turned his back to the village, and once more he faced the chalk pits and Bone Ash Works in the distance.

'I had such hopes, Little Leghorn.'

He had come to Ditchling to learn of his past. He'd wanted to make a few friends. Now he felt unbearable sorrow and pain from the betrayal of his ancestral home-land, and the people of England who spread their colonies around the world, only to turn their backs on their grand-children when they returned.

He set out with the Leghorn pressed to his chest. No longer did he desire to be known as an artist, or to have a stone memorial with his name on it for posterity. This was what his grandfather must have felt when he was dying, a man destined to fade into nothingness, far from home.

Cull carried the Leghorn down the dark side of Dicul's mound, past the crows, over the final stile. At the bottom he lost his footing and extended his right arm to balance himself, only to discover 'the hand' had fallen off. He peered inside the cast – there was nothing but a stump. His wrist wasn't bleeding, just numb and infected where it had been sewn onto a dead man's hand.

He unbuckled the Leghorn's collar and released her. She veered off into the shrubs, lured by the promise of food, leaving Cull to wander the night alone. Perhaps in the chicken's mind he would be remembered a few moments longer, an afterimage within her avian neural pathways – the tall American waving goodbye with his remaining hand, the stranger who appeared in her house one evening, told her stories at bedtime, and saved her from an early death.

It was time to return to the chalk, and to the pools of rain that shone luminescent in the craters. He would lie down in the pitted earth and rest before the next leg of his journey. He would fall asleep among the fossils, and over time become fine white powder and blow away. Maybe someone would gather up his bones, crush him into a paste, and embed him into a chalk figure staring down from the hills as a warning.

ACKNOWLEDGEMENTS

I would like to thank the numerous people in the United States and the United Kingdom who helped me bring about *Scorper*. In particular, I would like to express my deep gratitude to Clare Alexander, Richard Francis, Michael Pfaff, Max Porter and Leah Russell.

A NOTE ON THE TYPEFACE

This book was set in Golden Cockerel, a font designed by Eric Gill in 1931 for use by the Golden Cockerel Press. The font is used alongside Gill's engravings in *The Four Gospels*, acknowledged to be one of the typographical masterpieces of the twentieth century. The font combines the elegance and clarity of Gill's best-loved fonts with a strikingly hand-drawn quality.